D0253000

WITHDRAWN

Dear Reader,

Sharing this story with you was so much fun for me. Thank you for coming along and participating in the Secrets of the Blue Hill Library series, and getting to know Anne and her family.

I've always wanted a home similar to Aunt Edie's, and getting to explore the house and town a bit has been quite the ride. I'm glad you've come along with me and the other authors.

As an avid reader, I love to connect with other readers. Visit me on my Web site www.robincaroll.com and sign up for my newsletter. You can connect with me on Facebook at www.facebook.com/robincaroll or write to me via snail mail at: PO Box 242091, Little Rock, Arkansas 72223. I can't wait to hear from you!

Blessings,
Robin Caroll
writing as Emily Thomas

CHAPTER ONE

"Ready or not, here I come." Anne Gibson removed her hands from over her eyes as she yelled. She smiled as she took off in the direction of her bedroom. Her children loved hiding in Anne's closet every time they played hide-and-seek.

She opened the door to her bedroom, decorated much like her bedroom had been in New York. She lifted her voice. "Ben? Liddie? Are you in here?" She went through the motions even though she knew they weren't on the third floor any longer.

Anne had grown up playing in the eight-sided room in the cupola at the front of the house, around the spiral staircase, and in all the little nooks and crannies that had long ago opened the floodgates of her youthful imagination. This house held many of her favorite hiding places as a child.

Giggles sounded from the second floor.

Anne shut the door with a resounding click. The giggling stopped. "Where, oh where, are my Ben and Liddie?"

Muffled giggles answered.

With a smile on her face, Anne moved to the grand staircase with its hand-carved mahogany banister. The top stair creaked in response. Anne always loved the grand Queen Anne Victorian house with its white clapboard and slate blue shingles and the winding path down to the base of the hill. Now she lived in the house that perched atop Blue Hill, which she frequently visited as a child. The first floor and a portion of the second had recently been converted into a library, a legacy from her great-aunt Edie.

The afternoon breeze blew over the rolling hills and in through the open window of the second-floor landing.

"*Ah-choo!*" Her eyes watered from behind her large-framed glasses as she lifted a tissue to her nose. Late September brought bright, vivid colors to the leaves that adorned the beautiful old trees surrounding Blue Hill. And autumn brought seasonal allergies to Anne as well.

"God bless you." Five-year-old Liddie's singsong voice echoed down the hall.

"Thank you, honey." Anne pushed the tissue into her jeans pocket then headed toward the Fiction Room. The kids often hid in the Children's Room on the library's second floor, but lately they'd explored the Fiction Room. With the four walls each painted a different warm color, accented by white molding and trim, the room beckoned readers—and playing children—with its cozy aura.

Like fitting the genre to the reader, Anne had taken great pains with each room of the library, trying to reflect the book category each room housed. She was delighted with the final results of her fledgling attempts at interior decorating. Another gust of wind stirred the air and resurfaced the tantalizing aroma of the pot roast they'd had for dinner. Time to find Ben and Liddie and get them into bed. Wendy Pyle had agreed to help with the final indexing of the historical fiction books this evening, after she got her own kids tucked in and her husband situated in front of the television. It was nearly that time now.

Anne ducked into the Fiction Room. "Where is my Ben? Where is my Liddie?" Her daughter would probably be crouched behind the reupholstered wingback chair, her fist pressed against her mouth to squelch her squeal. Ben would either be hiding beside the armoire that held all the award-winning books or next to the shelves of newest releases.

Anne went for her daughter first. She jumped around the chair. "Liddie!"

But her daughter wasn't there. Giggles filtered up the stairwell from the first floor. Ah, so they'd somehow managed to sneak downstairs.

Anne crept down the stairs to the first floor and into the History Room. They hadn't hidden in here before; the dark walls and serious tone hadn't appealed to Ben or Liddie. Although there were still a few finishing touches to be done, it was Anne's favorite room so far. Maybe because she adored old record books and long-forgotten history.

"Where, oh where, is my little girl?" She inched around the dark leather, overstuffed chair. She jumped, popping her head over the top of the chair.

Liddie shrieked then leapt into her arms. "You found me, Mommy."

Anne buried her face in her daughter's neck, inhaling the baby-shampoo scent clinging to her. Little Liddie looked so much like her father, with her chocolate brown eyes, that it sometimes made Anne's heart ache. After three years, she still missed Eric something fierce.

"I'll always find you." She released Liddie, smoothing the legs of her pink pajamas. "Now, let's find that brother of yours."

Lately, Ben was having a bit of a hard time adjusting to small-town life. He missed Brooklyn, his friends. Her thoughtful nine-year-old hadn't yet connected with a Little League group in their new hometown, since they'd moved to town mid-season. Although, thankfully, he had befriended Alex's nephew, Ryan, whom Alex was raising following the death of his sister and brother-in-law.

"I think he's in the closet," Liddie whispered.

"Ah. Let's see."

She opened the closet door with a flourish and at the same time, yelled, "Found you!"

But Ben's round face didn't greet her with a smile. He wasn't to be found. "Ben?"

No response.

Anne swallowed the panic. This was Blue Hill, Pennsylvania — not exactly a place filled with crime. People left their doors unlocked here, for pity's sake. "Ben?"

Still no response.

She looked in the shadow behind the historical periodicals, but her son had gotten too tall to hide there without crouching. "Are you sure he came into the room with you?" she asked Liddie.

"Yes, Mommy." Her curls barely brushed the top of her shoulders as she nodded.

So where was he? Had he left the room after helping hide his sister?

Anne stepped into the hall and lifted her voice. "Ben? Hide-and-seek time is over. Come on out. You got me this time."

No response.

Anne's heart thumped wildly in her chest. "Ben, come out." She hardened her tone. "Now. It's time for bed."

Crash! The sound came from back in the History Room.

She spun in time to see a loaded book cart clatter over onto its side. Volume upon volume of books—plus Ben on top—skidded across the polished wood floor.

"Mom!"

She ran to him and helped him to his feet. "Are you okay?"

He nodded. "I'm sorry, Mom."

"Stay in the hall, Liddie," Anne said. "What happened, Ben?" She stepped over several leather-bound books.

"I was hiding against the wall, behind the book cart. I heard you coming, so I pressed against the side of the cart..."

Anne raised an eyebrow.

"I didn't mean to bump it...didn't even know I had, really." Ben frowned, reminding Anne of how much more of a loner he'd become since moving to Blue Hill. Back in Brooklyn, he'd been a smiling, popular boy. But now that school was back in session, he would surely make more friends.

Anne pressed her lips together. On one hand, she wanted to gather him in her arms and tell him everything was okay, but on the other hand, she knew he needed to stand on his own, so to speak.

He straightened and focused his gaze on her. "I'm sorry, Mom. I'll help pick everything up and put it all back the way you had it."

His gaze dropped to the books littering the floor. "I didn't mean to make a mess, honest."

"It's okay, sweetheart, I'll get it because I really need you to help your sister." Again she fought the urge to hold him. "Take Liddie and brush your teeth, then climb into your beds. I'll be up in a minute to listen to your prayers."

He turned, holding his hand out to his little sister. "Okay."

"Make sure Liddie uses toothpaste this time," she said.

Turning to the mess on the floor, she grabbed the first book and lifted it gently. Anne ran a finger down the front of the old copy of *Poor Richard's Almanack*. Its cover felt rough to her touch, taking her back to her childhood when she'd spent many summer days lazing on the creaky porch, immersed in a book right alongside her aunt. One at a time, she shelved half a dozen books. She loved the feel and smell of books, even the old dusty ones — always had. And she missed Aunt Edie. Although, since moving back to Blue Hill, Anne was discovering a number of details about her beloved aunt that she hadn't known before.

"Mom, we're ready!"

"Coming." She climbed the stairs, suddenly more tired than she'd been before. The renovations seemed to be a never-ending project, and the constant demands exhausted her. Not for the first time she wondered if could she do this. *Really* do this.

Yes, she could.

Even with losing Eric and then getting laid off from the New York Public Library system, Anne counted her blessings. God had it all worked out according to His will. Like this bequest from Aunt Edie — the timing was perfect for their little family to start over in her hometown. God had a good plan for her and for her children. She just needed to remember to trust Him all the time and in all things.

She'd barely finished tucking in the kids, reading Liddie yet one more bedtime story, and listening to their precious prayers when the front bell chimed. Anne rushed down to the first floor and opened the door.

"Sorry. Jacob and Ethan both had to have twenty glasses of water before bed." Wendy grinned as she stepped over the threshold. Her black, chin-length, bobbed hair was held off her face by a blue band that accented her big, blue eyes. To look at her, no one would guess she had seven children. How she found the time to read as much as she did, Anne couldn't guess, but the woman went through books almost as quickly as Anne herself.

"Come on in. I just got my two down for bed."

Wendy shut the door behind her. "I'm glad you decided to go with the Victorian doors. The ones you picked out are much more in keeping with the original architecture of the house."

Which was exactly why Anne had vetoed her first instinct to have strong security doors installed and went with those designed more for the 1896 house. Having grown up in Blue Hill, she knew the town was safe, even the quaint downtown area. She'd been away in the big city for years, following the career path Aunt Edie had encouraged her to take.

And now she was back in Blue Hill, turning Aunt Edie's house into a library. Everything always seemed to come back to Aunt Edie.

"So, what are we indexing tonight?"

Anne led the way up the stairs. "The rest of the historical fiction, after I clean up the mess."

"Mess?"

"Ben accidentally knocked over a book cart. Unfortunately, it was full," Anne said. She flipped on the History Room's light. The jumble of books sprawled across the floor was just as bad as she recalled. Maybe worse.

"Oh, my." Wendy nearly stepped on a book, sidestepped, then reached for it. "Is he settling in well at school? Christian is a year ahead of him, so they don't have recess together."

Anne pulled up the shelving cart and then knelt by the largest grouping on the floor. "He's really trying to fit in. It's hard for him, since he had so many close friends in New York."

"We'll just pray him through the adjustment period."

"Thanks." Anne smiled. "Becoming friends with Ryan has helped. And Christian inviting him over to play has helped too."

"What about Liddie? How's she settling in?"

"She's informed me she can outrun any boy in her kindergarten class."

Wendy chuckled. "So my Justin tells me. You'll have to keep an eye on that one. She's quite spirited."

Now it was Anne's turn to laugh. "That's a rather polite way of saying she's precocious."

Wendy only smiled as she carefully picked up the books and placed them on the cart. "Did Alex mention what time he'd be by to check out the measurements for the new doorframe?"

Alex Ochs. They'd been best friends even before they were high school sweethearts. But Alex had been so hurt when she'd left him after graduation to go to college that even when she'd returned to Blue Hill several months ago, he'd been somewhat reserved toward her.

She couldn't help that she'd met and fallen in love with her husband, Eric, when she'd been in college, no more than she could help when he'd died three years ago from a heart attack and she thought she'd never feel whole again. But now, tackling the renovation project seemed to have spurred her past the depression. She'd hired Alex as the contractor for the library renovations and being in his company on a regular basis had helped ease the coolness between them. Their friendship had finally been restored, and Anne was happy about it because she needed friends…now more than ever.

Anne reached for two books lying on top of each other. "He said he wouldn't have time to come by until tomorrow midmorning, which is okay. It'll give me time to get the kids off to school."

"I know the town is more than ready for you to finish and open," said Wendy.

"Once these last shelves are inventoried, I'll be able to open the doors at least. All the rooms won't be as complete as I'd like them to be, but the adult fiction, the children's, and this historical area should be ready." Excitement pulsed through her veins as she reached for another book. Aunt Edie's vision was within reach. "And Alex says he's almost done with the Blue Hill History Room. We're on schedule for the grand opening this weekend."

"I got the postcard announcement. You've made great progress." Wendy pulled the cart toward her just as Anne reached for it.

The book Anne held slipped from her fingers and thudded to the wood floor. "Guess this one is determined not to be shelved." Anne grabbed the spine and lifted the book.

A yellow piece of paper drifted from between the pages.

Oh, no. A page must have ripped out. It felt almost as if Anne's own heart had been injured. She opened the book's cover and tried to make out the name on the bookplate, but it had been partially torn off and most was missing. What little of the bookplate remained was very faded. All she could make out of the writing was *Isa,* then the large part was ripped out then *es.*

The yellowed page landed closer to Wendy. She picked it up off the floor. "What's this?" She wrinkled her nose as she perused the paper.

Anne carried the book to Wendy and looked over her shoulder as Wendy unfolded the yellowed paper. "A map?"

She turned the book in her hand to see the cover and read the title. "*The Journals of Lewis and Clark.*" After riffling through the first few pages, she found the copyright date: 1953.

Wendy handed her the yellowed map. "Looks like a state map. A very old one. With some writing on it."

Anne held the paper gingerly and studied it. "A map of Pennsylvania." It contained some scribbles, just in the corner. She couldn't make out the words, even though she squinted and pushed her glasses back to the bridge of her nose. However, she could make out the formal print: "By William Scull. 1775."

"That's from 1775?" asked Wendy.

"I'm no expert by any means, but by the brittleness of the paper, I'd say it could be an original, not a copy of a 1775 map."

Anne's heart thudded. She would need to take special care not to damage the document. And she'd have to get the map authenticated as well as appraised. There was so much to do…

"You know, when Chad and I moved to Blue Hill, the first person to befriend me was Coraline Watson. That woman loves to talk, especially about history."

"I've met her. She's sweet, but you're right, she does love to talk," said Anne.

"Among other things, Coraline told me all about Blue Hill's now defunct Historical Society. Evidently, at least one town ruckus originated there." Wendy sank to the arm of the leather chair.

"Ruckus?" Anne asked. "What kind of ruckus? Why?"

"According to Coraline, the society claimed to have an original state map that was the actual one used by Lewis and Clark at the start of their expedition."

"What happened to it?" Anne asked.

"The way the story goes, it was stolen from the society about a hundred years ago. But I don't know for sure," said Wendy.

Stolen?

"Knowing Coraline's penchant for details, I'm betting her story is pretty accurate."

Anne stared at the map. "Do you think this could be it? The stolen map?"

Wendy shrugged. "I don't know. You'd have to get an expert to validate its age, I guess, then go from there."

Anne nodded. How did it get into this book and onto Aunt Edie's shelves? What if it *was* the original state map that Lewis and Clark had used? Then this was an important piece of American history, and she would have to decide what to do.

But first, she had to find out if the map was real.

CHAPTER TWO

"Ben, if you don't hurry up, you're going to make us late for school." Anne took the empty juice glass from Liddie. "Go brush your teeth, sweetie."

"Yes, Mommy." Liddie skipped to the kitchen door.

"And please tell your brother to get a move on it," Anne said. She loaded the breakfast dishes into the dishwasher, set it to wash, and then wiped the counters. She stared at the bag of trash slumped by the kitchen door that waited to go into the outside bin. She glanced at the oven's clock. Maybe she should help Ben out just this once…

No, he'd never get in the habit if she kept letting him get away with sloughing off his chores. Now that summer was over, it was time for him to get back into a routine. Friday morning meant taking the trash out because pickup would be midmorning, and she had several errands to run to be ready for tomorrow's big day.

"Ben!" She turned around and nearly tripped over him.

"I'm right here, Mom." He slung his backpack over his shoulder. "I had to find my lucky pencil because I have my math test today." He lifted the trash bag. "I didn't forget I needed to take the trash down. I'll be right back."

Lucky pencil…just like his dad. Eric had been the same way, only his lucky charm had been a quarter, dated the year of their marriage. He'd taken it to every publishing board committee roundtable and important meeting since the day they'd married. He teased her that she was his good-luck charm, but since he couldn't slip her into his pocket, he'd make do with the quarter. Anne smiled at the memory.

The door slammed, jerking Anne's attention to Ben as he returned from outside. His frown seemed permanently etched into the softness of his face. She could understand, to a degree. Moving to a state where he had no friends and knew no one was hard on a nine-year-old. On the other hand, Ben hadn't exactly been trying to reach out and make new buddies. "Mom, we should get a dog," Ben challenged her from across the room.

Anne swallowed a sigh. "We've already had this discussion. I've already told you that your father was highly allergic to animal dander. Just walking by a pet store would stuff him up for days. You and Liddie are probably the same way. I'd hate for either of you to get attached to a pet, only for us to have to find a good home for it because you're allergic."

"We don't know if we even have the same allergies as Dad. We've never been tested," he said.

"Ben, being tested is very uncomfortable. Maybe when you're a little older, we can discuss it again," she said.

"But, Mom! A dog would be my best friend. He could sleep in my room, and I'd take care of him and everything." The pleading in his sweet eyes nearly had her nodding.

Liddie skipped back into the kitchen, catching the end of the conversation. "Ben's getting a dog? If he gets a dog, I want a kitten. A white one I can name Snowball."

Anne sighed. Now they'd both be constantly after her for a pet. She'd best nip this discussion in the bud right now. Anne shook her head. "Ben isn't getting a dog, and you aren't getting a cat." She kissed the top of Liddie's curls. "Head on out to the car, honey." She met Ben's sour look. "Wash your hands then hurry up. And don't forget your backpack."

Out in the car, she double-checked Liddie's seat belt, then started the engine and blew on her hands. The late September Pennsylvania air held much lower temperatures than just a week ago. She glanced at the trees, the leaves decorated in exquisite and beautiful shades of red and yellow. The air felt cleaner here. Even with the kids having to adjust, moving back to Blue Hill was the right decision, Anne knew. She'd come home. It was no longer Aunt Edie's house—it was hers and the kids'.

Ben slumped into the backseat alongside Liddie.

"Seat belt," Anne said. She slipped the car into reverse then backed out of the unattached garage.

His seat belt clicked, but his huff sounded louder. Anne opened her mouth to speak to him about his attitude—yet again.

Liddie's innocent voice split the silence first. "Jesus loves me," she sang, "this I know."

Anne swallowed her admonition to Ben and sang along with Liddie, but she eyed her son in the rearview mirror. She'd have to draw him out of his gloominess somehow.

But not with a dog.

Ben rode the rest of the way to school in his sullen silence and barely said good-bye when he broke free from the car once they'd pulled to a stop. Anne held Liddie an extra second when she hugged her.

After seeing the kids safely inside the building, Anne pulled away and headed toward Main Street to run her errands. She picked up the cookies and punch. At her next stop, the florist assured her he would have the centerpiece delivered before nine in the morning. She struggled against a heavy yawn as she slipped back behind the steering wheel again.

Leaves danced across the road as she turned down Bluebell Lane toward home. Anne unloaded the refreshments for tomorrow's grand opening. Then she headed back to the library's checkout area on the first floor. She had locked the map in the oversized desk drawer for safe keeping last night. With great care, she unlocked the drawer and, after slipping on a pair of latex gloves, she pulled out the map and ever so gently smoothed the paper on top of the desk. The creases where it had been folded for years, decades even, left blank patches in the map.

She grabbed a pen and paper and began to make notes about the map and the signature. She noted her observations of the markings and the crest and everything else she could think to document. Then she grabbed some acrylic sheets to protect the map before returning it to the reference desk's center drawer and locking it. At least it would be better protected lying flat and between archival-safe materials.

Once she was satisfied that the map was as safe as she could make it, she went to her personal desk and opened her laptop. With a few clicks, her favorite Internet browser loaded. She typed in the name *Scull*, along with the state and the year; then she clicked the search button. Seconds later, pages of results loaded. She clicked on the first one, which was a message board for antique maps.

Anne perused the site and found postings by many expert historians. She continued reading until she came across two specific posts about a Scull Pennsylvania state map dated the same year as the one she'd found. She read two posts from the message board members who claimed they each had such a map. Her pulse thrummed. If either of them owned the actual, authenticated map, then the one she found might simply be a copy.

She quickly posted private messages to the two members and clicked send.

The front bell rang, splitting the comforting silence. Anne nearly shot out of her skin. She jumped to her feet and turned to face the entry.

Alex grinned. "Hi, there. Open for business?" he asked.

She smiled back. "You startled me." She automatically smooth-ed her ponytail.

His smile widened. "I didn't mean to scare you. I told you I'd be by to check out the measurements for your new doorframe." He held up his measuring tape. "Must get everything cosmetic done today so it's beautiful for tomorrow's grand opening."

"I know, I know," she said.

"I thought you'd be busy decorating or something." He nodded at her computer. "Working hard already this morning?"

"Not really working, per se, but kinda." She pushed her glasses back to the bridge of her nose.

"Kinda working?" He stepped into the checkout area and peered over her shoulder. "How do you *kinda work*?" Humor tugged the corners of his mouth upward.

She welcomed his gentle teasing. When she'd first returned to Blue Hill, he'd been nothing but professional. Since they'd been working on the library renovations, though, little pieces of the old Alex had started to slip out every now and again. Anne liked that. It reminded her of their shared childhood friendship. She turned back toward the reference desk. "I've been doing some research. I have something I want to show you."

"Now you have me curious," Alex said. He set his tape measure on the front counter and followed her.

Anne carefully withdrew the map and removed the top piece of acrylic. "Look what Wendy and I found last night."

Letting out a low whistle, Alex leaned closer. "1775. Is this a copy?" he asked.

"I don't know yet," Anne said.

"Looks old, but you'd know more about this kind of thing I ever would."

Anne shrugged. "I was researching on the Internet when you came in. I need to take the map to an expert who will run tests to authenticate it. "

"And?" He straightened and met her gaze.

"I found a site of historians. There were two members who posted on the message boards that they have maps by William Scull dated 1775. I've sent them private messages. If either of them has had their maps authenticated, then this one might only be a copy," she said.

Alex's brows scrunched. "If both of them can have authenticated maps, why does this one have to be a copy? If there can be two, why not three?" he asked.

"As I understand it, only one can be the true map, but there might also be an authentic copy of the original. That's why I've contacted them to see if either of theirs has been authenticated as the original."

"So, this could be an authentic copy? Is that worth a lot of money?" Alex asked.

"The original would be worth probably upward of eight to ten thousand dollars. A copy..." She pressed her lips together and tried to remember the last article she'd read about values. She couldn't recall the specifics. "...I think a copy could run anywhere between fifty bucks to a couple of thousand, if I remember right."

Another whistle. "Where'd you find the map? In another of Aunt Edie's secret rooms?" His eyes lit up with the teasing.

"No, I found it in a book." She grabbed the book and passed it to him. "It was one of the books someone had donated to the library before I even moved in."

"Isn't there a listing of all the donors?" Alex asked.

There was, because she was having a plaque made with all their names engraved. "I left it for safekeeping with the law firm who handles Aunt Edie's estate until we got the house restored. I want to write personal thank-you notes once things are up and running," said Anne.

"Maybe you should ask someone there to look at the list and see who donated the book. Maybe they'll know something."

She nodded. "I'd love to find out more about the map and see if it's even worth the price to have an expert look at it." She took off her glasses, wiped them with the bottom of her shirt, and shoved them back on. "Wendy said Coraline Watson told her about a similar map that the Blue Hill Historical Society once had."

"I'm listening." He pulled out one of the chairs and sat.

Anne replaced the acrylic over the map and returned it to the drawer as she told him what Wendy had explained to her last night. She plopped onto a chair opposite Alex. "So, I don't know what to think," she ended.

"I don't recall hearing anything about a map being stolen. Then again, my mother was never active in the historical society," he said.

Anne held her tongue. Alex's parents worked with a program that trained missionaries, and they were often out of town. Even when Alex was a child, his parents were out of town at least two weeks out of every month. His mother had never been around enough to belong to historical societies, garden clubs, or even the church's ladies guild, but she had been busy helping make a difference out in the world for God's honor.

Alex cleared his throat. "Is it possible that this could be the allegedly stolen map?"

She shrugged. "It could be. I wish I could find out if the rumor is true. Maybe find out more details."

Alex rubbed his chin. "Why don't you check with the paper?" he suggested.

"The *Blue Hill Gazette*?" Anne asked.

"They've been publishing every week since before the historical society was formed," said Alex. "Seems to me if a map had been stolen, there'd have been a big write-up about it."

Very true. Blue Hill wasn't a metropolis where news of a theft at a historical society would be buried in the back of a society page, if reported at all. This was a charming small town known for its wholesome and close-knit community. A theft at the historical society would most likely be front-page news.

She nodded. "You're right."

"Grace would probably be thrilled to help you again," he said, referring to the *Gazette*'s editor, Grace Hawkins.

Excitement churned inside Anne. "Thanks. I'll do that."

Alex stood, pushing his chair back to its original place. "After we get the new doorway ready, I'll only need to finish up the trim work in the History Room."

A tingle started at her toes and worked up to her forehead. She saw the room in her mind—sunset colors and sepia photographs of the town's rich railroad history hanging on the walls. She'd paid top dollar to have the pictures made from damaged negatives. She had already planned a number of historical exhibits to be prominently displayed, and she already had a number of items ready to showcase that depicted the history of Blue Hill as well as Aunt Edie's house.

Alex nudged her. "In your head, you're inside the History Room, aren't you?" His gentle tone matched his soft smile.

"I am, but I'm also very curious about the mystery of the map."

Alex shook his head, his grin widening. "Just remember that curiosity killed the cat."

"Perhaps, but I'm determined to figure it out," she said.

"I know you will, Anne. There's no doubt in my mind."

Based on his smile, she couldn't tell if he was teasing her or not. It didn't matter. She'd find out the map's history. Digging through records and reconstructing history was one of her most favorite things.

She had a feeling this mystery would not disappoint.

Chapter Three

Early afternoon sun snuck through the branches of the live oaks lining Main Street and flickered against the cracked sidewalks. The *Blue Hill Gazette* was housed in picturesque Victorian architecture, as were many of the other businesses that lined the street. Less than four steps from the curb, the two-story, red-paint dwelling had a quaint porch covering the first floor, with a triangular gable just above the front door.

Anne pushed open the door. A bell rang overhead. The tinkling sound added a certain charm. She smiled to herself as she shifted her folder and purse to her other arm.

"Hi, there. Can I help you?" A bright-eyed girl behind the counter wore a smile as wide as Main Street. Her ponytail swayed as she moved.

Anne felt much older than her thirty-four years in the presence of the cute girl. "I'm here to see Grace, if she's available."

"Sure, she's here. Follow me." The girl led Anne behind the counter to a room without a door, only an arched entry.

As they entered the editor's office, Grace looked up from behind her desk, a smile already formed. The faint aroma of bacon, remnants of a recent lunch eaten in-office, filled the air.

"This lady's here to see you, Grace." With a bob of her ponytail, the girl was gone.

Grace stood and offered her hand. "Nice to see you again, Anne. What can I do for you?" she asked.

Anne shook Grace's hand as she gave another silent appraisal of the young woman. She had to be in her late twenties, maybe early thirties at most, with blonde hair, blue eyes, and skin so flawless and pale it almost looked translucent.

Anne took a seat in one of the overstuffed chairs in front of Grace's desk. The well-worn tapestry cover of the chair was soft to the touch and smushed around Anne quite comfortably.

"Alex said the library's renovations are coming along well," Grace said. "He just finished adding on a craft room to the back of my house." Grace's blue eyes twinkled. "He says the library is turning out to be beautiful."

"It is. We're almost to the final phase of the renovations. The grand opening is tomorrow," Anne said.

Grace nodded. "I'll be covering the opening for the paper. The citizens of Blue Hill are really excited to have a library. We've sorely needed one."

Grace's warmth nearly bowled Anne over. She was one of those people others were drawn to. "Thank you," said Anne.

Grace interlocked her fingers, resting her chin on her hands.

Anne shifted in her seat. "Alex actually suggested I talk to you."

"Why is that?" Grace said, dropping her hands to the desk and sitting back in her chair.

"I'm doing some research on the Blue Hill Historical Society. I'm interested in old *Gazette* articles."

"What about the society are you looking for?" Grace asked.

"Everything and anything that ran in the paper."

"From when to when?"

Anne opened her folder and scanned the notes she'd taken this morning following her online research. "Starting in 1912, when the society was formed, until it ended."

Grace's eyes widened. "Wow, that will likely be a good number of articles. Are you looking for anything specific?"

She didn't want everyone in town to know about the map, especially the local newspaper editor—at least not until she could figure out the map's history. "No, nothing specific," Anne said.

"Well, you're going to be wading through lots of microfiche." Grace stood and motioned for Anne to join her down the hall. "The early articles will be easier to find because we've had all editions through 1925 archived under a topical index."

She led Anne into a large room, complete with two microfiche machines and storage. Stopping in front of a shelf with large binders, she tapped the spine. "The years we have covered are noted here." She pulled out one of the binders and opened to the front page. "Each month has its own page, with the four issues broken down into headline, byline, and a one-sentence summary of each article. The microfiche reels are labeled by year and month."

"Thanks, Grace. This is really helpful," said Anne. At least the article about the formation of the historical society should already be indexed. Maybe the map was stolen before 1925, so it would be indexed as well.

Grace smiled. "I'm sure as a librarian you know how to use a microfiche machine and make copies."

"I do." Anne returned the smile.

Grace snapped her fingers then clapped her hands in rapid succession. "Well, I'd better get back to work. Let me know if you need anything else."

"I will. Thanks." Anne slipped her purse onto one of the chairs next to the microfiche reader and set her folder on the table.

Grace let her gaze drift over the room before giving Anne a final nod and heading back down the hall.

Letting out a slow breath, Anne grabbed the binder for 1912. She quickly found the month the society was formed — August — and pulled out that microfiche. Moments later, she found the article that announced not only the formation of the society but also detailed their most prized acquisition: a 1775 Pennsylvania state map by William Scull. A picture ran alongside the article.

Anne set the machine to print copies. Then she continued to the next article she had noted — February 1913, which detailed the missing map. She flipped to the article's headline: *Alfred Rhodes Accused of Stealing Historical Society Prize.* Anne pushed her glasses back up her nose and continued reading:

> *The Blue Hill Historical Society has reported their prized exhibit, a 1775 Pennsylvania state map by acclaimed cartographer William Scull, has been stolen. Unnamed sources close to the police investigation report Alfred Rhodes is the only suspect in the case so far.*

Wow. This was quite a scandal for the small town of Blue Hill.

Anne's cell phone vibrated. She reached for it from the outer pocket of her purse. She turned off the alarm and double-checked the time. Could it really be time to pick up the kids from school?

She set the machine to make copies of the article, then gathered her belongings. She'd have to come back later when she had more time. But what she had was a great start. Her mind kept running through scenarios. If Alfred Rhodes was publicly accused of stealing the map, had he been charged with the crime? Arrested? Once she had the kids settled in and doing their homework, she'd be able to really study the article instead of doing a quick skim.

After collecting her copies, shutting off the machine, and putting the area back as she found it, Anne rushed down the hall. When her kids expected her to pick them up from school, she liked to be there a good ten to fifteen minutes early so they would see her waiting for them when they came out of the building.

"Did you find everything you needed?" Grace smiled from her doorway.

Anne paused in her trek out the door. "I found a great beginning. I have to pick up my kids, but I'll come back again soon if that's okay."

"Sure. And if you give me a call before you head this way, we can have a cup of coffee." Grace's smile was contagious.

"I'd like that," Anne said. "Oh, I made some copies. How much do I owe you per copy?"

"We charge five cents for black-and-white, eight for color. If you're going to be working for a couple of days, just keep a running total and settle up when you're done," said Grace.

"Thanks," Anne replied. "I'll see you tomorrow at the grand opening."

She pushed open the front door. Sunlight flooded in. Anne blinked, only seeing dots. She took a step and ran right into someone. Anne's purse, notebook, and microfiche copies spilled onto the porch.

"I'm so sorry. Are you okay?" Anne reached out and steadied the woman she'd almost knocked to the ground. "I was in a hurry and didn't see you."

"I'm fine." The slender woman looked vaguely familiar to Anne, but she couldn't quite place her. "Anne? Anne Summers?" the woman asked.

"It's Anne Gibson now." Anne peered into the woman's small, round eyes and suddenly recognition hit her. "I went to school with you, didn't I?"

"Megan Rhodes. I was a few years ahead of you in school. You were always really nice to me."

"Oh, yes. I remember you now." Anne smiled. "How are you?"

"Good. I'd heard you were moving back to town. For the library, right?"

"Yes. The grand opening is tomorrow. I hope you'll come," said Anne.

Megan nodded. "I got the announcement in the mail. I plan to attend."

A breeze danced one of Anne's microfiche copies across the porch.

Anne darted for it.

"Let me help." Megan reached and grabbed one of the other copies from the porch.

Anne gathered the rest and stuffed them in her folder. "Thanks. I should've put them in the binder to begin with, but I'm rushing to pick up my kids from school."

"I understand." Megan straightened as well.

"Thanks." She held out her hand for the copy Megan had. "I guess I'll see you tomorrow."

Megan's gaze went to the copy for a moment; she held it out then slowly pulled it back. Her eyes widened as she read. "Why do you have this?" she asked.

"I'm doing some research on the historical society." Anne still held out her hand as she waited for the copy.

"You aren't looking into the theft of that stupid map, are you?"

Anne shook her head. "I'm researching the historical society."

Megan frowned. "It's ridiculous." Her stare almost went through Anne. "Why are you dragging all this up again?"

Anne grabbed the copy from Megan, the copy about the map being stolen. "Dragging *what* up again?"

"Accusations that smear the Rhodes name."

Anne pushed her glasses back up the bridge of her nose. "I'm not smearing anyone's name. I'm just researching."

Megan's scowl deepened. "Researching my great-grandfather's alleged involvement in that stupid map theft?"

Long-forgotten high school memories washed over Anne. Megan had tried so hard to be popular and do the right thing, but her family's reputation wasn't the best. For several generations, the Rhodes family had been in and out of legal trouble. The black mark covered the entire family name, including Megan, who, as far as Anne could remember, had never gotten into trouble once in her life — not even a referral to the principal's office. But many people didn't like Megan, simply because of her last name. One time, Anne recalled, Megan tried out for the spirit squad. Many of the kids whispered about her and virtually shunned her. And Megan hadn't made the spirit squad. Anne had felt sorry for her then and worked hard to be extra nice to her.

Looking at the paleness of Megan's face, Anne felt sorry for her now too.

"My great-grandfather was accused of stealing that stupid map," said Megan. "And my grandfather was accused of embezzling town funds. Yet neither of them had any proof against them, mind you, which is why neither was ever charged. But do you think the people in this town cared about that? Cared about the truth?" She shook her head, her hands trembling. "I finally have a chance to put all that behind me and find some happiness, and here you are, about to dredge it all back up again."

"No, I'm not," Anne insisted. At least, that wasn't her intent. "I'm just looking into past history because of something I found in one of the books someone donated to the library." Anne laid a hand on Megan's arm. "I would never intentionally set out to hurt someone."

"I know you always tried to be nice to me." Tears filled Megan's big brown eyes. "It's just that I'm engaged to someone now who isn't from Blue Hill. He hasn't heard all the nasty rumors, so he doesn't think my family is bad news." She sniffed. "Even marrying the first time didn't help erase the black mark on my family's name that has stuck with me."

How awful, Anne thought. "I'm so sorry, Megan. I remember how mean some people were," said Anne.

"When I lost Peter, I thought happiness was beyond my reach. But now, with Mark...well, I think I can help the people of Blue Hill see that the Rhodes aren't bad people. We just need the chance to do something good." A wrinkle of pain settled on Megan's forehead identical to what Anne sometimes noticed in her own mirror.

Anne reached out to squeeze Megan's shoulder. "You lost your husband? I'm so sorry. I'm a widow too."

"I heard that. I'm sorry. At least you have children." Megan's face sagged. "Peter and I tried, but it wasn't meant to be. He was a fireman and died in a fire three years ago."

"I'm so sorry," Anne said. She remembered how painful it could be, so she opted to change the subject. "Mark is your fiancé?"

Megan smiled and passed a photo from her own notebook. "Our announcement photo for the paper."

"Beautiful couple." Anne handed the photo back to her. She couldn't imagine marrying again. She loved Eric and knew that he'd want her to move on, but she couldn't see that. Not yet.

"I'm sorry for jumping to the conclusion that you were trying to dredge up all the old history. Every year or so, some reporter or tourist gets wind of the old story and looks it up." There was no mistaking the humiliation lurking in Megan's eyes. "Seems I never get a chance to prove to the townies that the Rhodes family aren't bad people."

Anne shook her head. "I'm not here to do that. I promise."

"Thank you." Megan smiled. "I'd better let you get out of here and get your kids."

"I'll see you tomorrow." Anne watched Megan step into the *Blue Hill Gazette*, the little bell ringing in welcome. She'd told Megan she wouldn't bring up the accusations against her great-grandfather in relation to the map, but what if she couldn't keep that promise?

What if the map she found proved to be authentic—and the one stolen from the historical society? And what if she found proof that Alfred Rhodes *had* stolen the map?

Could she still keep her promise?

Chapter Four

"Look how high I can swing, Mommy!" Liddie pumped her little legs.

"Ooh, don't go so high, Liddie-girl. You might scare me." Anne grinned at her daughter.

The afternoon sun shone over the Blue Hill Park. Families played, some even serving up early picnic dinners.

Ben shook his head and climbed the monkey bars. At the top, he slowly stood. "Check me out, Mom." He carefully walked down one side of the bars, then back up to the middle. "I'm amazing, right?"

Anne chuckled. "Yes, you're amazing," she said.

Liddie jumped off the swing and ran up to her. "Am I 'mazing, Mommy?"

Gathering her daughter into her arms, Anne inhaled deeply. Liddie smelled like sunshine and recess.

She'd been so busy with the library's renovations and the grand opening, she didn't want the kids to feel like they had to vie for her attention. And time. Anne released Liddie, who promptly sat on the grass and began running her fingers through the clover. Every few days, Anne had stopped by the park on their way home and let the kids play and have her undivided attention. It seemed to do them all a world of good.

Anne was determined to keep a close relationship with her children. Especially when she considered the group of truant boys she'd found hanging out last week at the old abandoned tree house at the bottom of Blue Hill.

She had discovered the gang of five boys, all around Ben's age or a little older, down at the tree house during school hours. She'd stopped a couple of times to see if she could recognize any of them, but they scattered as soon as she got close. One thing she had noticed when she stood under the tree house: it reeked of cigarette smoke.

She couldn't believe boys that young were smoking. She'd do her best to keep Ben and Liddie away from negative influences, but she couldn't help wondering who those boys were. Their parents must be worried sick if they'd gotten calls that their sons skipped school.

Right then, Ben jumped down from the monkey bars and ran over. "I keep forgetting to put my baseball glove in the car so I have it when we come to the park." He glanced over at a team of boys playing T-ball nearby.

Anne followed his gaze, and her stomach muscles tightened. Could they be the boys from the tree house? "I can always play catch with you, you know," she said.

Her son frowned. "You're a girl."

Anne laughed. "That doesn't mean I can't play catch."

Before Ben could reply, a boy of about twelve walked by leading a dog on a leash. Ben's gaze followed them down the path.

Anne helped Liddie up and dusted her off. "Come on, it's time for us to head home."

They loaded into the car and drove the short distance to the house.

"I ordered pizza for dinner because we have a lot to do tonight." Anne smiled at her children as they entered through the library's front entrance. "Who wants to help decorate for the grand opening tomorrow?"

Liddie hopped about. "I do, Mommy. Me, me, me!"

Anne chuckled and stared at her son. "How about you, Ben?" He'd been a little less sullen on the ride home from the park. He even told her he'd scored a goal in the soccer game during PE class. She'd whispered a quiet prayer of thanks for small steps in the right direction—as long as he stayed clear of those boys who skipped school and smoked.

He shrugged. "I guess I can help you. Until the pizza gets here."

"It should be delivered in an hour or so, so we have time." She pinched her lips together and nodded. If she made too big a deal out of his participation, he'd withdraw again. "The florist will deliver the centerpiece for the sign-up table and refreshment table tomorrow, but we can put out the tablecloth and plates and napkins tonight."

The side of Ben's lip drooped. "That's girl stuff, Mom."

"Well, if you help me with the tablecloth, then you and I can work on the book displays while Liddie sets out the plates and napkins."

He sighed but nodded his agreement. A lot of his seriousness of late was his determination to be the man of the house now. It seemed to Anne that since moving to Blue Hill,

Ben had taken on the weight of watching out for Liddie. And for Anne herself. It nearly broke her heart to see him shoulder that burden, yet she didn't quite know how to get him to ease up on himself without hurting his feelings or making him feel unappreciated.

"I guess I can help you with the displays," said Ben.

"Or you can set up the sign-up table for the people to fill out the library cards." She paused for effect. "But you'd have to move the chairs around the table, and those are pretty heavy."

"I can lift them." Ben's chest poked out a little.

Anne swallowed her smile. "Well then, that's why I need your help."

He nodded. "Okay."

She led Ben and Liddie to the kitchen in the back of the library, right off the checkout area. Having already gotten the tablecloth washed, dried, and pressed, she grabbed it and held it to her chest for just a moment.

The tablecloth was white damask linen with beautiful embroidered lace patterns along the edge. Anne remembered it from her childhood. Aunt Edie had covered the old dining room table every Thanksgiving, Christmas, and Easter with the tablecloth. Anne ran her finger along the lace embroidery as memories washed over her. Laughing with Aunt Edie. Sharing great family recipes. Talking about books.

"Mom, I want to play outside before dinner." Ben stood at the other end of the table, waiting to help with the tablecloth.

Anne shook her head to bring herself back to the present. "I'm sorry," she said to Ben. "I was thinking about all the fun times I had with Aunt Edie." She snapped the tablecloth, letting it flare across the table.

Ben caught the other end and together they smoothed it down over the old oak tabletop.

"Do you miss her, Mommy?" Liddie's innocent question tightened Anne's throat as she opened a pack of plastic plates.

She never wanted to diminish the importance of grief in the healing process, but she also wanted to let her children know that, as time passes, so does much of the pain. "I do, honey, but not in the way that makes me really sad. I spent a lot of time here with Aunt Edie, and I have so many wonderful memories that I welcome remembering my childhood."

"Like when we remember Daddy, it makes me and Ben happy, right? Because he was the funniest guy you ever met." Liddie's face lit up as if she'd just gotten a pony for Christmas—not that she even remembered Eric.

Anne smiled. "Yes, just like that, honey." She handed Liddie the plastic plates. "While Ben and I set up the book display in the checkout area, why don't you set these out and the napkins, in a pretty design like we did for your birthday party?"

Liddie bobbed her head, the overhead light catching the hints of blonde in her light brown hair. "I'll make it pretty, Mommy."

Anne motioned for Ben to join her in the next room. She'd set out several books she wanted to display: a nonfiction account of Blue Hill's roots in the rich railroad history, the latest children's Newbery award winner, the top two novels on the *New York Times'* bestseller list, the hottest new cookbook, and the newly released biography of the current US President.

"Where is the table?" asked Ben.

She tipped her head toward the six-foot table she'd had Alex help her bring into the checkout area. It leaned against the wall. "I'll need a little help setting it up."

"I can help." Ben reached for the end of the table. Together, they unfolded the legs and locked them in place, then set the table upright.

"I have another tablecloth for this table too," Anne said. She turned to reach for the cloth she'd set on the desk.

"But, Mom…"

"Just help me, Ben." She snapped the cloth to open it, and he helped smooth it in place over the folding table. "Now, bring in three chairs from the supply closet to go on that side of the table while I set up the book display."

Ben hurried from the room, and she turned to the counter. If she'd had time to get the map looked at, she would've known whether to insure and protect it or simply to have it framed and put out for display purposes. But she hadn't. With a sigh, she began arranging the display. She'd just finished setting up the children's book display on the primary-colored block book holder when Ben huffed into the room, carrying one of the sturdy wooden chairs. Anne had to press her lips together to keep from offering to help. Whether she liked it or not, her son was growing up.

He sat the chair carefully in the center, then raced toward the closet. Anne arranged the two best-selling novels on the red, satin scarf she'd swirled along the countertop for the fiction display. Ben placed the second chair as she finished standing the cookbook on end beside the wooden spoon and wire whisk.

As Ben went for the third and final chair, Anne propped the president's biography against the standing United States map she had picked up on sale at the local flea market. She'd just finished arranging the Blue Hill book among the town historical artifacts she'd found when Ben returned and placed the chair alongside the other two.

"Mom, I still think we need a dog. I could take care of it. I'd feed it and give it water and take it on walks and play with it and brush it and—"

"Ben, we aren't getting a dog, and that's final. I've explained this already."

"But Mom, I don't mind getting tested for allergies." His eyes widened with an innocence found only in children.

The memory of his last bout of vaccine boosters rushed through her mind. He'd almost hyperventilated at the size of the needle for the tetanus shot, and that was just last year.

"I told you we would discuss it when you are a little older."

His frown deepened, as if cutting permanent grooves on either side of his mouth.

"Besides, we're just getting the library up and open. Where on earth would we keep a dog? We couldn't just let one run around the library."

"We could use the back porch as a run during the day when I'm at school, and I'd take him for walks before and after school, and he could stay on the third floor with us, not even coming near the books," said Ben.

He was so intent and had clearly given the matter a lot of thought, but that didn't change the fact that she just couldn't take on another responsibility right now. "I'm sorry, son. The answer is still no, but I appreciate all the energy you put into thinking things over," Anne said.

His bottom lip quivered and, for a moment, Anne caught a glimpse of the sunny toddler Ben had been. In a split second, he stiffened his lip, squared his shoulders, and narrowed his eyes. "Is it okay if I go outside to play now?" he asked.

Anne desperately wanted her sunny boy back and knew a dog would go a long way toward achieving that goal. But for now anyway, she had to remain firm in her decision. She let out a long breath. "Sure. Just stay where you can hear me call you when the pizza is delivered."

He ran outside without replying. What was she going to do with this surly child who had once been the sweetest of boys?

"Mommy, come look at my napkins," Liddie said. "I made them all pretty."

Anne would figure out a way to reach Ben. Later. She smiled at Liddie and held out her hand. "Show me. I can't wait to see."

Several napkins sat wadded into tight balls. The rest were splayed beside the fanned plastic plates. She could easily straighten those.

"See, Mommy, I made flowers," said Liddie.

So that's what the wads were. "They're very lovely, Liddie." Anne tapped a finger against her pursed lips. "They're so pretty, I don't know if I want to share them with everyone else." She squatted beside her daughter. "Do you think it'd be okay if I took all these pretty flowers to my room so I can enjoy them all?"

Liddie's face lit up. "I can make you more, Mommy. I can make you as many as you want."

"No, baby. These are perfect. Can you run them to my room and lay them on the table beside my bed? That way they'll be the first thing I see every morning when I wake up and the last thing I look at after I say my prayers and go to sleep."

"Of course, Mommy." Liddie grinned as she scooped up the wadded napkins and raced to the stairs.

Anne straightened the napkins, then she moved to the sign-up table in the checkout area. After setting out the copies of the library floor plan, she placed the beautiful, Victorian-style library patron sign-up cards she'd had printed in neat stacks in front of the three chairs. Even in this day and technological age, Anne loved having the paper forms with a line for real signatures. It just made everything feel more in keeping with the style and tone of the library itself and the town of Blue Hill. She also believed that handwritten cards were simply more beautiful and portrayed Aunt Edie's gracious legacy.

Bam! Bam! Bam!

Anne jumped as Liddie jumped down the last step of the stairs. "Someone's here, Mommy."

"Probably the pizza delivery." Anne grabbed her wallet and headed to the front door. Sure enough, the delivery girl smiled back at her. Anne paid for the pizza, including a tip for the girl, and set the pizza box on the entryway table.

"Ben! Dinner!" Anne called out. She grabbed the pizza and smiled at Liddie. "Come on, let's go get the table set."

Once in their second-floor personal kitchen, Anne instructed Liddie to go wash her hands. While her daughter scampered to the bathroom, Anne pulled paper plates from the cabinet and set them on the kitchen table, then filled glasses with milk.

Liddie returned with a burst of the energy she never seemed to run out of. "Where's Ben?"

Anne had called him a good ten minutes ago. What could be keeping him? She opened the back door and yelled, "Ben!"

When she didn't hear a response, she stepped outside, onto the landing of the staircase leading to their personal entrance. "Time for dinner. Now!"

"Is he lost?" Liddie's big brown eyes widened.

"No, he just went farther than he should have." She turned back to the open door and raised her voice as loud as she could. "Ben!"

"Want me to go find him?" Liddie bounced from her chair.

"No, I do not." She stepped back inside and shut the door behind her. "I want you to get the forks and ranch dressing and put them on the table while I get the salad." If Ben didn't come back by the time she finished setting everything out, she'd have to go find him.

Why hadn't he listened to her? She'd told him she'd ordered pizza and not to go too far. Was it possible he'd met up with those boys at the tree house? Fear spread through her chest.

What was she going to do with him? In the last three years since Eric died, she'd managed as a single parent. Lately, however, Ben's attitude seemed to make the task of parenting more daunting than ever before.

The door downstairs slammed, followed by clomping.

Anne pressed her lips together as she pulled the tossed salad from the refrigerator. She'd told Ben multiple times to use their personal entrance instead of the library's. If he tracked in dirt after she'd spent the better part of the weekend cleaning, he'd be down there scrubbing that floor himself. Until it shone.

"Hey, Mom. I'll go wash my hands." Ben traipsed toward the bathroom.

"Where were you? I called you several times." Anne set the salad bowl in the center of the kitchen table.

The water's splashing was her only response.

Liddie set the bottle of ranch beside the salad bowl then scooted into her chair. "Can I pray, Mommy?" she asked.

Anne smiled and took her seat. "Sure, honey. Just wait for your brother."

Moments later, Ben took his seat across the table from Liddie, who bowed her head. "God is great, God is good. Let us thank Him for our food. By His hand, we all are fed. Give us, Lord, our daily bread. Amen."

"Amen." Anne lifted her head. "Thanks, Liddie. That was very nice." She used the plastic tongs to serve each of them a helping of salad.

The kids coated their salad in ranch dressing while Anne put a slice of pepperoni pizza on each of their plates. They ate in silence for a moment before Anne took a sip of milk and stared at Ben. "Where were you earlier? I called you twice and you didn't come."

"Sorry." He swiped his mouth with the back of his hand.

Anne automatically handed him his napkin.

"I was just playing down the hill," he said.

"And you didn't hear me calling?" Anne asked.

Ben shook his head. "As soon as I heard you, I came."

She nodded. "Next time, just stay closer to home so you can hear."

"Okay, Mom," he said.

"Mommy, what time does the library open in the morning?" Liddie scooped a big bite of salad coated in ranch dressing into her mouth.

"Ten. The florist should be here by nine," said Anne. Excitement circled her chest, filling her with warmth. At long last, Aunt Edie's vision would become a reality.

"I'm gonna wear my pink dress tomorrow."

"Don't talk with your mouth full, Liddie." But Anne couldn't stop the smile. "I think you'll look very pretty in your pink dress. I'm going to wear a dress as well." She faced Ben. "Do I need to iron some pants for you?"

Ben wrinkled his nose. "Can't I just wear jeans?"

"No, not for the grand opening." Anne cut a tomato wedge in half. "I want us all to look nice."

Ben sighed but made no further argument. For the rest of dinner, Liddie kept the conversation alive as she rambled on about school, dresses, and the grand opening. "...and all my friends will love my room."

Anne shook her head. "Liddie, I've told you before, people aren't allowed to come up into our private living areas. They have to stay down in the library sections." She reached over and grabbed her daughter's hand. "You may not invite anyone up here tomorrow, okay?"

Liddie nodded but said, "I know, Mommy. Only my friends can come visit."

"No, Liddie. Not even your friends. No one but me and you and Ben are to be up here tomorrow. Do you understand?" Anne said.

Her little head bobbed up and down, her sweet little-girl curls bouncing.

"I'm serious, Liddie. No one up here. Period." She turned to Ben. "Okay?"

He shrugged and frowned. "Who would I invite?" He slurped down the rest of his milk and swiped his sleeve across his mouth. "I'm done. May I be excused?"

Anne glanced at his plate. He'd only eaten half of his piece of pizza and probably no more than a bite of his salad. "Is that all you're going to eat?" she asked.

"I'm not hungry," said Ben.

"Okay." Maybe he'd eaten a big lunch at school. "Rinse out your glass and throw away your plate."

Ben jumped up. "Can I go outside for just a little while before bedtime?" He set his glass in the sink and turned on the water.

She glanced out the window. What if he had found those boys? "It'll be dark soon."

"Please? Just for a few minutes?" Ben asked. He flashed her one of his rare grins. "I promise to be back before it gets dark."

Anne couldn't resist his smile, so much like Eric's. "Okay, but you'd better be back in this house before it's dark," she said. And he'd better not come home smelling like smoke.

"Thanks." He raced across the room and opened the door, still holding his plate.

"Throw away your trash," she said.

"I'll put it in the can downstairs." He shut the door behind him.

"Can I go outside too, Mommy?" Liddie asked.

Anne shook her head. "You, my sweet, get to take a bubble bath!"

Within an hour, both kids were tucked into bed: bathed, teeth brushed, hair combed, and prayers said. Although she had a big day tomorrow, Anne couldn't get the map out of her mind.

She made herself a nice cup of tea, then went to the desk in the library's checkout area. She donned a pair of latex gloves and pulled the map from the center drawer of the reference desk, carefully smoothing it out from between the sheets of acrylic protection. She grabbed the copies of the articles and photo she'd made at the newspaper and laid the photo of the map beside the map she had.

She cleaned her glasses and slipped them back up the bridge of her nose. She settled on the stool as she compared the photo to the map. The name and date in the corner looked the same. The crest and markings...well, those were a little difficult to make out in the photo, so it was hard to tell if they looked the same. They *were* in the same place on the map. That probably counted for something, right?

She continued to compare, but the copy of the photo wasn't crisp, and the map certainly was blurred and aged.

Sighing, Anne squared her shoulders and rotated her head slowly until her neck popped. She took a sip of her tea, still staring at the map.

What's your story? She knew Meriwether Lewis had been selected as the commander of the expedition across the newly purchased Louisiana Territory in 1803, but he and Clark didn't actually begin their expedition until 1804. Could this have been one of the maps they'd carried along with them on their trip?

She might not know right now, but one thing was certain — she aimed to find out.

Chapter Five

The late September morning dawned clear, bright, and beautiful over Blue Hill. Anne smiled at the beams of sunshine sneaking past the curtain in her bedroom window. A perfect day for the library's grand opening. She glanced at the clock. Only five more minutes remained before her alarm would sound and she'd be up and in the shower.

She rolled onto her back and stared at the ceiling. Would Aunt Edie have been pleased with the way the library turned out? Was it what she envisioned? Anne snuggled her quilt under her chin and sent up a silent prayer that the townspeople would show up for the grand opening.

The alarm clock's buzzing filled the air and bit at Anne's ears.

She switched off the alarm and tossed back the covers. As soon as her feet hit the cold wood floors, a shiver slithered down her spine. She raced to the bathroom and hopped into the shower. Fifteen minutes later, Anne quickly dressed in a classic black sweater dress with comfortable flats. She pulled her hair back into a loose chignon, applied makeup with a light touch and then slipped on her glasses. She debated wearing contacts today but decided she didn't really want the hassle. She chuckled as she checked her appearance in the mirror. A bun. After all, she *was* the town librarian.

God, please let today be successful. Not just for my sake, and the sake of the library, but for Ben and Liddie too.

"Mommy, I got dressed by myself." Liddie stood in the doorway, wearing her frilly pink dress. Her white tights bagged at her ankles.

"You sure did, honey. But maybe you should eat breakfast before you get all prettied up. You don't want to ruin your dress with syrup, do you?"

Liddie's eyes went wide. "Syrup? That means you're making waffles or pancakes."

"We're having waffles for breakfast." It didn't matter to Liddie if the waffles came fresh from an iron or from the freezer to the toaster. Today definitely called for the frozen variety. "Tell your brother to get a move on, then change your clothes. I'll help you dress for the grand opening after breakfast."

Liddie ran down the hall. "Ben! Waffles. Mommy says to get a move on!"

Grinning, Anne headed to the kitchen. She tied on an apron and pushed the button to start the coffee brewing. Then she pulled a box of ready-made waffles out of the freezer. After gathering the butter and syrup and dropping the first set of waffles into the toaster, Anne filled her coffee cup. She'd barely gotten a sip down when Liddie bounded into the kitchen, this time wearing her pajamas. Wrong side out.

"I beated Ben, so I get the first waffle." Precious Liddie all but danced around the kitchen in her Sleeping Beauty fuzzy slippers.

"You sure do," said Anne. "And it's 'I beat Ben,' not 'I beated Ben,' honey. *Beated* isn't a word." Anne glanced out the kitchen window as she poured two glasses of milk.

The sun climbed across the clear sky, leaving tails of brightness in its wake. It was a perfect day for the opening.

The toaster popped up the two waffles. Anne coated them in butter and syrup, then set the plate in front of her daughter alongside a glass of milk.

Liddie bowed her head and offered up her rote mealtime prayer.

"Give us, Lord, our daily bread," Anne finished, then placed a kiss atop Liddie's soft waves. She popped two more waffles into the toaster. "Ben! Your waffles are almost ready."

She stole another sip of coffee, and the hot French roast spread warmth all the way down. She enjoyed her coffee black, just like Aunt Edie always had. As a matter of fact, it had been her aunt who'd given Anne her first taste of coffee at thirteen. She'd made two cups early one Sunday morning before church and slid one across the table to Anne. *If you're of the age of accountability and able to profess Jesus as your Lord, then you're old enough for a cup of java,* she'd said. At first, Anne hadn't enjoyed the rich, bold flavor, but she'd drunk the whole thing because it felt like a rite of passage with Aunt Edie.

The waffles popped up, the toaster making a loud springing noise.

Anne sloshed coffee from her cup. She wiped up the spilled coffee as she chided herself for being so lost in the past when today was a busy day. "Ben! Your waffles are ready," she called out.

She fixed his plate and set it on the table beside Liddie's place, then she set the milk on the edge of the placemat. "What's keeping your brother?" she asked.

Liddie shrugged as she stuffed another bite into her mouth.

Heading down the hall, Anne called Ben again.

No response.

She pushed open the door to Ben's bedroom. "Ben?"

He wasn't there. Nor was his bed made. His slacks and jacket lay across the desk chair, where she'd set them yesterday.

Her heartbeat kicked up a notch. No, she wouldn't panic. Not yet. But her pace quickened to match the pace of her racing heart as she headed to the bathroom.

The door stood wide open. There was no sign of her son.

Anne's heart shot to her throat, holding her breath hostage. *Calm down. Think. Where could he be?*

That was the problem; she didn't have a clue. The only thought that raced through her mind was the group of boys down at the old tree house. She clasped her hands together as she headed back toward the kitchen.

No, not Ben. He wouldn't. Would he? Maybe he'd gone downstairs to the library. For what reason, she couldn't imagine, but anything was better than her son just being gone or being around those boys. She'd just reached their kitchen again when the library's doorbell rang.

Ben!

"Stay in the kitchen and finish your breakfast," she instructed Liddie as she raced down the stairs.

She used the hand-carved, mahogany banister of the grand staircase to steady herself as she straightened and crossed to the library's front door and then swung it open.

"Morning, Ms. Gibson. Where do you want this arrangement?" The florist held a beautiful, large centerpiece of fall flowers and foliage.

"Oh. Put that one back over there, on the table where the napkins are laid out," said Anne, pointing the way. She peered past the front porch. No sign of her son. "The other one will go in the center of that counter." She motioned to where she'd set up the book display behind the patron sign-up table.

"Got it."

"I'll be right back," Anne said. She climbed the stairs, her heart pounding more in fear than in exertion. She stepped into the kitchen and stopped cold.

Ben sat at the table, eating his waffles. They were almost gone, as was over half of his milk.

"Where have you been?"

Her son looked at her with innocence brimming in those clear eyes of his. "Eating breakfast."

"Where were you before you came to eat breakfast?" she asked. Anne moved closer to Ben and sniffed the air around him. She didn't detect any cigarette smoke, but still...

He blinked several times. "I left something in the car, so I ran out to get it."

She narrowed her eyes. "What was so all-fire important that you had to retrieve it so early on a Saturday morning?" she asked.

"I-I—"

"Ms. Gibson, I need your signature," the florist called out from the foyer downstairs.

Saved by the florist? "We're not done," Anne said to Ben before heading down the stairs. She smiled at the florist and took the clipboard. "Sorry. There's so much to do this morning." She looked at the arrangement sitting on the counter. "They're beautiful." Anne signed her name in the blank space, then handed the clipboard back to the florist. "Thank you."

The florist smiled back. "You're welcome. I'll see you later at the opening." She tucked the clipboard under her arm and left.

Anne returned to the kitchen to find the room empty but the table cleared, the dishes already loaded into the dishwasher, and the butter and syrup returned to their proper places. The sound of running water drifted down the hall.

Ben's voice stopped her in the hall outside the bathroom. "No, Liddie, you have to brush for the whole timer."

"The sand's all in the bottom," Liddie replied.

"But you stopped brushing when it was only halfway filled. Mom said we have to brush the whole timer's length. No shortcuts," said Ben.

Anne pressed her fingers to her lips. He sounded just like her.

"I'll brush longer tonight," said Liddie.

"No, this party thing is important to Mom. She sent invitations to the whole town. So if everybody comes, you need clean teeth. Just brush them again, okay?" Ben sounded exasperated with his little sister.

Anne gasped. She hadn't realized Ben understood how anxious she was about the opening—about the library in general.

Perhaps he wasn't just sullen because of having to leave behind his best friends. Maybe part of his attitude change was due to his picking up on her stress levels. Maybe they should go to the park together more often.

"Fine. Just don't tell Mommy," said Liddie.

The water came on again, and Liddie began humming, a habit Anne had taught her to make the two-and-a-half minute brushing time go by faster—hum a favorite song and dance while brushing.

Anne silently eased into Liddie's room, where she put the pink frilly dress and tights right-side out again. In less than three minutes, Liddie skipped into the room. "My teeth are all shiny and white, Mommy. Look." She lifted her lips and smiled like a horse.

"So they are. Great job, sweetie. Now, let's get you dressed," Anne said. As Liddie prattled on about all the kids from her school she'd see at the opening and Anne helped slip the pink dress over her daughter's head, Anne's nerves bunched as bad as Liddie's tights had this morning.

What if the townsfolk didn't like the redesign of the house? They would all love Alex's work, of course, but what about her decorating? Had she used colors that were too bold? Too many colors? No. Mildred Farley, Aunt Edie's best friend, had loved the color selections.

Would some of the older town folk have problems with the new computer and filing system she'd incorporated? No. Surely not. And if they did, Mildred and Coraline Watson could help teach them.

Anne helped Liddie with the tights, smiling as her daughter's excitement shone in her eyes, but inside, Anne's stomach tied in knots. She'd just finished pulling Liddie's hair back with a headband when the library's door buzzer sounded.

"They're here for the party!" Liddie rushed to put on her little Mary Janes.

Mercy, I hope not, Anne thought. They'd be almost an hour early if so. She hadn't even set out the refreshments yet. And she needed to fire up the computer. And she had to make sure Ben wore what she'd laid out for him. And...

Anne let out a slow breath as she stepped off the final stair and moved toward the library's entrance. She unlocked the door and opened it wide.

"Hi there," Wendy said as she crossed over the threshold. "I thought you might need a little help this morning." She smiled. "I've got all my kids dressed and ready," she said. "Chad will bring them all here in an hour. I'll do whatever you need me to do, then once my crew arrives, I'll take all the kids to the Children's Room and keep them entertained."

Anne gave Wendy a quick hug and together they stepped into the foyer. "I was wondering how I was going to keep an eye on the kids and meet all the townspeople too. You are a lifesaver."

Wendy shook her head. "No, this library is a lifesaver for this town."

"Thank you, Wendy. For everything."

"Hey, what'd you find out about that map?"

Briefly, Anne told Wendy what she'd found at the newspaper office. Then she filled her in on her encounter with

Megan Rhodes. "I have to go back and dig some more, but I have to be careful. This could really affect some of the townspeople," she said. She saw no sense in alienating them without good reason.

Wendy rubbed her hands together. "Maybe you should talk with Reverend Tom. He is, after all, the keeper of all our town's secrets."

Hmm. She hadn't considered that.

"Hi, Mrs. Pyle." Liddie rushed down the stairs, interrupting them. "Mommy, Ben called me stupid."

"I didn't call her stupid, I said her dress was stupid," said Ben. He stood behind Liddie on the landing, wearing the slacks but not the jacket, with his arms crossed over his chest.

"Did too." Liddie spun and stuck her bottom lip out.

"I did not." Ben looked as stubborn as a mule.

"Did too."

Anne frowned. "We don't use the word *stupid*, Ben, and you know it. Apologize to your sister. And where's your jacket?" she asked.

He grunted something that sounded like an offhand apology at Liddie, then scowled at Anne. "The jacket's too tight across my shoulders," he said.

He'd worn it to a going-away dinner back in New York not very long ago. "Well, you didn't tell me it was too small when you wore it last, so you'll have to manage with it now."

"It's uncomfortable, Mom."

Wendy shifted toward Anne and whispered so the kids couldn't hear her. "How about I wrangle Ben into his jacket and keep Liddie from mussing up while you finish what you need to do down here?"

Although Wendy sometimes overwhelmed Anne with her direct and outgoing nature, at this moment, Anne wanted to hug Wendy with gratitude. "Thank you."

As Wendy led Ben and Liddie upstairs, Anne pulled refreshments out of the library's kitchen pantry and set them on the table. The cookies looked yummy, but Anne resisted taking a bite. She straightened the bowl of chips. And again. Then a third time. The grandfather clock in the History Room chimed loudly, ringing out notification of the half hour.

Anne rushed to finish putting the punch together in the big, crystal punchbowl that had been Aunt Edie's, and Anne's grandmother's before. The crystal design caught the light from the antique chandelier overhead and cast prisms of light over the table. Beautiful. Aunt Edie would have loved how the refreshment table and display turned out, with the perfect blend of antique Victorian and modern-day décor.

Anne washed her hands and set out the plastic cups. Then she heard heavy footsteps on the front porch. She hurried to the door to greet the first official visitor of Blue Hill Library.

Alex pushed open the door. His boots creaked comfortably on the wooden planks as he walked to the checkout counter. "You look nice, Anne. Almost as nice as my handiwork." He grinned and ran a hand over the smooth countertop.

She smiled. "You clean up nicely too."

Mildred Farley came in right behind him. "It all looks great, Anne. I'm so very glad you did this."

"Did what?" Anne asked Mildred.

"Honored your aunt's bequest to oversee the library. The town certainly needs it," said Mildred.

But did the town need *her*? Sometimes she felt like such an outsider, as though she hadn't lived here in her childhood. It was probably her imagination that she felt like this. "Thanks, Mildred. I do hope everyone loves what I chose for the library."

"Stop worrying, girl," Wendy said as she joined them. "Everything looks amazing. Everyone will love it." She gave Alex a quick hug. "You did a great job here."

"Thanks," he said.

"We're going to the Children's Room to pull some books for a read-aloud once the kids start showing up. As they do, send them our way." Wendy smiled as she took Liddie's hand and led her to the stairs. Ben, wearing his jacket, followed behind them.

One of these days, Wendy was going to have to share the secrets of her ability to get children to toe the line, but for now, Anne was grateful for her help. Ben wasn't always so sullen, but with his self-imposed responsibility of being the "man of the house" and his lack of a large circle of close friends, he'd withdrawn quite a bit.

"Anne, it all looks so wonderful. I feel like I've entered a room in heaven with all these books," said Mildred. Before Anne could answer, the front door swished open again and an elderly couple tottered into the library and made their way into the front entry. Right behind them were Wendy's husband and children; then the mayor of Blue Hill, Bob Bultman, and his wife, Betty; and Reverend

Tom and Maggie Sloan brought up the rear. A few other people straggled in behind them.

Anne put all the warmth from her nerves into her smile. "Hello. Welcome to the new Blue Hill Library. Please make yourselves at home." She lifted the stack of copies of the library floor plan and offered one to each of her guests. "Here's a copy of the library layout. As you wander about, remember we have refreshments in the back room past the checkout area. And please, everyone, fill out your information to receive your Blue Hill Library card." She waved toward the table. "Enjoy yourselves."

Reverend Tom's smile reached his warm brown eyes. "It's lovely, Anne. You and Alex did a marvelous job with the library." He clasped her hands in his. "Edie would love it."

"That's exactly what I've told her," Mildred said.

Emotions clogged Anne's throat. To hear someone who knew her aunt even better than she did say that Aunt Edie would love the library, well...it made the beautiful day all the more complete. "Thank you," Anne managed to whisper.

Mayor Bultman and his wife looked over their copy of the floor plan. "It's all so charming," Mrs. Bultman offered. "Well done, Anne, well done."

Another couple of townspeople whom Anne hadn't yet met wandered in and introduced themselves—not that she would remember their names. She had so much information coming at her from all directions. It was as if she'd never lived in this town...like it had all been a dream.

Wendy would be starting a children's reading time every other Saturday. One woman stated she was going to start a book club to meet at the library once a month. Another woman talked about the knitting club meeting at the library, and wouldn't the Reference Room upstairs be a lovely place to meet?

Anne was going to have to find a volunteer just to keep up with the library's event calendar. And volunteers to oversee the events. And people to setup and tear down for the functions. And someone to watch the library while she spent time with her children.

Finding it a little hard to breathe, Anne nodded at people as she wound her way to the refreshment area, keeping the smile firmly planted in place. She opened the refrigerator and let the air cool her flaming cheeks.

"Feeling a little overwhelmed?"

She jumped, shut the refrigerator, and then turned. "Reverend Tom!"

"I didn't mean to startle you." He smiled. "Feeling a little overwhelmed by it all?"

She nodded. "My, yes," she said. "Even though I am a librarian—and, granted, it was one of the smaller branches— still, I did work at one of the New York libraries…" Anne couldn't believe the way she was rambling on so. She shrugged and lifted her hands. "And yet, managing *all* of this…by myself…I don't know what Aunt Edie was thinking."

Reverend Tom laid a hand on her shoulder and squeezed. "She was thinking that you are perfect for this job. Perfect for this town."

She shook her head. "I don't know about that."

He squeezed her shoulder again before he released her. "I do. So did Edie. You're going to do fine. You'll do it just like you did the restoration — one manageable piece at a time."

Anne let out a slow breath, then nodded. "Thanks. I do believe I just had a little panic attack." She smiled, a little shaky but sincere.

"Understandable, but I have faith in you, Anne. You have a love of the town's history. You're a part of it. You're going to do well here in Blue Hill."

"Thanks." Speaking of Blue Hill and history…"Reverend Tom, can I come by the church later and speak with you? About some historical facts regarding the town?"

His eyebrows crinkled. "That sounds intriguing."

"I found an old —"

"Mrs. Gibson, my mom said to tell you that she's about to bring all the kids down for 'freshments." Wendy's six-year-old, Justin, sported a grin with a front tooth missing.

Reverend Tom tapped Anne's hand. "Sure. I'll be there from three o'clock until seven. We can talk then," he said.

She nodded then turned her attention to Wendy's son. She would see what Reverend Tom had to say about the history of the map once the open house was over. But right now, she was about to have a good dozen children traipsing in, and if cookies weren't ready for consumption, she just might have her first riot on her hands.

Mildred joined Anne. "Tell me how I can help," she said.

Together, Anne and Mildred set out cookies. Mildred paused as she spied the crystal punch bowl. "Your aunt loved that bowl," she told Anne. "I can remember the first time I saw it. I told Edie then that it was beautiful. She told me it had been a wedding present to her parents."

Anne nodded.

"I never grew tired of hearing Edie talk about her family's gatherings over the years. Good memories," said Mildred. "But I must stop rambling on. Today's grand opening is a good memory in the making—you making Edie's dream come true."

"I feel so honored she trusted me with this dream of hers," said Anne.

"Why, dear, who else would she trust? You and Edie were the two bookworms," said Mildred.

As the children clamored into the kitchen area, Wendy instructed them to go out into the backyard by the picnic table and she'd bring them all cookies and punch.

Mildred and Anne walked together back into the checkout area. Anne smiled at the large photograph of Aunt Edie hanging there, as if seconding Mildred's words.

"Thank you, Aunt Edie," Anne whispered at the portrait.

CHAPTER SIX

The afternoon sun dipped toward the west as Anne parked outside the Blue Hill Community Church. The late September breeze spread its chilly fingers across the town. Anne hunched her shoulders and ducked her head against the cold wind as she hurried toward the red brick building that had been constructed back in the late 1800s.

She slipped through the front door under a beautiful stained glass window. The setting sun caught the reds and blues of the stained glass, causing them to shimmer and glisten. Once inside, she relaxed her shoulders. Something about being in the church filled her with peace and comfort. She sent up a small prayer of gratitude for all her blessings as she walked down the passageway that connected the church to the fellowship hall.

She tapped on Reverend Tom's open door just off the passageway.

He glanced up from his reading, smiled, then stood. "Anne, please, come in and have a seat." He motioned her toward the two chairs opposite his desk. On either side, the walls sported floor-to-ceiling bookshelves. Each shelf overflowed with books, some looking quite old and well worn.

She shrugged out of her jacket and laid it in the chair beside her before sitting across from Reverend Tom.

"The grand opening was quite the success. I think most of the town made a showing today. That's great support."

Anne nodded. "I couldn't be more pleased. I'll be entering data for the library cards for a week, but it's worth it." She paused. How should she broach the subject?

In his keenly attentive way, Reverend Tom averted her discomfort. "I have to say, you've got me curious." He leaned back in his chair, holding a pen and staring at her intently.

Anne told him how she'd found the map and what Wendy had told her. She pulled out her copy of the *Blue Hill Gazette* article and handed it to him.

He slipped his reading glasses on and his gaze danced over the page. "I remember hearing about all this." Reverend Tom paused, took off his glasses, and handed the copy back across the desk. "It nearly split the town apart."

"How's that?"

He leaned back in his chair, which creaked slightly under his slim build. "As I understand, it all comes down to the historical society going defunct back in 1993. Half the town was in support of eliminating the society," he said. "They felt like the society had served its purpose, but the town no longer needed such a group."

Anne nodded, and Reverend Tom continued. "But the other half of the townsfolk…they fought the society's dissolving with everything they had. They believed the society could preserve the town's history and also bring some tourist funds to Blue Hill. Some of them still feel that way."

"Really?" Anne asked. Interesting. She'd never heard about this.

"Yes," he replied, fiddling with his glasses. "So, what are you going to do about the map?"

"Well, I need to get it authenticated. Now that the opening is over, I can take the time to find a good person to inspect it," said Anne.

"Might I make a suggestion?" asked Reverend Tom.

"Of course." She certainly respected his opinion.

"Take it to someone out of town." He tapped his glasses against his desk calendar. "If word of this map gets out, it's sure to stir up all the dissention regarding the historical society. Not to mention get people riled up about the reward monies still unclaimed."

"Reward monies?" asked Anne.

"Oh, yes. As I've heard tell, all those years ago when the map went missing, the staunch supporters of the society collected a reward for whoever provided information that led to the arrest of the person responsible for the theft of the map," said Reverend Tom. "Of course, no one could have the money since the map was never recovered. The money has been sitting in an escrow account at the bank all this time."

"How much are we talking about, Reverend?" Anne asked.

He set aside his glasses and ran a hand through his gray-touched brown hair. "Back then, it was about twenty-five thousand dollars. With interest all these years, I'd guess it'd be close to forty-something thousand."

Forty-something thousand? That was a lot of money. "Wow."

He chuckled. "Wow is right. So you can see why I recommend you take the map out of town to be inspected. It wouldn't do to get community talking about the historical society and the theft and the reward without even knowing if your map is a real one."

"Right." She would just find someone in a neighboring town to appraise the map. It would take her a little longer, but there wasn't any real rush—unless the map was real and someone found out she had it. Especially when there might be over forty thousand dollars at stake.

Reverend Tom cocked his head to the side. "What have you heard about the town's reaction when the map went missing?"

"Only what I told you—what Coraline Watson told Wendy." She shook her head. "Let me guess, there's more to the story?"

"Oh, yes. I believe Coraline sugarcoated her version, as is her way. She is the type of person who leaves out details she thinks might hurt someone's feelings." He offered a pastoral smile. "You understand this is hearsay on my part, but from what I gather, when the map first went missing, people were interested in the society because they believed there might be other valuable items on display. People came to see what the society had, hoping for some history-rich artifact. The society had items from Blue Hill's railroad history, but not really anything of any great value."

She'd read up on the history of the town before deciding to move back. "Back in 1899, a booming company acquired, consolidated, and abandoned the town's railroad track, right?" At least, that's what she'd read.

He nodded. "That's my understanding, yes. Most of the town's population left then, looking for work. It was a hard time in Blue Hill's history."

Anne could only imagine. So many railroad towns dried up when acquiring companies abandoned their tracks. Blue Hill had managed to survive, outlasting the dark times. Yet remnants from the town's rough patch were still reflected in the back alleys of the town and on the faded advertisements on some of the buildings. The once vibrant downtown wore a weathered look.

In recent years, many of the town's old buildings had been restored to their original condition, which added to the historical depth of Blue Hill.

Reverend Tom cleared his throat, pulling her attention back to the present. "The tourists who came, hoping to find a treasure, were disappointed to find nothing as interesting or popular as the map. Word got out and visitors stopped coming at all.

"For a town that had already endured such an economic hit with the abandonment of the town's railroad, a lack of visitors all but squashed what was left of the townspeople's gumption. Soon enough, the society began to flounder financially. Most of the few tourists who trickled into town slowly migrated their attentions — and their dollars — to the Railroad Museum on Main Street. They basically left the historical society's displays unwanted and unneeded."

And probably deepened the town's bitterness over the missing map.

Reverend Tom let out a heavy sigh. "So, in 1993, due to lack of funding and interest, the Blue Hill Historical Society folded. Just the mention of the map, the society, or Alfred Rhodes gets most of the townspeople all stirred up," he said. "The items that had been owned by the historical society ended up being sold or donated. It was a trying time for the townsfolk."

"I had no idea." She must have been pretty oblivious to have never heard this story. Of course, she'd been absorbed in living her own life at that time.

"You can see why I recommend you take the map out of town to be examined," he said.

"Of course, and I definitely will." She slipped the copy of the newspaper article back into her purse. Her mind continued to race as she stood. "Thank you, Reverend Tom. I really appreciate your being so candid with me."

He stood, came from around his desk, and helped her put on her jacket. "Anytime, Anne. I look forward to seeing you and the kids in church tomorrow."

She nodded, then took the passageway back to the church and out into the parking lot. The sun had all but disappeared, leaving a void of cold darkness in its wake. Anne hadn't meant to stay so long. She hurried home.

"I'm sorry I'm so late," she told Wendy as soon as she walked up the back stairs to the third floor. The house was quiet.

Wendy laughed. "Don't worry about it. We made grilled cheese sandwiches and heated up the vegetable soup you had in the freezer. We had a lovely dinner together, and then we cleaned up the kitchen. Chad left with my crew, and I just got Liddie out of the bath. She's brushing her teeth, and Ben's ready to take his shower."

"Thank you," Anne said. Wendy Pyle could very well be a miracle worker. "I can't tell you how much I appreciate it."

Wendy scrunched her nose and waved her off, in her unique way. "Don't be silly. That's what's great about being part of a community. We pitch in and help each other. You're the one who grew up here. Don't you remember?"

Back in New York, she and Eric had been so busy with their careers, each other, and the kids that they'd rarely had time for anything community-minded. There certainly hadn't been an inviting feeling among the New Yorkers she knew. Sure, she and Eric's coworkers were friendly, and they did visit socially on occasion, but nothing like back here in Blue Hill. It wasn't as if they didn't have friends in New York—they did, but all their close circle of friends either had children who played ball with Ben or were in the book industry.

Maybe Aunt Edie, in her infinite wisdom, understood the core of what Anne needed most after losing Eric: a much stronger circle of community, a sense of belonging,...being connected to her past. Maybe that's why Aunt Edie had left her house and bequest the way she did.

Wendy interrupted Anne's wandering thoughts. "Oh, the Miller girls, Remi and Bella, called. They wanted to know if you'd be interested in allowing them to volunteer here at the library." Wendy grabbed her jacket as Anne discarded hers.

"Didn't they just graduate? Aren't they going to college?"

Wendy shook her head. "They're taking off a semester or two. Neither one is sure of what they want to do, so their mother told them they should have an idea before they enrolled. She says she won't pay for them to be professional students."

Anne grinned. "I sure need the volunteers. But I don't know them well."

"They're good girls, in spite of growing up amid their parents' constant absenteeism." Wendy snagged her purse from the end of the couch.

While Anne could picture the girls she'd met at church, she couldn't pull up the image of their parents. "I guess I don't remember meeting their folks."

"They do mission work with Alex's parents." Wendy shifted her purse strap high up on her shoulder. "Matter of fact, they're a lot like Alex's parents."

Enough said. They were busy doing good, but they were gone all the time.

"I'll vouch for the girls. I have an idea that Remi might be leaning toward some type of career in English," said Wendy.

"Mommy!" Liddie rushed toward her, arms extended as if she hadn't seen Anne in days. She hugged her like there was no tomorrow.

Her daughter's unabashed affection always warmed Anne's heart. She squeezed Liddie back. "Hi, sweetie. Did you and Ben behave for Ms. Wendy?" Liddie nodded, the ends of her hair still a little damp. "We had samiches and soup for supper. I ate bunches. Ben loaded the dishwasher, too." She spun around, as if to model her pajamas. "I already had my bath."

Anne ran a hand over her daughter's silky curls. "I'm glad to see you've had your bath."

"I'm ready for prayers," Liddie said.

Wendy chuckled and reached for the doorknob. "I think that's my cue to leave. I'll see you both at church tomorrow."

"Thank you again, Wendy. For everything." Anne gave her friend a quick hug before Wendy disappeared into the cold darkness.

Liddie tugged at her hand. "Come on, Mommy. I'm ready for prayers." She pulled Anne to her room, then knelt beside her bed. "Dear God," Liddie began, "thank You for a good opening for Mommy's library, even if I didn't get to have my friends to my room to play cuz Mrs. Pyle made us stay in the Children's Room. And thank You that Ben came home without Mrs. Pyle having to send Mr. Pyle out to find him. Amen." She jumped into her bed.

With her pulse spiking, Anne tucked the covers around her daughter. She didn't want to use prayer time as a time to gain information on her kids. She'd taught the kids to talk to God about everything. But something her daughter had mentioned in prayers turned her insides cold. She couldn't just ignore it. She brushed Liddie's bangs from her forehead. "Liddie, did Ben go missing again this afternoon?" Anne asked.

Liddie's eyes went wide and she clamped a hand over her mouth. "Uh-oh. I wasn't 'posed to say anything. He wasn't missing. He just couldn't hear Ms. Wendy yelling for him," Liddie said.

"It's okay, honey." Anne swallowed, forcing her voice to remain steady as she smoothed the comforter. "And where had he been?" If she found out he'd been hanging out at the abandoned tree house with those other boys...

Liddie shrugged, flipping to her side. "I dunno. He told Ms. Wendy he'd been checking on something down the hill and just didn't hear her." She yawned as wide as a cat.

"When was this, honey?" Anne asked.

Liddie blinked slowly, barely able to keep her eyes open. "After dinner." She pulled her teddy bear to her and yawned again. "G'night, Mommy. I love you."

"I love you too, sweet girl." She pressed a kiss on her daughter's temple, turned out the lamp on the bedside table, and then pulled Liddie's bedroom door closed behind her.

She moved across the hall to her son's room, pushing the door open. "Ben?" She sniffed the air but only caught the scent of shampoo and soap.

He knelt beside his bed, eyes closed in prayer. "Amen." He stood and smiled at her. "Hi, Mom."

So angelic looking, yet she couldn't allow his vanishing act to go unaddressed. "Ben, I understand you were missing again this afternoon and Ms. Wendy couldn't find you."

He scowled and crawled into bed. "I didn't think she'd tattle on me," he said.

"She didn't." Maybe she should talk to Wendy about Ben's actions. If he'd been down there with those boys who smoked, surely Wendy would've noticed the stench. "This is the third time you've pulled this disappearing act. What's going on?"

"Nothing."

His silence was colder than the air outside.

If only he would talk to her and open up about what was going on inside that head of his. "Ben, where do you go when I can't find you?" Anne asked.

He shrugged. "Only down the back of the hill. It's just hard to hear you calling if the wind's blowing."

"But why? Why do you go there? What are you doing?"

His frown grew more prominent. "I just go to be alone. To think," he said.

Now it was her turn to be silent. She remembered all the times as a child, here in Aunt Edie's house, she'd gone to the little balcony off what was now her room, just to be alone. To think.

"Mom, I don't have anyone to play with and talk to."

"You have Liddie," Anne said.

He snorted. "She's a baby. And a girl." As if playing with his sister was a form of punishment. Well, she could see his point.

"You have friends you can play with. You like Wendy's son, right?"

Silence hung in the air and accentuated their stalemate. She knew she was stubborn, she just hadn't realized Ben had inherited that trait from her.

Anne sighed. "Why don't you go play with Ryan? You two are friends," she said.

"I do play with him, Mom. But he sometimes visits his grandparents out of town and isn't at Alex's."

Alex and Ryan lived only a short way from them, just down the hill and right off the road. He couldn't hear Anne call him from Alex's, but at least if he went there, he'd have to tell her where he was going, and he was only a phone call away.

Then again, he'd have to pass the tree house to get to Ryan's. Maybe she shouldn't have made that suggestion.

But the mention of grandparents scraped against Anne. It had only been since the summer, when they moved to Blue Hill, that they'd seen her parents, who were now actively retired in Florida. And Mom and Dad would be up for a visit before the end of the year. She simply couldn't feel guilty because Ben didn't live near his grandparents. Besides, they hadn't lived any closer to them back in New York.

"You'll just have to figure it out, Ben, but the disappearing act has to stop," she said. "I don't care what you have to do to hear your name being called, but if you can't come when called, you won't be allowed out of the yard."

"Mom!"

"No arguing, young man. You make your choices."

He glared at her with his stony silence. She met his stare with a hardness of her own.

"Yes, Mom."

Standoff diverted. "Good." She leaned over and brushed a kiss across his forehead. "Good night. I love you," Anne said.

"'Night and love you too." He rolled over, punching his pillow.

She turned off the light and shut the door. Anne leaned against the wall in the hallway, resting her head. She let out a long, slow breath. Sometimes this single parenting thing was much harder than she'd ever imagined it could be.

Chapter Seven

Anne ran into the Miller girls in the parking lot after church. She invited them to the library to discuss the possibility of their volunteering. At home, she made a quick lunch for her and the kids out of leftover pizza, then she left Liddie playing with her dolls in her room.

"Mom, can I go see Ryan?" Ben asked.

"Well…" Anne could hardly refuse since she'd been the one to make that very suggestion last night. "Okay. But you have to be home before dinner."

"Okay," said Ben. He grabbed his baseball glove and raced down the back stairs. Anne checked on Liddie and her dolls before heading to the library. While she waited for Remi and Bella to arrive, she began entering the data from the library card applications into the computer. She loved the application cards she'd ordered and hated to throw them away. Actually, now that she thought about it, she'd keep them. Maybe she'd think of some way to use them down the road. She could have a library patron of the month or something. For now, once she had all the information loaded into the computer, she filed the pretty cards in a plastic container, which she would later slip onto the shelf under the counter.

Yet, even with the excitement of the library and the successful grand opening yesterday, Anne couldn't stop thinking about the map and what Reverend Tom had shared with her about its history.

She stopped uploading information for the library cards and opened her e-mail program to find an e-mail from her mom and dad, along with four junk e-mails, two from friends from New York, and one from Eric's mother. But there was nothing from the message boards in response to her inquiry about the map.

With a sigh, she closed her e-mail program and took out her notebook. She put her notes in chronological order then scanned what she'd found. The Blue Hill Historical Society was formed in August of 1912. One of the founders, Isaac Jones, had authenticated the society's prized possession—a 1775 Pennsylvania state map by William Scull, believed to have been used by Lewis and Clark at the beginning of one of their expeditions. In February of 1913, the map disappeared. Alfred Rhodes was accused of stealing it, at least in the public's eyes.

A reward had been established back in 1913, payable to the one who provided information that led to the arrest of the person responsible for the map's disappearance. This reward money is still in an escrow account controlled by the city council. In 1993, the town's historical society was dissolved.

Pushing her glasses back up to the bridge of her nose, Anne chewed the end of her pen. She didn't have a lot of information from 1913 to 1993. A lot could have happened in those eighty years. She needed to find out the rest of the story. She needed to do more research at the newspaper office.

The front doorbell rang.

Anne startled, then smiled at herself. When would she ever get over her jumpiness? She closed the notebook and headed to the front entry. Remi and Bella Miller stood on the porch. She unlocked the door and brought them inside. "Hello, girls," she said. "Come on in."

"Hi, Mrs. Gibson. Thanks for inviting us over." Remi, the older of the girls by a full three minutes, stood a good five feet eight, an inch taller than Anne. Her brown hair was woven into a French braid as thick as a three-ply rope. Her eyes were as deep brown as Liddie's, and as unguarded. Anne liked her immediately.

"Come on in. Would either of you like a bottle of water?" Anne asked. She led the way to the back of the library.

"No, thank you. We just finished lunch," said Remi's twin. Bella Miller was much shorter than her older sister. Shorter by at least six inches or so. Her hair, much lighter than Remi's, hung in loose, wavy curls past her shoulders. Her eyes were as blue as Alex's as she stared intently at Anne. No one would guess they were twins.

"Then let's sit here in the checkout area and talk a bit." Anne sat behind the reference desk, letting the girls sit beside one another at the counter. "Wendy tells me you're interested in volunteering here at the library..."

"I know some people are talking about us, about us not going right to college after graduation. Let me assure you, it's not because we're not smart. We both graduated with honors in the top five percent of our class. Both of us had a 4.0 grade point average," Remi began.

"But neither of us are sure what we want to major in, so Mom thought it best we take a semester to explore all of our options," Bella finished.

Anne smiled. "I'd actually heard you both were very smart."

Remi smiled wide, revealing a row of teeth so straight they had to have benefited from braces. "I've thought about becoming a librarian myself," she said.

"Really?" Anne asked. She loved her career. She was forever grateful to Aunt Edie for encouraging her to pursue her dream of becoming a librarian. Over the years, she'd tried to do the same for others with a heart for the industry. Maybe this was a perfect opportunity to share her passion with the next generation of librarians. And the fact that Remi was a native Blue Hill... well, Anne felt like she'd almost stepped into Aunt Edie's role. "I love being a librarian. There's just something comforting about being around books all day."

"I love to read," Bella interjected. "I love to lose myself in a good story."

Anne nodded. "My late husband was an editor at a New York publishing company, did you know that?" she asked.

Both girls shook their heads in unison, their grace matching. Maybe it wasn't such a reach to find them twins.

"He was. A senior acquisitions editor. He loved to read a story that transformed him. Loved to help the author make it even better than they'd imagined." Images of Eric's face, flushed with excitement, danced across her memory. "It was one of his favorite things — to see an amazing story come to print and shared with the world. He thrived on it."

"I think that'd be the coolest thing ever. Exciting." Bella's eyes twinkled with the same sparkle Eric's had.

Anne recognized that look. She had a feeling Bella was destined for things beyond Blue Hill. "Eric loved being an editor." And he had, so very much. It was part of who he was. His passion for books, for stories that could transform people, was one of the attributes that attracted Anne to a man twelve years her senior. She'd met him at a coffee shop close to campus while she was still in college. He'd been reading a manuscript over a latte, and she'd been enamored with him, regardless of their age difference.

She'd had a wonderful marriage. They were happy.

"We both love books, so you can understand why we'd like to volunteer here," said Remi, her smile drawing Anne back to the present.

"You do understand there'd be responsibilities, so you would have to treat it like a job?" Anne asked.

"Yes, ma'am." Bella's waves brushed around her shoulders as she nodded.

"A lot of it would be pretty boring stuff like shelving books, entering information in the computer, checking people out. Sometimes helping someone find a book or show them how to use the computer system."

Remi's smile widened even more. "We both took advanced computer classes, so mastering computer programs quickly is easy for us."

"And we like to help people. And we know most everybody here in Blue Hill," Bella added.

Anne crossed her arms over her chest. "On occasion, you might have to help with an event or set up the library's public calendar."

"I love scheduling. I can even set up a page for the library on all the social media sites and load the events there too." Remi's excitement shone on her face.

"Starting out, I can't afford to pay you. Your work would be strictly on a volunteer basis, but the experience would look great on your resume. I'd need someone on Mondays, Wednesdays, and Fridays," said Anne.

Bella laughed. "We share a full-time babysitting job, so we could swap our volunteer times and babysitting shifts."

Anne stood. "Thank you, girls. I must say, I see you two as a real answer to prayer." She nodded and smiled. "Well then, the only thing left for me to ask is—when can you start?"

"Tomorrow," the girls said in unison.

"Great. How about nine?" Anne asked.

Both heads bobbed.

Remi pointed at the computer. "Maybe you could go ahead and show us the system, since we're both here now. Unless you're busy?"

"No, that's a great idea," Anne said.

Less than an hour later, both girls were fully trained on the computer system, as well as familiar with the filing system and the layout of both floors of the library. Anne felt so confident with the pair that she gave them a key to the library.

She asked if whichever one of them volunteered tomorrow morning would open up for her. She was determined to head to the *Blue Hill Gazette's* office as soon as she dropped the kids off at school.

After showing the girls out and locking the library door behind them, Anne headed upstairs to check on Liddie. She poked her head in her daughter's bedroom. "Whatcha doing, Liddie?" she asked.

"Playing with my babies," said Liddie. She held up her loved-almost-to-pieces Raggedy Ann doll Eric had given to her in the hospital when she'd been born. "Look, Rags likes the new dress Grandma sent her."

"She looks so very pretty in it too." Anne couldn't resist dropping a kiss on Liddie's crown. "I'm going to start making dinner. How does spaghetti sound?"

"Yea! I love s'ghetti." A predictable reaction, since spaghetti was Liddie's favorite meal. "With cheese bread?"

"I know you love *spaghetti*," Anne said, gently correcting her daughter. "And of course we're having cheese bread. What is spaghetti without it?" Anne laughed. "You play while I make dinner. I'll call you when I put the bread in so you can wash up, okay?"

"Okay, Mommy." Liddie turned back to her dolls.

In the kitchen, Anne quickly chopped an onion, half a green bell pepper, and half a red bell pepper, then she dumped them into the skillet with the hamburger meat to cook. She grabbed her cell phone and quickly dialed the number Grace had given her. Grace's voice mail picked up.

Anne waited until the tone sounded. "Hi, Grace. This is Anne Gibson. I'm planning to come by the paper tomorrow and do a little more research. I thought maybe when I was done we could grab that cup of coffee, if you don't have plans. I understand if you can't. Well, okay. I'll see you tomorrow. Bye."

She stirred the hamburger, onion, and bell pepper mixture. Then she opened the French loaf, cut it in half, slathered both sides with butter, and coated each in shredded cheese. The hamburger meat was nicely browned, so she drained it and dumped it into a pot, to which she added two cans of spaghetti sauce.

After putting water on to boil to cook the pasta and pre-heating the oven, Anne again reached for her cell phone. This time, she dialed Alex's number. He answered on the second ring. "Hi, Anne."

"Hey," she said. "Could you send Ben back this way, please? Dinner's almost ready."

"Sure. He and Ryan have been playing outside all afternoon. It's been good for both of them."

"Thanks for letting him come over. He's having some growing pains."

"Oh, they've been having a grand time, playing ball and ripping and roaring about. You've made Ben very happy."

Well, who knew her suggestion for Ben to go play with Ryan would be such a big deal? And who knew a thirty-four-year-old mom could make a nine-year-old boy so happy?

The water boiled. "I've got to get the bread in the oven. Please tell Ben to come home right away," she said.

"I'll tell him now. Bye, Anne."

Anne hung up and dumped the pasta in the boiling water. Then she put the bread on the baking stone in the oven. She went to the hallway and called up the stairs. "Liddie, go wash up for dinner. It's your turn to set the table."

She stirred the pasta and heard water running in the bathroom sink. Minutes later, Liddie appeared. "Tell me again what should I do first, Mommy?" she asked.

Anne had just begun to let Liddie help set the table. She handed her the napkin holder. "Put a napkin at each of our places. Then put our forks on top of the napkins."

As Liddie did as instructed, the back door slammed and Ben whisked by them, muttering a quick "be right back" on his race up the stairs. He must've run all the way from Alex's. Anne remembered those times as a child that she got too busy to play to tend to nature's call until the situation became desperate. She smiled.

Anne heard the bathroom door shut as she turned back to pull the bread from the oven. She cut it and placed the slices in the bread keeper, then handed it to Liddie. "Put the bread on the table, honey."

Liddie took the bread keeper while Anne stirred the sauce.

She checked the pasta, then drained it. "Can I pour our milk?" Liddie asked.

"No, honey. Just set the glasses out. I'll do the pouring," said Anne. She stepped into the hall and listened up the stairs. The sound of water running came from the bathroom. "Ben, hurry up. Dinner's ready."

"Can I have a big glass, Mommy?" asked Liddie.

"No. Get your and Ben's regular cups." Anne grabbed the milk out of the refrigerator and reached for her own glass. She poured all three. "Put these on the table," she said to Liddie.

Anne pulled three plates from the cabinet. "Ben!"

"I think he's out of the bathroom. Do you want me to go get him, Mommy?"

"No. Just sit down. I'll fix our plates. He'll be here in time for grace."

She finished fixing Liddie's bowl, then Ben's, and finally her own. "Ben!" What could be keeping him?

He rushed to his seat. His hair was wet and he wore his favorite Spider-Man pajamas. "Sorry," he mumbled.

"Did you take a shower?" asked Anne.

He opened his eyes wide. "Yeah, Mom. I wanted to go ahead and get my shower out of the way before dinner. Is that not okay?" he asked.

Aside from the point that she usually had to beg him to take a shower? "Um, no. Just a little unexpected."

"I'll pray, Mommy." Liddie bowed her head and said her sweet prayer as always. She lifted her head. "Can I have two pieces of bread?"

"It's *may I?* And start with one piece. If you eat all of that with your spaghetti, you can have another piece."

Anne stared at Ben, who began eating like he was a starved man. "What happened to your manners, Ben? You're going to need another shower," she said.

He paused, his fork mid-bite. Spaghetti sauce surrounded his mouth. He swallowed loudly.

"Ben eats like a pig. Ben eats like a pig," Liddie sing-songed.

"Shut up." Ben glared at his sister.

"Ben, we don't tell each other to shut up. That's rude," Anne said. She faced her daughter. "Liddie, that's not nice. Where would you even hear such a thing?" she asked. The mean things kids came up with never ceased to rub against Anne's heart.

"The older kids at school say it all the time in the cafeteria," Liddie replied.

"Well, it's rude. Apologize to your brother," Anne said.

"But he's being sloppy on purpose, Mommy. Look how messy his face is. He knows how to eat right," said Liddie.

Ben jerked his paper napkin across his mouth. "Shut up, Liddie."

"Ben!" She set down her fork. "Liddie, you're being rude. Apologize to your brother."

"I'm sorry, Ben," said Liddie.

Anne looked at her son. "And it's very rude to tell your sister to shut up. You know we don't use that phrase in this family. Apologize to Liddie."

"Sorry."

Liddie's bottom lip protruded. "He didn't mean his 'pology, Mommy. He just said it cuz you made him."

Anne had to agree with her daughter, but Liddie had provoked Ben. "That's enough, both of you. Eat your dinner," she said.

She pushed a bite of cheese bread down past the lump in her throat. Maybe her fears were founded and Ben had connected with those boys. That would explain his recent change in attitude.

She took a long sip of milk. She'd have to think about how she could find out for sure, and put a stop to it, if that were the case.

The rest of the meal was eaten in a most uncomfortable silence. Neither Liddie nor Ben wanted to talk to each other at all, and Anne didn't want either of her children to think she'd chosen the other's side.

As soon as they'd finished eating and cleaned up the kitchen, she sent Liddie to get ready for her bath. Ben started to leave the kitchen.

"Ben, wait a minute," Anne said.

He stopped, turning to face her.

"Is anything wrong?" she asked. If only he would talk to her. She knew he'd had a hard time with the move, but he'd made some friends. His attitude should be improving, not getting worse.

"You mean other than having Liddie as a little sister?" he asked.

"That's not very nice. You and Liddie usually get along better. What's changed?" Anne asked.

He shrugged. "She's just a baby."

Could it just be that Ben had gotten too grown up for his little sister? "Are you sure there's nothing else wrong?" she asked.

Anne took a step toward him and mussed his still-wet hair. "You know you can talk to me, right? About any problem you have."

He nodded.

She smiled, grabbing his chin in her hand. "And you are sure there's nothing you want to talk to me about?" she asked.

He grinned, his smile almost identical to hers. "Can we get a dog?"

CHAPTER EIGHT

Where were the highs of sixty degrees she remembered from the early fall days of childhood? The temperatures were cold, and with the crazy wind whipping about, the windchill made Blue Hill seem downright frigid.

Anne pulled her jacket tighter around herself as she made her way into the office of the *Blue Hill Gazette*. The cold breeze followed her inside, sneaking down the back of her neck. She shivered as she smiled at the young receptionist. "Hi."

"Hi. Are you back to look at the microfiche?" the young woman asked.

Anne nodded. "I am. Is Grace in?"

"Not yet. Can you find your way by yourself?"

"I'm good. Will you let Grace know I'm here when she comes in?" asked Anne.

The girl bobbed her head, her ponytail as bouncy as before.

Anne headed back to the microfiche area. She pulled the records where she'd left off before and loaded the machine. In minutes, she was flipping through articles. She paused when she caught a certain headline: *Paul Rhodes Accused of Embezzlement of Blue Hill Funds*. Rhodes. Like Megan.

Like Alfred.

She enlarged the 1990 article and read about the missing town funds. Apparently, over thirty thousand dollars of the town's funds earmarked for future town purchases had disappeared. Most believed Paul Rhodes, then the town's chief financial officer, had embezzled the money. No evidence had ever surfaced linking him to the crime, but most of the townsfolk believed he was smart enough to cover his tracks so well that no one could ever connect the money to him.

Anne took off her glasses and rubbed her eyes. Paul Rhodes and the town's missing money didn't have anything to do with the map or historical society, but she couldn't help but see the similarities: valuable assets belonging to Blue Hill going missing, a member of the Rhodes family being accused, the assets never being recovered. No wonder Megan had been so upset to think Anne was digging into her family's questionable past.

She put her glasses back on and changed out the microfiche. She skimmed through articles in 1983. She stopped when she read the headline about the society receiving a new curator. Anne leaned closer to the screen. September 1983, the Blue Hill Historical Society hired Garret Jones as curator. A brief bio of Garret was listed in the article. Only twenty-five, he was one of the younger curators in the industry. He was a Blue Hill native, only leaving the area long enough to attain his degree.

Garret Jones. Garret Jones. Why did that name sound so familiar to her? Maybe she remembered him from her childhood?

No, she had no memory of a Garret. That was an unusual name, and she would've remembered someone by that name.

"Hey, Anne."

Smiling, Anne turned to face Grace. "Hi. Did you get my message?"

"I did. I could so use a cup of coffee." She nodded toward the machine. "You about ready for a break?" asked Grace.

"Am I ever! Let me put all this up." Anne removed the microfiche from the machine.

"Just leave it. I'll lock the room's door. You can just leave everything out so you don't have to get it all back out when we come back," Grace said. "Nobody ever comes in here anyway."

"Are you sure?" Anne asked as she grabbed her purse. She had her notebook and notes spread out all over the table, as well as the index book and various reels.

"Sure, it's fine," said Grace. "Let's go."

Anne followed Grace out of the room. Grace locked the door, then led the way down the hall. She told the bubbly girl she'd be back.

"The coffee at the diner is good. Is that okay?" asked Grace.

"Sure."

Grace pointed at the Jeep parked on the street. "I'll drive."

Anne settled in the passenger's seat and secured her seat belt.

"I'm really glad you called." Grace eased the Jeep into traffic. "It's rare that I get to share a cup of coffee with someone and just visit." She smiled as she pulled up to a stop sign. "This is a treat for me."

"Me too. It's been a long, long time." *Actually, since before Eric died,* Anne thought. After his death, she'd been busy trying to allow herself to grieve while putting hers and the kids' lives in some kind of order. Soon after, she'd lost her job and wondered what she was going to do. Then Aunt Edie died, and left the strange request about the library. She'd been so busy moving and getting settled, she hadn't really had a lot of time to share a cup of coffee with a friend, other than a few times at her kitchen table with Wendy. She didn't think that really counted, since Wendy always seemed to be working on a project and coercing Anne to join in on her schemes.

Grace whipped her Jeep into the parking lot of the little diner. They hurried inside.

The mouth-watering aroma of coffee brewing wrapped around them like a warm shawl. Anne inhaled, pulling the smell deep into her chest. Her mouth watered.

"Come on, let's sit back there," Grace said. She led the way to a booth in the back corner. The worn vinyl crackled as they slid across the cushions.

A waitress appeared, coffee carafe in hand. "Coffee, ladies?" she asked.

"Yes, please." Grace's voice was husky and filled with reverence as she flipped up the cup.

Anne's fingers were so cold, she could barely turn over her own cup. "Black, please," she said.

Once the cups were filled and the waitress gone, Grace reached for the sugar container. "I like a little coffee with my sugar," Grace said, laughing.

The waitress set a small pitcher of cream on the table, and Grace poured enough to change her coffee from brunette to a light blonde; then she picked up the sugar again and added another round. Anne couldn't stop staring at Grace, who didn't even use a spoon to measure the sugar she added to her cup. She just kept pouring it in.

"You weren't kidding — you do add coffee to your sugar. How do you drink it so sweet? That would make my teeth ache," said Anne.

Grace chuckled. "I only allow myself coffee when I'm out, so I can drink it the way I like it. I don't even have a coffee pot at my house."

Anne shook her head. She'd never make it without her daily java. She took a sip of her coffee. It tasted as amazing as it smelled. She almost sighed with contentment.

"It looked like you had a great turnout for the library's grand opening," Grace said.

"I think so. We had at least a couple of hundred people come through," said Anne. "Most filled out the information cards to get a library card, so I hope that means they intend to be steady patrons."

"We got some good quotes from people to use in the article. I really want to interview you as well," Grace said.

"Oh, I don't think that's such a good idea. Let it be all about the library." Anne had always been uncomfortable drawing attention to herself.

"But the librarian and renovator is part of the library," said Grace.

"I'd rather you talk more about Aunt Edie and her generous donation. And all the books that people have donated," said Anne.

Grace set down her cup and appraised her over the table. "You don't like to be in the limelight, do you?" she asked Anne.

Anne shook her head. "Not really."

"Okay. I won't make you." Grace took another sip of coffee. "Hey, did you close the library to come today?"

"No. I've acquired two volunteers: Remi and Bella Miller," Anne said.

"Oh, those girls are sweethearts. I have hope that Bella might become a journalist in the future. She has a love of words," said Grace.

Anne took another drink of the java. The taste intensified with the heat. She set her cup on the table and traced the rim with her finger. "Grace, what can you tell me about the historical society and a stolen map?" she asked.

"Ah. I wondered when you'd get around to just asking me," Grace said.

"You knew what I was looking for?" Anne asked.

Grace chuckled. "It's not hard to figure out. I am a journalist. It's kinda my job to figure stuff out."

"Well, I'm caught." Anne tapped her nail against the ceramic cup. "So, what do you know?"

"I know what was reported in the paper. I know what the rumors say."

"But?" Anne asked.

"To be honest, I haven't really looked into it myself. Perhaps I should. Uncovering what happened to that map would be quite the article. Might even garner some state attention." Grace stirred her coffee again—probably to get the last inch of sugar from the bottom of the cup. "I know that while people accused Alfred

Rhodes of stealing the map, there was never enough evidence to link him to any crime."

Anne paused as the waitress came by and topped off their coffees, then rushed to the next table. "Why was he accused?" Anne asked.

Grace shrugged. "Well, supposedly, he had access to the map."

"But?" Anne scrutinized the editor. Grace wore an odd expression. Similar to the one Eric used to wear when a plot had a fatal flaw. "You don't think he did it."

Grace shook her head. "It just doesn't make sense to me. Why steal a map you can never sell? I mean, why bother?"

Good point. Anne took a sip from her cup. "Maybe he stole it to hurt the society?" she asked.

"I don't know. Hmm, maybe I *should* dig a little deeper. See what I can find out." Grace set down her cup and pointed at Anne. "Now, tell me why you're so interested in the map."

Anne desperately wanted to trust Grace, but she wasn't sure. The only person she'd made real friends with was Wendy, who had initiated their friendship. Or was that demanded? She and Alex were slowly but surely getting back to a comfortable friendship, and that was good. But a close friendship with Grace would be new. Could she trust Grace completely?

"Anne?" Grace peered at her over her cup. "If you can't tell me, I understand, but if you do, I won't blab. If that's what you're worried about." She set down her cup and grinned. "I am a journalist and we protect our sources, you know."

Eventually, she'd have to venture out and trust her own judgment. "Last week, while Wendy and I were indexing the historical books, I found a map." Anne went on to tell Grace everything: the message boards, talking with Reverend Tom, the run-in with Megan, and matching what she found archived in the paper's microfiche. When she was finished, she wrapped her hands around the ceramic mug.

"Wow. No wonder you're doing the research," said Grace.

Anne took another sip of coffee and nodded.

"I'll do some digging of my own and see what I can find out." She shook her head. "Poor Megan."

"How's that?" asked Anne.

"Well, you read that her great-grandfather was Alfred, accused of stealing the map, right?"

The waitress came by and refilled their cups.

"Well, Paul Rhodes, Blue Hill's chief financial officer who was accused of embezzling the town's funds, was her grandfather." Grace poured more sugar into her fresh cup of coffee. "Even if the town could just let it all drop, her father still sits down with the other old-timers in front of the general store and, at least every other week, brings up how his family is so innocent and how their name has been slurred without cause. He won't let it go."

"Oh, my." Anne looked at Grace and then stared at her reflection in the black liquid of her coffee cup.

Grace nodded. "There's some serious bitterness between Paul and Garret, that's for sure."

"Garret Jones? The curator?" Anne asked.

"Yep. He was the curator when the society dissolved. From what I can recall, he pretty much placed the blame for the society folding squarely on Paul's shoulders," said Grace.

Anne frowned. "Was Paul involved in the society in some way?"

Grace shook her head. "Not hardly. Garret's great-grandfather was one of the founders of the society. There's been bad blood between the Jones family and the Rhodes family ever since the map went missing and Alfred was accused of stealing it."

"I can understand that, but I don't get why Garret would blame Paul."

"Oh." Grace set her cup on the table. "Because Garret had applied to use some of the funds earmarked for future town purchases to buy an artifact for the society to return the society to the level of prestige it once had. The town council was considering the application, and then it was discovered the money was missing."

"And Paul was accused of embezzling it," Anne said.

Grace nodded. "Right. Although there was never enough official evidence to charge Paul, the townsfolk all believed him to be responsible. He was, after all, the town's chief financial officer with access to the money at all times."

"What a mess."

"Yeah." Grace took a final sip of her coffee. "Like I said, I'll do some digging around on my own and see what I can find out." She tossed some bills onto the table.

Anne did the same, then they both slipped on their jackets and headed outside. A blast of cold air slammed against them.

"I remember the highs in September reaching into the sixties," Anne said. "Maybe my memory's worse than I thought."

Grace chuckled as she fastened her seat belt. "Every few years, we get a really early and hard winter. Looks like this year is going to be one of them."

"You'd think I'd be used to cold weather, coming from New York, but here...I don't know. It's like the cold sinks right into your bones."

"It does feel like that sometimes." Grace turned the Jeep onto Main Street. "I really enjoyed this. Thank you for calling."

"I enjoyed it too. We'll have to plan to do it again soon. Maybe for lunch," Anne said.

"Ah, now you're speaking my language." Grace parked her Jeep on the curb in front of the *Gazette*. "I wake up planning my lunch."

Anne laughed as she headed to the building. "I like to eat, but I don't think I'm that bad."

They paused for Grace to unlock the research room for Anne. "I should be in my office all morning if you need me."

"Thanks, Grace." Anne turned to her work again once Grace had headed to her office. She pulled her notes and started back through the microfiche.

After an hour, she'd found nothing of any importance. She cleaned up the area, put the microfiche and indexes back in their place, and then headed to Grace's office. She wasn't there.

Anne stopped at the front desk and spoke to the energetic receptionist. "Let Grace know that I left, please. Tell her I'll call her later," she said.

"Sure will. Have a great day, Mrs. Gibson."

* * *

After settling in at the library and sending Remi out for a lunch break, Anne was pleased to find that Remi had finished inputting all the information from the application cards into the computer. Not only that, but the application cards were filed alphabetically in the plastic container. It looked like signing Remi and Bella up had been a great decision.

She ran her fingertips over the cards. She hated to put the lid on and store them on the shelf, they were so pretty. Even the feel of the cardstock was nice. She looked through them. Grace Hawkins had filled one out. So had Alex Ochs. Mildred Farley. Coraline Watson. And Reverend Tom Sloan. And...

Anne sucked in air. So had Garret Jones.

Now she remembered why the name sounded familiar — she'd met him at the grand opening yesterday. Tall and stately, he'd introduced himself to her as Mr. Jones soon after she'd spoken with the mayor and his wife. He was the man with a rather pointy chin and groomed moustache. Yes, now she remembered. He had hazel eyes, but their color was almost nondescript. It was his hair she recalled. A beautiful shade of gray that made her wonder if he'd grayed prematurely or if he had his hair dyed.

She stared at his application. His house wasn't too far from the library. Maybe when Remi got back, she should pay him a visit. He had, she recalled, told her at the opening that they should meet and discuss the option of him speaking on Blue Hill's history as a library event.

Anne returned the card to the plastic bin. She worried a lecture on the town's history might not be much of a draw for the townspeople, but she'd need to be open to any and every suggestion. She'd have to keep the library in people's mind, garnering their patronage and their support. Anne couldn't let Aunt Edie's legacy down. Not only did she owe the success of the library to her aunt's memory, but she'd become reconnected to Blue Hill. She'd begun to think of it as a sanctuary for herself and the children. She'd made friends with Alex again, and with Wendy and Grace, not to mention Mildred. She felt at peace at Blue Hill Community Church.

She'd come home.

CHAPTER NINE

There was no e-mail response yet from the private messages she sent the two people who claimed to have authenticated maps.

Anne tried not to let her frustration choke her. She went back to the message boards and posted, querying if anyone knew how to get in touch with either of those two specific people.

The library door opened.

She closed out the webpage, then stood, smiling, ready to help the newest patron of the Blue Hill Library.

Megan Rhodes faltered only a little when she saw Anne standing there. She recovered after a moment. "Hi, Anne," she said.

"Hello, Megan. Thank you for coming." She leaned against the counter. "I don't think I saw you at the grand opening on Saturday."

"I didn't make it. I'm sorry," said Megan.

"No problem. What can I help you with? Would you like to fill out the application for the library card?" Anne asked.

"Actually, I came to talk to you." Megan glanced around the library. She took the few steps to stand next to Anne. "I wanted to apologize for coming across so harsh the other day at the *Gazette*."

"Come on. Let's go have a cup of tea, shall we?" Anne asked as she led the way to the refreshment room. After she put on the kettle of water, she sat across the dinette table from Megan. "You don't really have to apologize. You've already explained," she said.

"I just am so tired of living under this black cloud of my family's reputation. I know you read all about my great-grandfather Alfred and the stupid map. You probably know about my grandfather, too, and the missing money," Megan said.

Anne nodded and cut her eyes to the kettle on the stove. Now would be a really good time for it to whistle.

Megan's eyes shimmered. "I can't vouch for my great-grandfather, because I have no memories of Alfred. He could've stolen the map. I don't know." She swiped at her eyes. "But I can honestly say I don't believe my grandfather had anything to do with the missing money. I remember he went to his grave denying having any involvement in the embezzlement."

Anne jumped up when the teapot whistled and hurried to turn off the stove. She poured the boiling water over the tea bags in each cup, then set a cup in front of Megan before sitting back down. "You don't owe me any explanation, Megan. It's none of my business," Anne said.

"But there was a reason you looked into the map's disappearance." Megan shook her head. "I'm sorry. I'm trying so hard to keep the peace in my family with the upcoming wedding. Every time someone even mentions that stupid map or missing money, my father goes on a tirade. He rants and raves. I don't want him stirred up just before my wedding. You can understand that, right?" Megan wore such hope of acceptance in her eyes.

Anne's heart nearly broke. "Of course. And I assure you, I have no intention of stirring up anything. As I mentioned before, I was only doing some research for the library. For the History Room," she said.

"But if you do something with the history of Blue Hill's Historical Society, you'll have to bring up the map. That's enough to put my father in a tailspin," said Megan.

Oh, if only she could trust Megan with the news about the map. But Megan and her family had too much at stake if the map was the same one. Anne couldn't take the chance of building up false hope, not without knowing if the map was the same one or not.

She reached across the table and laid her hand over Megan's. "I do understand, and it's not my plan," Anne said.

"Then what is your plan? What does the map have to do with the library? You made a copy, so it wasn't just random," said Megan.

Anne simply couldn't tell her. Not yet. "I've always loved mysteries." Wasn't that the truth? Alex would more than agree to that statement. She'd dragged him into more mystery chases in their childhood than she cared to admit. "A missing map is similar to a treasure hunt to me. I just wanted to see if I could figure out what happened to it." All true. Not the whole truth, but she'd stated facts.

"And your treasure hunt led you to my great-grandfather, right?" Megan asked. The lines around her eyes seemed to deepen.

"On the surface, of course," said Anne.

The hope returned to Megan's face. "But?" she asked.

Anne shrugged. "I don't know. We'll probably never know the truth."

Megan's shoulders sagged.

"But I'm not going to do anything to bring attention to the alleged connection between your grandfather and the map," said Anne.

Megan eyed her warily for a moment. Then two. Then three. Finally, she stood. "Well, I thank you for that. And I appreciate your time. And the tea." Although she hadn't even taken a single sip.

Anne put both cups in the sink, then followed Megan the short way to the front entry. "Come back soon, Megan. I welcome your visit."

Megan stopped and stared at Anne, as if she couldn't quite figure out how to read her. After a long moment, she gave a curt nod, then headed out the front door.

Back at the checkout desk, Anne couldn't keep her mind on possible library events. The map. Everything came back to the missing map. The crux of why the society had folded. The first smear on the Rhodes name.

Anne opened an Internet browser and initiated a search for someone to authenticate the map in a neighboring town, as Reverend Tom had advised. The suggestion was a good one, so that word wouldn't spread around town and get Megan's dad riled up. Anne desperately wanted to help Megan. Being a widow herself, she had a soft spot for other widows trying to rebuild their lives. Megan deserved happiness.

In less than thirty seconds, Anne found a name, number, and address of a respected professional expert qualified to examine the map. She placed the call.

"Midtown Antiques, how may I help you?" the cheery voice asked.

"I'd like to speak to Mr. Bridges, please," Anne said.

"One moment." Elevator music flooded the connection.

Remi returned to the library, all smiles as usual. Anne gave her a little wave.

"This is Mr. Bridges." The man's voice indicated he must be in his later years, and the gruffness bespoke of a former smoker.

"Mr. Bridges, I'm Anne Gibson, the librarian over in Blue Hill. I have a map I'd like you to examine." She briefly gave the information from the map itself: the name, year, markings, and crest.

"I have to admit, I'm curious, Mrs. Gibson."

"So, you would be willing to look at it for possible authentication?" Anne asked.

"Of course. I will need to evaluate the map's overall style, the printing technique used, the paper type, the supposed date, color, and the map's condition before I could make any determination," said Mr. Bridges.

"That sounds wonderful." She eyed the time on the computer. "I can bring it to you now," said Anne. She had just enough time to drive over, drop it off, and get back to pick the kids up from school. But she had to leave right now, or she'd be cutting it awfully close.

"I'm sorry, Mrs. Gibson, I can't take it yet. I'm leaving in the morning for a two-week vacation."

Anne's heart fell to her toes. Two weeks?

"I'm happy to receive it upon my return and analyze this map for you. Why don't we go ahead and set up a time?" asked Mr. Bridges.

"Yes. Let's do that." Although she hated to wait, Anne and Mr. Bridges worked out the day and time she would deliver the map to him.

"I look forward to seeing you then. In the meantime, I suggest you handle the map as little as possible and that you put it in a safe place," he said.

"Thank you again, Mr. Bridges, and have a lovely vacation." A safe place? She hung up the phone just as Remi returned to the front counter.

"Is there anything specific you'd like me to do now, Mrs. Gibson?" Remi asked.

It wasn't as if there were people milling about. "Didn't you say something about setting up the library on social media sites?" Anne asked.

Remi smiled. "Yes, ma'am."

"Why don't you start on that? I've got a few things I need to do before I pick the kids up from school." Anne stood up from her seat at the checkout desk. "Use this computer," she said.

Once Remi was settled, Anne ran to her room, grabbed her digital camera, and then returned. She pulled a key from her pocket and unlocked the desk drawer. She slipped on a pair of latex gloves and slowly pulled the map from the drawer and out from between the pieces of acrylic. She took various photos of the map, some close-ups of different attributes, at all different angles. When she'd shot more than fifty pictures, she carefully returned the map to the drawer, locked it, and slipped the key back into her pocket.

"Mrs. Gibson, come look at this." Remi turned the computer monitor so Anne could see. A lovely, clean, and concise information page popped up on one of the popular social media sites.

"Wow, you did that already?" Anne asked.

Remi nodded at her camera. "If you'll go take a couple of pictures of the library right quick, I can get those uploaded."

Glancing at her watch, Anne shook her head. "I don't have time before I pick up the kids."

"If you're okay with it, I can take some pictures and upload them," Remi said.

Anne handed the girl the camera. "Thank you. I'll be back soon."

"No rush." Remi was already moving from behind the checkout desk.

She drove to the school and parked in the student pickup line, but her thoughts were still on the map. Having to wait two weeks was going to be hard. Really hard.

Anne pulled out her smartphone and opened a search browser. This time, she typed in 'William Scull' in the search bar. Maybe he'd drawn more than one map. If so, perhaps she could view his cartouche. Most cartographers had a distinct cartouche, or title area, that they utilized on each of their maps.

The result page for William Scull loaded. She followed the link for his biography, then skimmed the information. It seemed Mr. Scull was not only an American cartographer but also an officer in the Revolutionary War. Even more interesting was the fact that he was the son of Nicholas Scull, the colonial Surveyor General of Pennsylvania. Apparently, according to the online information, William Scull was rumored to have drawn several maps that Lewis and Clark used during the expedition period.

Could she possibly have an authentic William Scull map in her possession? Was it the same map the Blue Hill Historical Society once owned but went missing?

The backseat car door opened, pulling Anne's attention. She cleared her smartphone as she twisted to help Liddie buckle her seat belt around her booster seat. "How was school today, honey?"

"I'm learning patterns. I'm good, Miss Reed says."

"Repetitive numbers in a row forming a pattern? Those are fun. I always loved patterns. They're almost like figuring out a puzzle," said Anne.

Liddie nodded. "Miss Reed says I have a knack for them." She kicked her backpack to the floorboard. "What's a knack, Mommy?" she asked.

Anne chuckled. "That means you're able to understand them easily."

"Oh." Liddie smiled. "Yep, I have a knack for patterns."

Ben opened the front door and started to sit.

"Backseat, Ben," Anne said.

He groaned and moved. "I'm tall enough, Mom. I don't want to sit in the back like a baby."

"I sit back here," Liddie said.

"Exactly." Ben stared at Anne. "All the other guys' moms let their kids my age ride in the front seat."

"I'm not other guys' moms, I'm yours. Buckle up." She inched out of the line and onto the street. "And I'm sure that's not true. It's not just something I decided to do to make you miserable, Ben. It's the recommendation of the state police." She pointed at the warning label on the underside of the sun visor. "And the recommendation of the company that manufactured this car."

Ben let out a loud and obvious sigh as he turned to stare out the window.

Anne's sullen son had returned. "I'm not a baby, am I, Mommy?" Liddie asked. "I've got a knack for patterns."

Ben didn't answer his sister, just continued to stare out the window.

Liddie stuck her tongue out at her brother's back. Although Anne caught it in her rearview mirror, she pretended not to see. *She* wanted to stick her tongue out at him too.

She really needed to figure out what to do about Ben. How could she confirm if he'd gotten mixed up with those boys at the abandoned tree house? Anne was almost positive he had. That was the only logical explanation for the change in his attitude and his recent disappearing acts.

At the house, the kids climbed the back stairs to their living quarters. Anne followed behind them. "You can have a snack of an apple and peanut butter, then you may both play for an hour or so before you have to start on homework."

"I don't have no homework," Liddie chimed as Anne opened the door.

"You don't have *any* homework. And if you don't have any assigned homework, you can practice patterns. Show me your knack for them," Anne said.

"Okay." All smiles, Liddie dropped her backpack on the cabinet Anne had set up for such items; then she rushed to the kitchen.

"What about you, Ben? Have a lot of homework?" Anne asked. She shut the door behind them.

Ben tossed his backpack beside Liddie's. "Not really." He strode into the kitchen as if he had a purpose.

He's purposefully trying to avoid talking to me, Anne thought.

Anne followed and pulled two apples from the bowl to the cutting board. "What do you mean by *not really?*" She reached for the apple slicer.

Liddie got the jar of peanut butter and set it on the counter.

"Thanks, Liddie. Why don't you get juice boxes for Ben and yourself?" Anne asked. She spooned a tablespoon of the creamy peanut butter onto each plate.

Her daughter did as she was told while Ben silently grabbed two napkins.

"Ben? Homework?" Anne asked.

"I just have to write sentences with my spelling words." He took the two paper plates with the sliced apples from Anne, placing one in front of Liddie and keeping the other as he slouched into a chair at the kitchen table.

"That's not too bad then." She rinsed the slicer and cutting board, setting them in the draining rack. She needed to keep Ben engaged in conversation while she could. "How many spelling words?"

Liddie dropped into her chair.

"Twenty." Ben took a slice and jerked it through the peanut butter.

"Ben ate without saying grace first." Liddie crossed her little arms over her chest.

"It's okay, Liddie. He just forgot. Why don't you go ahead and say grace for the both of you?"

Anne dropped her head as her daughter prayed. She sent up her own silent prayer. *Lord, I don't know what's going on with Ben, but I pray You guide my words and discipline to help him in a way that will bring honor to You.*

Ben choked down a huge mouthful. Then another.

Anne struggled not to lecture, but where had her son's manners disappeared? He'd never before eaten so fast, or so sloppily. A change was happening in her son, and Anne didn't like it. Was it part of growing up, or had he taken on too much self-imposed responsibility in acting as the "man of the house"?

Liddie, on the other hand, nibbled on her slices right up to the edge, without eating the apple skin.

Ben sucked down the juice box until it caved in on itself. He shoved the last slice of his apple into his mouth. "Can I go play with Ryan?" he asked with his mouth full.

She wouldn't lecture, but she just couldn't ignore bad manners, either. "Don't talk with your mouth full."

He made three more chews, then swallowed loudly. "Can I go play with Ryan?"

"It's *may I*, and you have homework," Anne said.

"I'll be back in an hour or so. Please, Mom?" He shot her the smile that always tugged at her heart.

"Be back here by five thirty. No excuses," she told him.

"Okay." He jumped so fast from his seat that the chair nearly toppled over.

"Clean up your mess first."

He tossed the paper plate and empty juice box into the trash.

"And carry your jacket. It's still cool out," Anne said.

"Okay." He headed toward the back door.

"Five thirty, I mean it. I'm making sloppy joes for dinner," she said.

"Okay." And then the conversation was over as the door slammed behind him.

Liddie finished her last piece, sucked her juice box until she slurped, and then threw away her trash.

"What do you want to do, Liddie-my-girl?"

"I want to play with my dollies."

Anne smiled. "That sounds like a good idea. I'm going to go down and check on the library. Come down if you need me, okay?"

"'Kay, Mommy."

Anne dropped a kiss on the top of her daughter's silky hair before heading down the stairs.

Such a sweet girl. Ben was usually a sweet boy also. What had gotten into him lately?

CHAPTER TEN

A nne finished uploading the pictures of the map from her camera after she dropped the kids off at school. Returning to open the library, without Remi's smiling face, was a very lonely business. She stared at the beautiful page Remi had created for the library on all the social media sites. She'd have to figure out some events soon to add to the calendar page—anything to draw people to the library.

She would make the library a success, not just for Aunt Edie's memory but for her own sake as well.

After saving the pictures of the map into a private folder, she deleted the pictures from the camera's memory card. She put the camera in her purse, then stood in the empty entryway of the library.

Silence surrounded her, wrapping around her in a suffocating grip.

Anne slowly exhaled. Libraries were supposed to be quiet.

But not this quiet.

She turned to the staircase and reached for the banister. When she closed her eyes, she was taken back in time. A time of playing hide-and-seek with friends in the house. Using the stairs as a get-away route when found. If she stood still long enough, she could almost hear Aunt Edie calling out to them to be careful.

She wasn't a child any longer. Anne opened her eyes. She might not be young any longer, but mysteries still intrigued her. And she had quite the mystery on her hands.

Anne made her way to the History Room, and she went straight to the shelf that held the book she'd found the map inside. A cloth hardcover with no dust jacket. *The Journals of Lewis and Clark.* She eased open the brittle cover and again noted the copyright date—1953. She turned the page.

Edited by Bernard DeVoto. Houghton Mifflin Company, Boston, The Riverside Press Cambridge was listed as the publishing company.

She turned the book over but found no other identifying factors. Going back to the nameplate, she noted that, even faded, the bookplate itself looked distinctive. A blue-silver color... But what was this, the edge of some family crest, perhaps? And the writing...

Isa. Isaiah? Isabel? Isabella?

es. Foxes? Or...Rhodes?

But *Isa* doesn't fit the Rhodes family members she'd come across: Alfred, Paul, and Megan. And wasn't Megan's father named Donald?

Carrying the book with her, Anne returned to the checkout desk and accessed the computer Internet. She loaded a popular ancestry site then initiated a search on Megan Rhodes's ancestors.

The fears Megan had expressed to Anne now clawed against her conscience. Surely an online search wouldn't hurt.

Anne also put out an open query to the ancestry message boards regarding searches of residents who resided in Blue Hill over the last one hundred years. If she could find the owner of the book, maybe she could learn how the map came to be inside it.

When the community of Blue Hill learned of Aunt Edie's bequest, many of the town's senior residents donated old books pertinent to Pennsylvania and their town. There were boxes upon boxes that had been donated. Mr. Merrill, the administrator of her aunt's estate, had inventoried all the donations for the donors' tax purposes. Anne had requested the administrator keep the list on a flash drive and in his office for safekeeping, since the library was undergoing so much renovation and reconstruction.

She should've retrieved the records as soon as the major reconstruction was completed. It had slipped her mind. She reached for the phone and dialed the number.

Mr. Merill's assistant took Anne's message that she would like a copy of all the documents and inventory lists from Aunt Edie's estate that pertained to the library.

As Anne hung up the phone, Wendy came through the front door, smiling as she made her way to the checkout desk. "How's it going?"

"Slow," Anne sighed. She'd hoped for more traffic in and out of the library than they'd seen over the last couple of days.

"Give it time." Wendy shrugged out of her jacket. "But I have good news."

"What's that?"

"A couple of ladies called me today. Seems there are quite a few wannabe writers in the area. They want to form a writers' group. And guess where they want to meet?"

A writers' meeting at a library? Perfect. "When do they want to meet?" Anne asked.

Wendy grinned. "That's why I'm here. They'll be here within the hour. Have you got coffee on?"

An hour? "Oh, there's so much we need to do." Anne started to straighten the items cluttering the checkout desk.

"I'm going to put on a fresh pot of coffee," Wendy said. "You figure out the logistics."

Anne chewed her lip. She hadn't really considered where to put groups that wanted to use the library for their meetings. But she needed to have a place for them. Where would be the most feasible location?

The Reference Room on the second floor had plenty of space to put up at least three six-foot tables without crowding the room. It was close to the stairs — and the elevator should someone need it. Perfect.

"Coffee's on."

"We'll set up some tables in the Reference Room. We have plenty of space there. That's where we can plan for groups to meet."

Wendy nodded. "I like it. So, where are the tables?"

"In the storage room," Anne said.

Wendy grinned. "Well, thank goodness they're on the same floor as the Reference Room." She led the way up the stairs. "So, have you found out anything more about that map?" As they set up the tables, Anne brought Wendy up to speed on everything she'd learned.

"You know, I remember hearing the rumors about some people being really upset about the society folding. It was like it was personal to a few of the townsfolk. At least, that's the way I remember the story."

"That was back in 1993. Garret Jones was the curator. Do you know him?" Anne asked.

Wendy nodded. "He's a strange bird, that one." She laughed. "Well, not really. I just think anybody who believes they're nothing but intellectual is eccentric. And full of themselves."

"Garret's like that? Full of himself?"

"Well, he's always telling anybody who'll listen how he's such an expert on Pennsylvania history—as if his degree is so much better than everyone else's because he went to an Ivy League college." Wendy shook her head. Strands of her black hair slipped from her cute bob cut and brushed against her chin. "He's just a little stuffy for my liking."

Anne could easily see that. Wendy was always in motion, either with the kids or without. It was like she was incapable of just sitting still. Unless she was reading. Then, well, then she could stay still and be lost in a story for hours on end.

They descended the stairs slowly.

"I want you to look at the book we found the map in. I think the bookplate has some sort of crest. Maybe you'll recognize it." Anne pulled the book from under the checkout desk counter and handed it to Wendy.

Very gently, Wendy opened the book to the opening page. She ran her finger over the torn bookplate. "It does look a little familiar…the coloring. But—" She shook her head. "I can't place it. Sorry." She closed the book and handed it back to Anne. "Maybe it'll be on the inventory sheet you get from the administrator."

Anne's response was interrupted by the library door opening. A flood of voices preceded the group of women into the front entrance. Anne smiled at the aspiring writers, then greeted them and offered them a fresh cup of coffee.

Ten, she counted. Ten people in the library. That was the most since the opening. Progress. Slow, but sure. She'd take it.

* * *

By the time she finished washing the supper dishes, Anne was so tired she wanted nothing more than to take a hot shower and fall into bed. Unfortunately, she still needed to get the kids down.

"Liddie, time for your bath," Anne said. She headed to the bathroom and began drawing her daughter's bath water.

"Can't I play a little while longer, Mommy? I practiced my patterns."

"No, honey. It's time for bath and bed," Anne said. "Come on, put your dollies up and grab your pajamas."

She nudged Ben's bedroom door open and said. "Your turn in the shower as soon as Liddie's out," She was still very pleased with the test paper he'd brought home this afternoon. A ninety-eight on his science test.

No response came from Ben, not even an argument.

Anne pushed Ben's bedroom door open all the way. No Ben. Her heart shot to the back of her throat.

"No, calm down, Anne," she said to herself. "Don't jump to any conclusions."

She rushed back to the bathroom, where Liddie was setting her pajamas on the counter. "What's wrong, Mommy?" Liddie asked.

"Nothing, honey." She turned off the water. "Do you know where your brother is?"

Liddie shook her head. "Is he losted again?"

"No, of course not. Go ahead and start brushing your teeth. Use the timer too." She stopped in the hallway, thinking. After dinner, he'd helped clear the table. It was his turn to sweep the kitchen while Liddie dusted the living room. She'd finished loading the dishwasher. Liddie had asked to go play until bath time. Ben had...

He'd taken out the trash because of the strong onion skins. She'd told him to empty all the trashcans and carry the bag down to the garbage bins.

Her heart raced. That was a good fifteen or twenty minutes ago. She hadn't seen him come back inside.

"Liddie, finish brushing your teeth. I'll be right back," Anne said. She went to the back door and opened it.

And nearly knocked over her son.

"Ben! Where have you been?" she asked. Her hands were trembling. She didn't know whether to hug her son or discipline him.

His eyes widened. "Carrying out the trash like you told me to," he said.

She pulled him into the house then shut and locked the door. "That was fifteen minutes ago. It shouldn't take you that long to carry out one trash bag," Anne said.

"I, uh, knocked over the garbage can and had to pick it all up."

Anne stared at Ben. Everything in her wanted to believe her son, her precious child. But in her heart, she recognized the look of her son's deception. "Ben?"

"I did." His protest only confirmed what her heart already knew.

She moved toward him, but she got a whiff of him. He smelled like spoiled milk and rancid meat…awful, but thankfully not like cigarette smoke. "You stink."

He took a step back. "I know. I told you, I knocked over the garbage can and had to clean it up," he said.

This time, Anne believed him, and she felt incredibly guilty that she hadn't before. She'd been so sure he'd been wearing his deceptive face…to think she almost punished him for telling the truth.

She tried to swallow the lump in the back of her throat. "I'll hurry Liddie's bath so you can hop in the shower," Anne said.

True to her word, she had Liddie out of the bath and in her pajamas in less than fifteen minutes. "The bathroom is all yours, Ben," she hollered as she followed Liddie into her room.

"Mommy, are you mad at Ben?" Liddie asked.

"No." She ran the brush through Liddie's damp hair. "Why would you ask?"

Liddie shrugged. "Cuz you're always using the *mean voice* when you talk to him." She knelt beside her bed and began her nightly prayers.

Anne couldn't concentrate on the sweet prayers of Liddie. The *mean voice?* Last year, Liddie began calling Anne's stern tone the *mean voice.* Had she been too stern with Ben? So much so that Liddie would notice?

First, she found herself thinking her son was lying when he wasn't. Now, using too much sternness for no good reason. What kind of mother was she becoming? Certainly not the kind of mother she wanted to be.

Lord, please help me to be the mother they deserve.

"Amen." Liddie stood.

Anne put the brush on top of Liddie's dresser. "Scoot into bed so I can tuck you in," she said.

After Anne read a bedtime story, Liddie snuggled under her covers. Anne tucked them around her shoulders as she sat on the edge of her daughter's bed. "Can you keep a secret?"

Eyes wide, Liddie nodded.

Of course, Liddie couldn't keep a secret, but it was okay. There would still be elements of surprise for the kids.

She leaned forward and lowered her voice. "Since you and Ben have been so good and have done so well in school this week, I'm going to take you both on a special outing tomorrow after school," Anne said.

Liddie sat upright. "Really? Where?"

Anne chuckled and gently pushed Liddie back into bed. She re-tucked the covers around her daughter. "It's a surprise."

"Is it to a movie?" Liddie asked.

Anne shook her head.

"Out to eat? Are you taking us out to eat?"

Again, Anne shook her head.

"A park? Is it a park?"

"No, silly." Anne leaned over and gave Liddie a kiss. "You'll just have to wait until tomorrow to find out. Now, get some sleep. Good night. I love you."

Liddie wrapped an arm around her teddy bear. "G'night, Mommy. I love you."

Anne turned off the lamp, then pulled Liddie's bedroom door closed behind her. Ben headed toward his bedroom sporting his Spider-Man pajamas. Anne followed him.

Ben knelt beside his bed and began his prayers. As he prayed, Anne got a flash of the man he'd become. Strong, the spiritual leader of his family...like Eric had been. If only Eric were here now to see the potential in their son.

Ending his prayer, Ben slipped into bed. Anne sat on the edge beside him, pulling the covers up around him. "I'm really proud of your science test grade," Anne said.

He nodded.

"I'm so proud of the great work you and Liddie have done this week, so I've got a surprise for you."

"We're getting a dog?" The expectation...hope...happiness in his expression almost had her agreeing. But she couldn't.

"No. We're going on a special outing," she said.

Disappointment washed the hope and happiness right off his face. "Oh."

Unlike Liddie, he didn't seem to be excited. Didn't even ask where they were going.

"Well, okay." She gave him a brief kiss. "Good night, sweetheart. I love you."

"'Night, Mom. I love you too," he said. Ben rolled over to his side, facing away from her.

Her throat tightening, Anne turned off the light and shut the door. It seemed like lately, every day, in some way, she felt like a failure as a parent.

CHAPTER ELEVEN

A perfect day for an adventure. Even the weather cooperated, the temperatures climbing into the mid-sixties. Anne couldn't wait to pick up the kids and take them for their outing. She sat in the student pickup line, counting the minutes until the final bell rang at Blue Hill Elementary School.

Her cell phone rang.

"Hello," said Anne.

"Mrs. Gibson, this is Bella."

"Yes, what's wrong?" She'd been so happy to have Bella scheduled to work at the library today. She'd updated the events calendar with the writers' group's newly set monthly meeting.

"Nothing's wrong. I just wanted to ask if you have a copier on order," Bella said.

"A copier? What's going on?"

"The Garden Club ladies are here, researching how to create hybrid plants. I know you said you didn't want people to check out the volumes in the Reference Room. They'd like copies of several pages of one of the books you have, but there's no copier here."

"Ah. I see. Well, yes, we'll be getting a copier."

That was something else she'd planned to order but hadn't yet found the time since the completion of the renovations. "If you'll write down the book's title, the pages they'd like copied, and how many copies they'd like, I'll make the copies and have them ready for them to pick up in a couple of days," said Anne.

"Great, Mrs. Gibson. Thank you."

At least the library was being put to good use.

The bell rang and children spilled from the building. Liddie and Ben jumped into the backseat.

"I'm ready for our surprise, Mommy." Liddie struggled with the seat belt on her booster seat. Before Anne could turn around to help her, Ben had the belt fastened.

She smiled and pulled the car onto the road. That's the son she remembered. Maybe he'd just had a bad few weeks. Anne drove slowly down Main Street until they reached the flea market.

"We're going shopping." Liddie unfastened her seat belt and bounced out of her booster. "I love shopping."

Ben even wore a smile as he got out of the backseat.

Anne stepped out of the car. Both the kids seemed to love the flea market the first time they'd visited. Ben especially had loved going from booth to booth, scouring for little treasures. Each of the kids had picked out a lovely planting pot, and they'd spent an afternoon together planting two ivy plants in them to keep in their living room. By their expressions, it looked like today would be another successful outing.

Being a weekday afternoon, the flea market wasn't too terribly busy. The first booth held a variety of garage-sale type of items. Old clothes and shoes. Mismatched glasses and other dishes. A couple of coffee urns. Anne made a mental note to buy a couple of coffee urns for the library. It looked like she was going to need one up in the Reference Room.

The next booth had various odds and ends, but Anne found two sets of bookends that would be perfect for her living room. She purchased them, then tucked the bag's handles over her arm.

Liddie tugged at her hand. "There's a dolly store. C'mon, Mommy, I want to see the dolls." She led Anne, and Ben by proxy, across the wide aisle to a booth housing handmade rag dolls.

The woman behind the table worked on a doll in her lap, sewing on buttons for eyes. "Hi, there, sweetheart," she said to Liddie.

Liddie, normally outgoing and vivacious, clung to Anne's leg.

"Mom, can I go look around over there?" Ben pointed to the booth across the way. The one with trains and various depictions of Pennsylvania. "Please, Mom. I can't be here. It's all dolls." His voice cracked on the last word.

"You like dolls?" the woman behind the table asked Liddie.

Liddie nodded, but she didn't let go of Anne's leg.

Anne turned back to Ben. "Yes, but you stay right in that booth. I mean it," she said.

Ben smiled, relief beaming from him, and he ran across the walkway to the booth.

Anne squatted beside her daughter. "Are you okay?" she whispered.

"She's kind of scary," Liddie whispered back, her words barely audible even though Anne was very, very close.

What? Anne put her lips close to Liddie's ear. "She's just very old, Liddie."

"She looks all wrinkly like the sheets when you forgot to get them out of the dryer."

"Those wrinkles are from living so long, honey," Anne whispered.

Liddie's eyes widened. "Oh," she whispered.

"She's one of God's children too." Anne stood and smiled at the woman. "You make lovely dolls."

"Thank you. I started making them for my girls. Then my granddaughters, and now for my great-granddaughters," the woman said.

"I like that one." Liddie pointed to a newly finished doll beside the woman.

"You do?" The woman lifted her. "What kind of dress do you think she needs?" She pointed at the basket of handmade doll dresses at the end of the table.

Liddie let go of Anne and dug through the basket. She pulled out a red dress. "This one," she said, holding it up proudly.

"That one it is then." The woman took it from Liddie and slipped it on the ragdoll.

Liddie tugged on Anne's hand until Anne bent down to her. "Can I have her, Mommy? Please? I'll be really, really good the whole rest of my life."

"The whole rest of your life, huh?" Anne chuckled and straightened. "I don't know how I can turn down such an offer." She nodded at the woman. "How much?"

"Five dollars for the doll and two for the dress," the woman said.

Anne paid the vendor while Liddie admired her new baby doll. "I'm going to name her Betsy."

"Thank you," Anne told the woman, then she turned back to Liddie. "Betsy sounds like a fine name. Come on, honey, let's go see what Ben found."

Ben stood in the booth across the way, holding a train car. As Anne approached, she recognized the twinkle in his eyes — a twinkle she hadn't seen since they'd moved to Blue Hill. It was the same look Ben used to get on Christmas morning. Pure, unadulterated joy and excitement.

"What have you got there, Ben?" Anne asked.

He stared at her with eyes wider than she'd ever seen. "It's a Lionel caboose, Mom. A real Lionel."

Lionel, in train talk, usually translated to expensive. Very expensive.

The man standing beside Ben, the apparent booth owner, chuckled. "It's actually a Lionel and Western Northeastern caboose." He held out his hand to Anne. "Caleb Granderson, avid collector of trains and Pennsylvania history memorabilia."

She shook his hand. "Anne Gibson, librarian of the new Blue Hill Library."

His narrowly oval face widened. "Ah, yes. Edie's great-niece. It's a pleasure to meet you. I adored Edie."

"How did you know my great-aunt?" Anne asked.

"Edie and I had many a discussion regarding Blue Hill history. Matter of fact, when I heard of her bequest, I donated a couple of books to your library on Pennsylvania history," he said.

"Why, thank you." Could it be so easy? That he'd donated the book in which she'd found the map? "Do you remember which titles?" she asked.

"Of course. One was a 1976 edition of *A History of Pennsylvania* by Philip Shriver Klein and the other was a 1988 copy of *History of the Pennsylvania Railroad* by Timothy Jacobs." He nodded at Ben, who hung on the man's every word. "You should check that book out since you love trains. Wonderful information in that book."

Ben nodded, his eyes still glazed over. He held up the caboose to Anne. "Isn't it beautiful, Mom?" he asked.

"It's lovely." And probably very, very expensive. Anne smiled at her son, then turned her gaze back to Caleb Granderson. "That's quite the memory," Anne said.

He laughed again. "I have an almost photographic memory on most topics, but especially on topics I love, like Pennsylvania history."

A photographic memory of history? "Well, since you seem to have known my aunt so well, and speaking of history, I wonder if you recall anything about the Blue Hill Historical Society," said Anne.

"The Historical Society... that whole debacle hasn't been filed as historical just yet," Mr. Granderson said.

"Mom, can I have it? Please?" Ben asked. He hadn't let go of the caboose. Every ounce of his pleading shimmered in his eyes.

She knew the question would come, but knew she'd probably have to deny him. And today had been such a good afternoon. She looked at Caleb. "I almost hate to ask. How much is the caboose?"

"That one's priced at forty dollars." He noticed Anne's face going slack. "But for a true collector, like Ben here, I can sell it for twenty-eight," he said.

That was still a lot of money for a single train car.

"Can I have it? Please, Mom?" Ben asked.

Eric had loved trains too. He'd said that when Ben got older, he'd buy him a complete Lionel train set because Lionels only appreciated with time.

"I'll even throw in some old tracks so young Ben can at least make a loop," said Mr. Granderson.

"Please, Mom?"

She nodded.

Ben let out a whoop and jumped up and down. He hugged Anne, nearly squeezing her so tight it hurt. But it was the best kind of hurt.

"Let me get that wrapped up for you, young man. I'll make sure it's safe and secure for you." Mr. Granderson took the caboose, set it on the table, and rummaged behind the counter.

Ben took Liddie's hand and began pointing out train cars, telling her all about them.

"So, Mr. Granderson—" Anne began.

"It's Caleb, please." He pulled a handful of train tracks and banded them before slipping them into a plastic bag.

"Caleb. About the society debacle?" she asked.

"Ah, yes." He wrapped the caboose in delicate tissue paper with the Lionel logo all over it. "It was a mistake for the society to dissolve, if you ask me. Of course, no one did. Had they, I would have told them they could have revived the society if they'd just expanded their artifact collection." He shrugged. "Then again, they might very well have done that very thing, and saved the society, had Paul Rhodes not stolen the town funds."

He shook his head and tsk-tsked. "Without those funds, Blue Hill couldn't even consider purchasing more items for their collection. It's a sad thing, really. The society had such promise," he said.

"I heard about the missing map." Anne dug in her purse for her wallet.

Caleb placed the wrapped caboose into a box then put the box in the bag next to the track pieces. "Yes, the stolen map. I'd love to see the map found. I'd love to own the map myself, but I'd loan it to Blue Hill for exhibiting, of course." He handed her the box.

Anne counted out the bills to him. "Do you think the map's recovery would help in the healing of rifts in the town?" she asked.

"Possibly." He took the money from her with narrowed eyes. "Why the interest? Have you found the map?" His voice rose.

"I'm just curious, of course. Because of the library." She turned to her children. "Here, Ben."

Ben rushed to take the bag from her. "Thanks, Mom."

"Anne, if my intuition is as good as I believe it to be, I suspect you've found a map that you think is *the* map," Caleb said. "I'd be more than happy to inspect it and give you my opinion on its validity."

She took Liddie's hand. She couldn't lie. "I did find a map, but I've already made arrangements for someone to inspect it for authentication. Someone out of town." She motioned for Ben.

"Thank you, Caleb. Ben will love the caboose and the track." She started out of the booth.

"But I could look at it and see if it's the map that was stolen from the society. At least rule out that possibility." Caleb followed her into the aisle, but she kept walking at a fast pace.

Too many people knew about the map. Wendy. Alex. Reverend Tom. Grace. Mr. Bridges. Now Caleb Granderson.

She couldn't wait until Mr. Bridges returned and she could get the map to him. The sooner she knew if it was *the* map, the better off they'd all be.

Anne led the kids into the parking lot.

"We're leaving, Mommy?" Liddie clutched her new doll to her chest.

"Yes, honey. I'm sure you both want to get your new toys home."

"I do." Ben's eyes still danced. "I can't wait to show Ryan this caboose."

Now *that* sounded like the son she knew! Maybe he hadn't connected with those boys by the tree house after all.

She unlocked the car and the kids climbed into the backseat. Anne opened the trunk and set the bag with the bookends inside. She closed the trunk and jumped.

Megan Rhodes stood there, hands on hips and wearing a horrified expression.

"Hello, Megan," Anne said. "You startled me."

"You have the map?" Megan asked.

"What?"

"I overheard you and Caleb. You have the map?"

"I don't know. I found an old map," said Anne. "It matches the description of the map stolen from the society about a hundred years ago."

Megan took two steps, closing the distance between them. "What are you going to do with it?" she asked.

"I'm taking it to an expert out of town who will be able to tell me if it's the missing map."

Megan dropped her hands from her hips, letting them fall to her side. "If you found it, then that clears my family's name."

"I don't know anything yet, Megan. Just that I found a map that sounds like the same one. It could be a totally fake map for all I know. That's why I'm taking it to an expert," Anne said.

Megan nodded. "Do you intend to keep your promise not to drag my family's name through the mud?"

"I'm not out to hurt anyone. I've told you that." Anne pushed her glasses back up her nose. "I just want to find the truth. I think this town's been ripped apart enough by rumors and misconceptions. I only want the truth to come out so healing can begin."

Megan studied her for a long, silent moment. Then, she nodded. "I believe you, Anne. You're the first person who's been truly interested in finding out the truth and not just believing all the old stories."

Anne reached out and squeezed Megan's shoulders. "I meant that I don't want to hurt anybody. I think there's been entirely too much hurt in this town owing to the shadows of the past. I just want to help with uncovering the truth so everyone can move on," she said.

"Thanks." Megan smiled. "I'm sorry for confronting you like this. I just heard you and Caleb, then Caleb was on the phone with somebody talking about the map being found and I, well, I just got upset thinking it was all starting again."

"No need to apologize."

"Well, I'd better let you get your kids home." Megan waved to them in the backseat. Both Liddie and Ben had turned around to see what kept Anne.

"Come by the library, Megan. We'll have a cup of tea and you can tell me all about your upcoming wedding," Anne said.

All smiles, Megan nodded. "I'd like that. I'll see you soon. Bye." She gave the kids a little wave then walked back toward the flea market's entrance.

Anne stared after her for a long moment. Caleb was calling people and talking about the map? Mercy, but she'd forgotten how fast rumors spread in a small community.

If only Mr. Bridges hadn't been leaving on vacation. She needed to find out if the map was the same one that had been stolen, and as soon as she could—so Blue Hill could finally have some answers.

CHAPTER TWELVE

Monday brought a beautiful late September morning to Blue Hill. Gorgeous shades of yellow and red highlighted the changing leaves. The weather wasn't bitter cold, but cool, and soon the autumn season would give way to October and all the fall festivals.

Anne opened the library after dropping the kids off at school. Getting Ben away from his beloved caboose had been a slight challenge. It was good to see him excited about something again.

Still, she couldn't help but wonder...those boys at the abandoned tree house... Their mothers probably thought they were on the right track also. What if Ben had actually left the school grounds and headed to the tree house? Kids had been playing hooky for generations, after all.

She lifted the receiver and dialed the number for the school. This wasn't really checking up on her son; this was being a diligent mother. Parents had to stay on top of kids these days.

"Blue Hill School, this is Ms. Oxford."

"Hello, Ms. Oxford, this is Anne Gibson." For a moment, she regretted calling. Would this tell the school staff that she was worried about her son, maybe make them think Ben was a troublemaker? "I just need to verify that my son made it to school with his lunch," said Anne.

Ms. Oxford chuckled. "It's been one of those mornings, eh? Hold on just a minute and I'll buzz his homeroom teacher."

"I don't want to embarrass him," Anne said.

"Don't worry. I'll have his teacher pick up the intercom. Hold on a moment."

Anne tapped her pencil against the counter. If he wasn't there, she had no clue what she'd do. She'd march down to that tree house, first, and see if he was there.

"Mrs. Gibson?"

"Yes," Anne answered.

"His teacher says he has his lunch."

"Oh, thank you so much," said Anne.

"You're welcome. We get these calls quite often," Ms. Oxford said. "You have a nice day."

Anne had barely hung up the phone when a couple of elderly women strolled into the library. "Hello, dear. Could you point us in the direction of the romance novels?" one of them asked.

Suppressing a chuckle, Anne directed them to the Fiction Room on the second floor. She made herself a quick cup of tea then returned to the desk.

The mayor's wife teetered in on heels way too high for her balancing abilities. "Hello there, dear. How are you this glorious morning?" she greeted Anne.

"Wonderful, and you, Mrs. Bultman?" Anne asked.

"Couldn't be better. Couldn't be better." She leaned against the checkout counter. Her flowery perfume engulfed the space. "I wonder, do you have any new suspense novels? I've got a hankering for a good, edge-of-my-seat read," she said.

Stifling a cough, Anne nodded. "Yes, ma'am. Check the new releases shelves in the Fiction Room. Top of the stairs, directly across from the Reference Room. Or you're welcome to take the elevator if you'd like," Anne said. She watched to see if Mrs. Bultman would take her up on the offer of a ride.

"Thank you. But the stairs are fine. Good exercise, you know." She patted the counter and turned to make her way to the stairs.

Anne smiled. This library just might work without her worrying or trying to plan. Along with that thought, one of her favorite scriptures came to mind. Matthew 6:34. *"Therefore do not worry about tomorrow, for tomorrow will worry about itself. Each day has enough trouble of its own."*

Maybe she needed to be reminded of that today. She really shouldn't worry so much about the future of the library. Instead, she should trust in God and deal with each day as it came.

"Hello, Anne."

Anne looked up and smiled. "Hi, Mildred. How are you today?" she asked.

"Fine. I'm just running by to pick up a couple of books for Coraline. Her gout's acting up again, and she's about bored silly. I told her I'd run by and pick out a couple of cozy mysteries to keep her company since she can't get out and about."

"We just got a couple of new releases in. You'll find them on top of the new releases shelf," Anne said.

"Thank you, dear," Mildred said as she turned toward the direction of the Fiction Room.

Smiling, Anne moved to the computer and opened her e-mail. She quickly answered her mother's message. The kids would be thrilled to know Mom and Dad were coming to Pennsylvania for Christmas. Liddie especially missed her grandparents. She would also have to plan a trip to see Eric's family soon.

The second e-mail, she didn't recognize the sender's address, but she did recognize the subject line: 1775 Scull map of Pennsylvania. It had to be one of the people from the message board she'd private messaged.

Her pulse racing, Anne opened the message and read:

Mrs. Gibson, I do have a 1775 Pennsylvania map with the cartouche of William Scull in my collection. It's been verified that Mr. Scull drew several maps during this time period. Would love to meet with you and let you see. If interested, please verify you can meet me at the main Pittsburgh library at ten on Saturday morning. Front lobby.

Anne quickly hit REPLY and typed:

I'm very interested. I will meet you at the Pittsburgh library at ten this Saturday morning. Am looking forward to meeting you and seeing your map.

"You have quite a good collection of these romance novels," one of the women said as she made her way to the checkout desk, her arms loaded with books.

Anne smiled, closing her e-mail program. She pulled up the woman's information in the computer, set the system to print out a library card that she'd had custom-designed to match the application cards, and then handed the card to her. She checked out the half-dozen books, slipped them into a plastic bag, and handed them to the woman. "Thank you, Mrs. Lacey. These are due in two weeks," Anne said.

"Two weeks?" Her companion chuckled. "You'll be lucky if she isn't back here in two *days* to swap out books."

"Well, that's fine too. I'm a fast reader myself." Anne smiled as the two women left, still giving each other a good, fun rattling.

Mrs. Bultman came to the desk, carrying two hardbacks. "I'm delighted with your inventory, Anne. Newest releases." She passed the books across the counter.

Anne went through the procedure to print the mayor's wife's library card then checked out the books. "Since these are new releases, Mrs. Bultman, they're due back next week," she said.

"Oh, I'll read them both this weekend. The mayor's going out of town on business so I'll have time to catch up on my reading."

"That sounds lovely." Anne couldn't remember the last time she'd been able just to sit down and read a novel in one sitting. With the renovations, grand opening, and getting the kids settled, there just hadn't been a lot of free time for Anne to spend on herself.

"You know, Anne, I heard that you might have found a map that once belonged to the Blue Hill Historical Society..." Mrs. Bultman said.

Word travels fast. Anne smiled. "I found an old map, but I have no idea how old or its origin. I'm taking it to an expert over in State College to have it examined," she said.

"Good, good." Mrs. Bultman hugged the hardbacks. "My husband and I just like to keep up with everything going on in our town, you understand."

Anne nodded. "Thank you, Mrs. Bultman. I'll see you next week."

She let out a long breath after the mayor's wife left. She took off her glasses and cleaned them with a pre-moistened lens cleaner.

A young man rounded the corner.

Anne slipped her glasses back on. "Hello. May I help you find something?" she asked.

"My dad said you might have something on rebuilding carburetors," he said.

Nodding, Anne moved to the other side of the counter, to the computer for patrons. She showed the young man how to search for what he needed, then helped him find the book in the Nonfiction Room.

After he filled out the application for a library card, Anne entered the information in the system, issued him a library card, checked out the book he'd found, and sent him on his way in a matter of minutes.

Footsteps creaked on the entry. Anne recognized the gait and smiled as Alex came into view. "Hi, Alex," she said.

"Hey, Anne. How's it going?" His smile was quick and easy. And familiar.

"Great."

He raised his brows. "Is that mysterious excitement I detect in your voice?"

She grinned and rested her chin in her hand, her elbow sitting on the counter. "Am I that transparent?" Anne asked.

Alex shook his head. "Maybe not to most folks, but, well, we were best friends, back in the day..." A shadow momentarily darkened his smile.

He cleared his throat. "So, anyway, what's the news you're dying to share?" He could still read her well—and was gentleman enough to change the subject when he sensed he was straying into uncomfortable territory.

"Well, there's a lot to tell." Starting back with her first research expedition at the *Gazette*, Anne spilled out everything that she'd learned since. She ended with the e-mail and her upcoming meeting on Saturday.

"You've been a busy little bee, I see. As usual," he said. This time, there was no discomfort in his smile.

"I think I'm actually closer to getting to the truth," she answered. "This town deserves some answers."

He nodded slowly, in that cautious way of his. "It does that, but, Anne, I don't think it's such a good idea for you to go meet this stranger alone, out of town. For safety's sake. You know nothing about him, not even his real name. All you know is what he's e-mailed you. It could all be a lie."

"But he could have the map that was supposedly stolen," she said.

"If he does, why hasn't he come forward in all these years and claimed the reward money?"

"He might not know. It was so long ago...unless you live in Blue Hill, there's no way for that information to be common knowledge."

Alex lifted a casual shoulder. "Maybe. But still, going to meet a stranger is a bad idea. What about the kids? Surely you aren't planning on taking them?"

Well, she had, but now that Alex brought up the possibility of a safety issue...I'll ask Wendy to watch them. If she can't, then I'll ask Remi or Bella Miller."

"That's fine. But you aren't going alone," said Alex.

Now wait just a minute. Who was he to tell her what she wasn't going to do? She'd been doing just fine on her own for three years now...she didn't need anybody stepping in and making decisions for her. He couldn't —

"I'll go with you." A shyness seeped into Alex's voice as he continued. "For safety's sake, of course."

Well. Hmm. She couldn't very well argue with a friend volunteering to go with her to make sure she was safe. "Okay."

He nodded. "Good. I'll bring Ryan over to play with Ben while we're gone, if that's okay."

"Sounds like a good idea," she said.

"Maybe after we get back from State College, Ryan and I could help Ben set up that track you got him. I have a spare piece of wood that would make a great base. It wouldn't take up much room if I can suspend it from the ceiling with a chain. It'd give him plenty of space to collect more pieces."

She smiled. "Thanks. He'd really like that," she said. "Thank you for offering."

"Well, I'd better get upstairs. There are a couple of windows I need to replace the latches on. Want to make sure they're airtight before winter hits." With a brief nod of his head, he was on the stairs and out of view.

Pulling her cell phone from her pocket, Anne dialed Wendy's number. She answered immediately.

"Hey, Wendy. I was wondering if you could watch the kids, and the library, on Saturday morning for a few hours," Anne said.

"Sure. What's up?" Wendy asked.

"I have an errand to run in State College. I'll need to leave about nine thirty."

"Not a problem. I have set up the kids' reading program to meet on Saturday anyway. This will just be a little earlier," said Wendy.

"Um, is it okay if Ryan is here too?" Anne asked.

"You *and* Alex have an errand in State College? Does this have to do with the renovations?"

Anne briefly explained the situation.

"Oh. I see. Sure. It's fine," Wendy said.

"Thanks, Wendy." Anne put her cell back in her purse and tucked it in the desk's bottom drawer just as the landline phone on the desk began to ring.

Anne fumbled for the receiver. "Blue Hill Library, how may I help you?"

"May I speak with Anne Gibson, please?"

"This is Anne, how may I help you?"

"My name is Dana Munroe, I'm an antiques collector. I heard you've been telling people you've found a 1775 Scull map of Pennsylvania."

"I haven't been telling people that," Anne said.

"So it's just a rumor?"

Well. Ahem. "I have found a map, but it hasn't been authenticated by an expert yet. I have an appointment to do just that very soon."

"Yours is a fake."

"Really? How do you know?" Anne asked. Was this woman a crack? Should Anne be concerned? Maybe she should call Alex down.

No, that was silly. She was a grown woman and entirely capable of handling such nonsense.

"Because I have an authenticated 1775 Scull map of Pennsylvania."

Anne recalled what Caleb had said about Scull, and what she'd read herself on his online biography. "It's been verified William Scull drew many state maps during the late 1700s. It's entirely possible, likely even, that he drew several that are probably very similar," Anne said.

"That is possible, but it seems quite coincidental that you *find* such a map just as your library opens."

Anne gripped the phone tighter. "What are you saying, Ms. Munroe?" she asked.

"Just that it's entirely possible that you are trying to pass your map off as an original so you can display it in your library and get attention. And money."

Anne swallowed the snort. "That's absurd."

"I don't think so. I plan to prove you're a con artist to everyone in Blue Hill."

Anne's words were held hostage by her mouth being drier than the Mohave. She'd never been so personally accosted before, and she didn't know how to respond.

"I think you're only spreading these rumors just to get attention for the library. And yourself."

"That's simply not true." Anne found her voice. "I found a map and have an appointment to have an expert examine it. If he authenticates it as an original, so be it. If it's a fake, that's fine too. I have no control over that."

Anne tensed her muscles to stop her trembling. "Either way, I can assure you that I've done nothing to draw attention to the map, and I'm certainly no con artist. I resent the implication," she said.

"Maybe you didn't even find a map. Maybe you're just spreading rumors to get the attention, then playing all sweet and innocent."

"I did find a map." Anne spoke from between clenched teeth.

"Prove it."

"I owe you no explanation, much less any proof."

"So you *are* making it all up. I thought so."

"Maybe you don't have a map and you're simply interested in mine," Anne said.

"Oh, so it's *your* map now. I have a map and I can prove it. Just tell me where to send copies of the papers of authenticity and a photo." Only breathing could be heard over the phone. "I can back up my claim. Can you?" Dana asked.

"I have photos too."

"Then let's swap them." Dana rattled off her e-mail address.

Anne did the same. "You know, it's quite possible both of our maps are originals. It doesn't have to be either/or," said Anne.

"But it usually is. I'll send you an e-mail soon." The connection went dead.

Shaken, Anne hung up then turned to the computer. She opened the private folder with the map pictures. Selecting one of the shots of the whole map, Anne e-mailed it to the address Dana had given her. As soon as she hit SEND, she wondered if she'd made a mistake.

Who was Dana Munroe, really? Had Anne just fallen for some sort of con?

CHAPTER THIRTEEN

"Anne? I've got something to tell you." Wendy's voice was lower than usual. More serious.

Anne pushed the cell phone closer to her ear. "What's wrong?"

"I don't know how to tell you this except to come right out and say it."

A knot twisted in Anne's stomach.

"There's a lot of talk around town about you and that map you found," said Wendy.

Anne groaned out loud. News traveled faster than the speed of light in such a tight-knit community.

"I've heard some talk."

"What kind of talk?" Anne asked. Surely nothing like Dana Munroe. Or, well, what if Dana Munroe *had* gone through with her threat and started telling people Anne was a con artist?

"Some of the people are saying you're just trying to stir up trouble by dredging up the past."

"I'm not. Wendy, you know I'm not."

"Sure, I know that. And I've told people that, but some of them aren't so sure."

"What can I do?" Anne asked.

"I don't know, but Anne, some of them are talking about boycotting the library all together."

Anne felt like she'd been punched in the gut. "What?"

"I don't know what else to say to them," said Wendy. "I've told everyone you aren't like that. I've told them I was there when you found the map and that you were as surprised as me."

"What do they say to that?" Anne asked. Surely they had to understand. They couldn't boycott the library! That was ridiculous.

"Some of them said you planted it there and *found* it when I was there to witness it." Wendy hesitated.

"You know I didn't do that."

"I know that, Anne, but some of these people...they don't."

"Why would anyone believe that about me?" Anne asked. "I'm from Blue Hill, for pity's sake. I'm one of them. Us. Whatever."

"You went off to college, Anne, and didn't come right back. You got married. Had a career. In New York. You were gone almost a decade."

Tears burned her eyes. "So that makes me an outsider? Someone not to be trusted?" Anne asked. She couldn't believe this. After the opening's success, she finally felt like she'd be accepted back into the town's fold again. But now...

"It just makes people a little wary of you is all. Some of them are calling you 'that New Yorker' again," Wendy told her.

"What should I do, Wendy?"

"I don't know." A long breath sounded over the phone. "I'm praying for you. I just didn't want you to hear the rumors from anybody else."

"Thanks, Wendy. I do appreciate it." Anne disconnected the call but continued to hold her cell phone.

What would she do if they boycotted the library? She had too much time and money tied up in the library restoration, not to mention this was Aunt Edie's legacy.

God, what am I supposed to do?

If the library failed, where would she and the kids go? She couldn't uproot them again. Not when they'd settled in and were doing well in school. It wasn't fair.

The stupid map!

Anne shoved her cell into her purse, then slammed the desk drawer closed. What was she going to do? She needed to figure something out, and pretty fast.

"Mrs. Gibson?"

Anne looked up. She'd recognize that moustache and hair anywhere. "Mr. Jones?" she asked. Anne slowly inhaled through her nose, forcing her blood pressure to decrease.

"So you do remember me?" He smiled and approached the counter, resting his arm along the smooth surface. "How are you this fine Friday afternoon?"

"Well, and you?" Anne said. She took note of the time. Remi would be back in thirty minutes so she could go pick up Ben and Liddie from school.

"Lovely, just lovely." He tapped his finger on the counter. "I came by to get my library card. I heard you had them in now," he said.

"I do." She pulled up his profile on the computer, then set his card to print. In less than two minutes, she handed him the card. "Here you go," she said. He needed to leave. She needed to think. To figure something out.

He took the card and tucked it into his wallet. "Thank you." But he made no effort to move.

She fought the urge to sigh long and heavy. "May I help you with something else, Mr. Jones?" Anne asked.

"Well...uh...I've heard some rumors around town that you've found a map. A very certain map." He stared at her.

But of course. The map. Was it always the stupid map? Now she knew how Megan felt, like the map hung over everyone's head like a dark cloud. "You and everybody else in town, it seems, has heard that rumor. Let me assure you, I don't know if the map is authentic or not yet, but I will soon," she said.

"Why don't you let me take a look at it for you? After all, I am a professional, and I was once the curator of the Blue Hill Historical Society who, technically, still owns the map," he said.

"Only the society no longer exists," Anne said.

"True, but I'm happy to look at it for you."

He might actually be the one person in town who could shed some light on the map's authenticity and be able to stop the townspeople from boycotting the library. "I really appreciate—"

Remi rushed in the door. "Mrs. Gibson, there's a man here to see you." She led the way to the checkout counter, the administrator of Aunt Edie's estate behind her, carrying an expandable folder.

Mr. Jones smiled at her, then ducked his head. "I can see you're busy, Mrs. Gibson. I'll come back later," he said.

"Oh. Okay." She'd let him look at the map later. She turned her attention to the administrator of Aunt Edie's estate as Mr. Jones left. "Hello, Mr. Merill. You didn't have to come all the way here," Anne said. "I would've come to your office."

When he smiled, he reminded Anne of her grandfather. Warm and sincere. "I wanted to come see what you've done with the place anyway." He passed her the large package, which she placed under the counter. He looked around. "Care to give an old man the full tour?"

"Of course." She stood. "Remi, can you watch the front for me?"

"Sure, Mrs. Gibson," said Remi.

She would have to make it quick, so she could pick up the kids. "Right in here is the History Room," Anne said. She stepped across into the room boasting two windows for natural light. "Then right through here is the Nonfiction Room." She led Mr. Merill over the threshold into the room that not only had two windows, but also the back door, as well as a working wood-burning fireplace.

"It's beautiful, Anne," Mr. Merill said.

"Thank you." She stepped back into the checkout area and pointed toward the back of the house. "The refreshment area and restroom is back there." She reached for the stairs. "Come on, I'll show you the second floor."

He followed her up the stairs to the second-floor landing.

"Our personal living quarters are back there," Anne said, pointing to the closed door that led down a short hallway to their living room and kitchen. "Here's the Reference Room, which we're also using for groups who want to meet at the library. We already have a writers' group on the calendar."

She stepped across the hall into the room with an aura of whimsy with its multicolored walls. "This is the Fiction Room.

One of my favorites." A couple of comfortable chairs sat in the middle of the room, with shelves all around.

"I can see why," he said. "It's quite inviting."

Anne smiled at his praise. She moved to the next room. "And this is the Children's Room."

"I love the bright colors." He smiled at the mural she'd had painted on the back wall. "A perfect place for a child to get lost in Story World."

She nodded as she stepped back into the hall. "Down there is the storage area." Anne crossed her arms over her chest, feeling like a preschooler holding up a first drawing to a parent for approval. "That's it," she said.

Mr. Merill held onto her shoulder. "Anne, you've done an amazing job. This is more than Edie ever envisioned. She'd love it."

Happy tears welled in Anne's eyes, blurring her vision. "Thank you," she managed to choke out.

It was as if Aunt Edie herself had spoken her approval and warmth poured like a balm over Anne's anxious heart.

After seeing Mr. Merill out, Anne left the library in Remi's capable hands and rushed to pick up Ben and Liddie. As it was Friday night — movie night at the Gibson home — they stopped by the DVD kiosk in front of the supermarket. A couple stood in front of the kiosk, scrolling through the movies.

A woman whom Anne recalled seeing in the library stared at her as Ben and Liddie argued over which movie to rent at the outside kiosk. Anne continued to walk up and down the sidewalk as they waited for the couple to complete their rental transaction, the woman's eyes never leaving her. Finally Anne stopped and faced the woman. "I'm sorry, do I know you?" she asked.

The woman shook her head. "Are you trying to stir up trouble in town?"

That map again. Anne shook her head. "Contrary to what you may have heard, I'm not trying to stir up any trouble."

"Did you find the map?" the woman asked.

"I found *a* map. I don't know if it's the map that went missing from the historical society, though," Anne said. "I've got an appointment with an expert to examine it and make a determination. Once that's done, we'll know more, I suppose."

The woman stared at her again. Hard. Even tilted her head to the side. "Well, okay then. I guess everybody will just have to wait to hear if the map you found is *the* map."

Anne gave a nod. "Yes."

The woman turned and walked away, heading to her car parked in the supermarket's parking lot.

The couple took their DVDs and walked away, too.

Realizing she'd probably just withstood her first confrontation, Anne felt almost giddy. She was still standing. She'd come through, no worse for wear. "Ben, Liddie, come on. It's our turn," she said.

After renting the movie, they returned home. Darkness streaked against the sky as they entered their living quarters.

"I've got to go let Remi leave," Anne said. "I'll be right back."

"Mom, I need to run over to Ryan's for just a minute. Okay?" Ben set the movie on top of the player.

"I don't know, Ben. It's movie night," Anne said.

"I know. I'll be back soon. It's important."

She crossed her arms over her chest. "What's so important?" she asked.

Ben stared at his scuffed sneakers. "It's guy stuff, Mom." He met her stare. "I'll be back really soon. I promise."

"Okay. Thirty minutes, that's it," Anne said.

He raced out the back door.

Anne turned to Liddie. "I'm going to go lock up the library, okay?"

"I'll get the cereal out," said Liddie. Movie night also meant cereal for supper, followed by popcorn and cuddling on the couch to watch the movie.

"I'll be quick." Anne headed down the stairs. "Hey, Remi. Did you think I forgot about you?"

Remi laughed. "No, ma'am. It's actually been rather busy," she said.

"Really?" Anne asked.

Remi nodded. "I had about twenty or so people come in and pick up their library cards. Most of them checked out books." She pointed to the computer printout she'd just taken off the printer. "Here are the requests for holds, and these are the interlibrary requests."

"So many?" Anne asked. So much for a boycott of the library. Anne let out a breath of relief.

"Bella and I will both be here tomorrow to help Mrs. Pyle. Good night, Mrs. Gibson."

"Good night, Remi," Anne said. "And thank you." She locked the door behind the teen after making sure Remi got into her car safely.

She turned off the computers, then headed up the stairs.

Liddie sat at the kitchen table, a large bowl of cereal sitting in front of her.

Anne chuckled. "You couldn't wait?" Anne asked.

"I prayed first."

Shaking her head, Anne laughed louder. "It's okay, honey. Is Ben back yet?"

Liddie shook her head, her mouth full.

Anne checked the clock. He should have been back a few minutes ago. What was with him? Did he really lose track of time so easily? Maybe she should get him a watch.

Then the old fear came over her. The boys at the tree house. Maybe she should check it out. Or maybe ask Alex or Wendy if they knew the kids who hung out there.

She poured hers and Ben's cereal, then added milk and spoons. He'd be here any second now.

Anne ate slowly, trying not to stare at the clock. Two minutes passed.

Three.

Five.

If he wasn't back in another five minutes, she'd go searching for him.

Finally, Ben burst through the door. "Sorry I'm late," he said. He dropped into the chair.

Sorry? That was it? No explanation? No reason? Just a *sorry*?

He took a bite. "Eww, it's soggy."

"You should have been here on time," Anne said. She finished her bowl and took it to the kitchen. She rinsed it, then placed it in the dishwasher. Liddie did the same.

"Let's start the popcorn, Mommy," Liddie said. She danced around the kitchen, holding the doll she'd gotten at the flea market.

Anne put the popcorn bag in the microwave as Ben emptied his bowl down the garbage disposal. She noticed he dumped a lot of the cereal. She refused to feel guilty. He should have been on time.

"Why were you late, Ben?" she asked.

"I just got to talking with Ryan about stuff," he said.

Stuff. Guy stuff, apparently.

The microwave dinged.

"Movie night! Movie night! It's time for movie night." Liddie skipped into the living room and plopped down on the couch.

Anne followed with the bowl of popcorn. Ben put the DVD in the player, then sat on the other side of Anne. The movie started — Ben had talked Liddie into watching one about a boy and his hero dog. The popcorn didn't outlast the movie.

An hour and forty-eight minutes later, the movie was over. After their bedtime routine, Anne tucked them in, turning out their lights and shutting their doors.

Anne made herself a nice cup of tea and sat down in the living room. She'd brought up the package from Mr. Merill. With her laptop sitting on the coffee table, she rummaged through the folder until she found the flash drive with the book inventory. She hesitated only a second before she popped it in the computer.

She ran a quick search for the title *The Journals of Lewis and Clark* and the selection was highlighted in the spreadsheet. The book had been donated by someone named Brenda Hodges.

Anne chewed the end of her pencil. Brenda Hodges. Brenda Hodges. Brenda Hodges. That name rang a bell. Something about Brenda Hodges and Aunt Edie.

But what?

Chapter Fourteen

I t's a beautiful day," Anne said. She stared out the front windshield of Alex's truck.

He nodded. "It is. I love weekends."

Anne had always loved Saturdays, too. Years ago, when Eric was alive, Saturdays had been a time for family. They'd gone to the park. Gone to a museum. Gone out to eat. Ever since Eric died, the days sometimes ran together. She tried to keep weekends special for the kids, but sometimes—like today—she had to take care of business.

"Thank you for driving me," she said. "I really do appreciate it."

"You're welcome. I still think you're wasting your time, but at least it's a pretty day and we get to visit," he said.

"Alex, I just wanted to tell you how great I think you are with Ryan. He's a good kid."

He flashed a self-deprecating smile. "It's trying at times, that's for sure," Alex said. "Sometimes I wonder what my sister was thinking. But then other times, I'm glad I agreed to custody in the event anything happened to her. I can barely remember what life was like before he came to live with me."

"It's very noble of you," Anne said. "Not many men would step in like this to raise their nephew."

"It's what my sister and brother-in-law wanted. It was part of their will. I'd agreed back when Ryan was born to step in as guardian should the need arise." His voice grew husky. "I really never thought the need would arise ..."

"I can't imagine." Anne reached over and squeezed his arm. "I'm so sorry. I know how close you and your sister were."

"I miss her. Every day."

She squeezed his arm again, then dropped her hand back into her lap. "How are your parents? I haven't even seen them since I moved back to town."

"You know Mom and Dad, always busy with training missionaries." He turned onto the road connecting Blue Hill to Pittsburgh. "They actually just got back into town this week. They're having me and Ryan over for lunch after church tomorrow." He glanced at her, then back at the road. "You should join us," he said.

Anne shook her head and chuckled. "I don't think so."

"Why not?"

"Because." Because Anne had always felt like his mother judged her for being such a bookworm. Anne remembered overhearing Mrs. Ochs tell Aunt Edie that Anne was a strange child, always living in her own head. Anne hadn't known what his mother had meant back then, but her words had hurt Anne's feelings.

"Well, maybe some other time," said Alex.

"Yes," Anne replied. "Another time."

"So, I think it's a nice thing you're doing for Ben," he said.

Now Anne was confused. "Doing for him?" she asked.

"Yeah. You know. Ranger."

"Ranger?" she asked, hating sounding like a parrot, but she was totally lost.

"Your stray dog. That's what he named it."

Anne shifted in her seat to face him. "What are you talking about?" she asked.

"The stray dog he found that is staying at my place until you finish all the renovations, which I have to say is just about done. And maybe Ben can take the dog home now," Alex said. "I can help you build a dog run in the backyard, if you'd like."

Dog? "Alex, I have no idea what you're talking about. Ben's been asking for a dog, but I'm not ready for him and Liddie to undergo the allergy testing. Eric was so allergic to animals. I keep telling Ben that. He—"

"Wait a minute. You didn't know Ben found a stray dog?" Alex asked.

"No. He's been asking me relentlessly for a dog, but I've explained how allergic his father was, so before we could think of getting a pet, he and Liddie would have to be allergy tested," she said.

"So, you didn't tell him he could keep the stray he found, but couldn't keep it at the house just yet?" he asked.

"Of course not."

Alex stared at her for a brief second, then returned his attention to the road. "Oh, boy." He turned off the road in State College.

The enormity of the situation slammed against Anne's heart. "Let me get this straight," Anne said. "Ben found a stray and told you I said he could keep it, but that he couldn't bring it home until all the renovations were done?"

Alex nodded, keeping his eyes on the road.

"And you believed him?" she asked.

Alex shot her a look of innocence. "Hey, don't shoot the messenger. How was I to know you hadn't given permission? I was going merely by what I was told."

Going by the lie her son had told. She simply couldn't wrap her mind around that. Ben had never lied to her before.

Well, she couldn't say that with one hundred percent accuracy, now could she? It made her sick that he lied. Made her heart ache that she'd have to punish him.

A lot made sense now, though. The constant disappearing was to go see the dog, the taking a shower so she couldn't smell the dog on him. So sneaky. She'd never have expected it from Ben.

She hadn't had to worry even for a second that Ben had gotten in with the wrong crowd and might be skipping school or smoking. No, he just did something she deliberately had said no to, and lied about it.

Alex made eye contact after stopping at a stop sign. "Hey, it happens. Kids are gonna lie on occasion as they start growing up. Ryan went through a stage last year where he kept telling little lies. Not even for good reasons. He just lied to be lying."

"But Ben's never fallen into that. What does this say about him?" she asked. And what did it say about her as a parent? Had she failed her son? Had she been so wrapped up in the library and map that she'd downplayed the changes in her own son?

Alex pulled the truck into the parking lot of the Pittsburgh main library. He turned off the engine then reached out and took her hand. "Look, don't beat yourself up about this. It happens. Kids learn their limits by pushing them. It's not your parenting."

Was he reading her mind? "How—"

He chuckled and squeezed her hand before releasing it. "Remember, I know you, and it's all over your face."

"Maybe Ben's having to lie to get attention," she said. "I've read that kids will act out just to get their parents' attention."

"That's true. But Ben, and Ryan, have different reasons to act out, now don't they? Both of them have endured a great loss, and both are now living in a one-parent family. Their adjustments are even heavier," he said.

"So because Eric died, and Ben has to only have me as a parent, he'll act out more?" she asked, then shook her head. "That doesn't give him an excuse to lie. What's next? Stealing? Worse?" She'd seen so many shows on television that started with a young man lying. Then stealing. Then cheating. Before long, they were murderers on a rage because their father died.

She couldn't let that be Ben!

"Anne, Ben's going to be okay. He's a good kid."

"But he lied," she said.

"Yes, and you'll get on him about it and lovingly correct him." Alex smiled gave her an encouraging smile. "It's not like he's telling lies just to see how many he can tell or how far he can push. He lied about your saying he could keep a dog. Sounds like he probably hoped he could wear you down so that you'd agree he could have a dog, and then he'd already have one waiting in the wings."

"He still lied," she said. How was she supposed to accept that? This wasn't Ben.

Alex pulled the keys from the truck's ignition. "And I imagine you'll see to it that it doesn't go unpunished." He chuckled. "I actually feel a little sorry for Ben."

She laughed. "Thanks a bunch, Alex."

He grinned his mischievous grin. "Now, come on, let's go see this guy's map."

Once inside the main branch of the Pittsburgh library system, Anne moved to the lobby. She didn't see any man with a map. She checked her watch. They were right on time.

"Here, let's sit down." Alex led her to one of the couches. "Do you have a description of him?"

Anne shook her head.

"Well, we'll just keep an eye out for anyone looking like they're here to meet someone."

Nerves bunched in her gut. Maybe Alex had been right and this was a waste of time. Like she'd told Dana Munroe, there could be several maps by William Scull during the same time period.

But they wouldn't be exactly the same, and that's what she needed to see for herself. If this man's map looked identical to the one she'd found, and his was authenticated, then she could ascertain the one she'd found wasn't an original…wasn't the one the Historical Society had owned.

Alex nudged her.

She followed his eyes and saw the man entering the library. About mid-thirty, wearing jeans and a beatnik cap, he carried a cardboard tube. The kind of tube used to protect a large document.

Anne stood, leaving Alex sitting on the couch, and met the man in the middle of the lobby. "Hello. Are you the gentleman I messaged with?" she asked.

"Mrs. Gibson?"

She nodded, then pointed at the tube. "Is that the map?" She asked.

He led her to the little bistro-sized table and chairs right across from the couch Alex sat on. "First things first. Do you have a similar map? Did you bring it?" His pupils were practically dilated and he leaned closer to her as he spoke, invading her space.

Anne didn't sit. She took a step back. "You said you were bringing your map for me to see." The way he kept shifting his eyes so quickly made her very uncomfortable.

"I thought maybe you had brought your map," he said. "To compare, of course."

"I didn't," she said. "Let me see yours, as we agreed, please."

He opened the container and pulled out a map. Even to her eye, she could tell the map was a fake. The paper wasn't nearly old enough. He unrolled it and laid it flat on the little table. The ink wasn't even faded.

"That's not even a good copy," she said.

"I haven't really had it appraised just yet," he said. "But the man I purchased it from said it might be real."

Anne took another step back, right into a person. Without even turning around, she knew it was Alex.

The man's face paled. "Is this your friend?" he asked.

Anne nodded. "I can't believe you thought for one moment that map could be authentic."

His face turned redder than the dress for Liddie's new doll. "If this one is a fake, as you say, I'd be very interested in purchasing a real one," he said.

She could tell by his tone that he knew his map was a fake. He'd probably bought it at some souvenir shop. Wasn't this just the day for lies?

Anne faced Alex. "Come on, let's go back home," she said.

Alex took her elbow and they headed for the door.

"I'm serious about wanting to purchase a map. Message me if yours is authenticated," the man hollered after them.

Anne marched to Alex's truck, her frustration emphasizing every step. She slammed the truck door after her.

"Hey, my truck hasn't done anything to you," Alex said softly as he started the engine.

"I'm sorry. And I'm sorry you wasted your time and the gas to bring me here. You were right. I shouldn't have come," she said.

"Hey, stop beating yourself up," he said. "You're trying to figure out something from the past to set things to right. That's admirable." Alex backed the truck out of the parking space, then eased onto the road.

Admirable? Seriously? She felt foolish.

"Come on, Anne. At least you're trying to find things out. You aren't just listening to rumors and gossip. You're digging around for the truth."

Megan's image filled her mind. "But am I hurting people with my digging? Should I just let it drop?" Anne asked. "Let the people of Blue Hill forget about the map and society again?"

"They never forget, Anne. It's always there, right under the surface, waiting to bubble up. You're trying to fix it permanently."

"I'm not doing so great at it," she said.

He laughed as he turned the truck on the street back to Blue Hill. "You'll get there. At least you're trying."

The rest of the ride home was in silence, but a very comfortable one. With hers and Alex's past, they didn't need to fill time with chatter.

"Thanks again for coming with me, Alex. I appreciate it."

He parked outside Aunt Edie's. No, her house. "No problem," he said.

She stopped him at the entry. "I'm sure you can understand that today's not a good day for you and Ryan to set up Ben's track."

He nodded. "I thought I'd grab Ryan and we'd head home. I have to figure out something to do with a dog," Alex said.

"No, that's Ben's responsibility. He shouldn't have ever brought you into it."

"He's a good dog, if that's any consolation," said Alex.

It wasn't. "I'm assuming he has no collar?" she asked.

"Nothing."

"I'll help Ben make up some flyers."

"When I get back home, I'll take a couple of pictures of him and e-mail them to you for the flyers," he said.

"Thanks, Alex. I appreciate you."

Alex grinned and nudged her. "Cut the boy a little slack. He just wants a dog."

They found all the kids in the Children's Room of the library with Wendy. Ryan and Ben rushed to the hall as they spied Alex and Anne.

"Can we put up the train tracks now?" Ben asked.

Anne hardened her heart against the pure joy in her son's face. "Not today," she said.

He glared at Alex. "But you said …"

Anne put her hand on Ben's shoulder. "*I've* made the decision."

He stared at her, confusion easily readable on his little face.

"Tell Ryan good-bye. You and I need to have a talk," she said.

Alex led Ryan down the stairs. Anne motioned to Wendy that she was taking Ben out, and to keep going with the kids, then led Ben to her own room.

"What's wrong, Mom?" Ben asked. He sat on the bench at the foot of her bed, but he wouldn't meet her stare.

Lord, give me the words and curb my own anger and irritation at him.

"Is there something you'd like to tell me, Ben?" she asked.

"Tell you?" His expression was unreadable. "What do you mean?"

She ground her teeth and counted to five. Slowly. "I mean, is there something you need to tell me?" She leaned against her dresser, crossing her arms over her chest, and stared at him. Hard.

His eyes widened and his face turned ashen. "Alex told you about Ranger, didn't he?" he asked. His voice was weaker than she'd heard it in a long time.

"Yes, Alex told me about the dog you found. He told me about the lie you told him." She shook her head. "I would've never taken you for a liar and a sneak, Ben. I'm so disappointed in you."

Tears filled his eyes. "I'm sorry, Mom. I just found Ranger and he looked as lonely as me, so we became friends," he said.

She refused to feel sorry for him.

"I kept asking you for a dog, but you kept telling me about Dad's allergies," he said. "But I already knew I didn't have them. I've been around Ranger for weeks now, and not even a stuffy nose." He stared at her with such openness.

While he had a point, it made no difference. "You lied, Ben. You know better. You know lying is wrong." She pushed off the dresser. "And you snuck around to cover up your lie. Taking showers so I wouldn't smell the dog odor." She shook her head. "You know better, yet you deliberately lied."

"I'm sorry, Mom. Really, I am." The tears finally escaped the confines of his eyes, sliding down the roundness of his cheeks. "I didn't want to lie to you, I didn't, but I wanted Ranger."

"You know you can't always have what you want. You're old enough to know lying's not an answer," she said.

"I know. I'm sorry." He bent his head.

She fought not to pull him in her arms. He had to learn. She swallowed several times to get the lump to move. "We're going to make flyers about the dog and put them up around town to try and find his owners," she said.

He jerked up his head. "But, Mom, he's—"

She held up a hand. "Just because he doesn't have a collar doesn't mean he doesn't have a family. Alex says he's a good dog.

He probably belongs to someone. You'll make up the flyers and we'll take them around town."

He hesitated.

"It's the responsible thing to do, Ben. It's not right if there are people out there missing their dog," she said. "It's not fair for Alex and Ryan to take care of him, either." Anne held Ben's gaze for a long moment. "You'll use your allowance to pay for dog food that you'll take to Alex. And you will apologize to Alex for lying to him."

He nodded.

"This isn't a reward, Ben. This is a responsibility. He isn't your dog. This will only be for a few days longer."

His smile disappeared. "A few days?"

"Yes. If no one claims him after a few days once the flyers are put out, we'll take him to the humane society," she said.

"No."

"Yes." She pointed a finger at him. "You can't just take what you want, nor can you manipulate a situation to get what you want. Under no circumstances are you going to keep that dog. Do I make myself clear?" she asked.

His bottom lip quivered.

"I'm serious, Ben. Do you understand?"

"Yes."

"Your punishment for lying is you'll do the dishes and the dusting and the sweeping for the next two weeks. And you aren't allowed to play with your train for a week," she said.

"But Mom—"

"No buts, Ben. You lied. You went out of your way to be deceptive. I can't tolerate that. I won't." She let out a breath. "I love you, Ben, and I want you to learn from your mistakes."

He stood, as sullen as she'd ever seen him. "May I go to my room?" he asked.

She shook her head. "No. Alex is e-mailing me a picture of the dog for the flyers. We need to go design them so we can put them out after church tomorrow."

He pressed his lips together and refused to make eye contact again.

That was okay. He'd get over being angry.

Anne did what a parent could only do at this point—she prayed.

Chapter Fifteen

There." Anne taped the last flyer on the pole outside the diner. "That's all of them."

After church and lunch, Anne had taken Ben and Liddie around Blue Hill to put up the flyers about the lost dog. Anne had made Ben pay for the fifty copies out of his allowance. He'd been quiet the entire time they'd put flyers in business windows and in prominent places around town.

Anne prayed the owners would come forward. She really didn't want to take the dog to the humane society, but she'd have no choice if someone didn't claim him. She had to follow through with the punishment, otherwise, Ben wouldn't learn to "say what he means and to do what he says." That had been one of what she'd called *Eric-isms*, sayings her husband was fond of repeating. Over and over again.

Ben had to learn his lesson.

She couldn't have asked for prettier weather, though. Sun shining brightly overhead, temperature holding steady at sixty-six degrees, and only an occasional gentle breeze pushing through town.

"Mommy, can we go play with Ranger now?" Liddie asked as Anne fastened her seat belt around the booster seat.

Anne wondered again at her judgment in letting Liddie see the dog when they'd delivered the bag of dog food to Alex's last night. She'd been as immediately enamored with the dog as Ben.

"No, honey. We're going home," Anne said. "Remember, Ben has some chores he has to get done." She shut the back door, then slid behind the steering wheel.

"But I don't," said Liddie.

"No, you don't. You can play with your dolls. Or maybe you can swing on the big tire swing Mr. Alex put up for you." Anne started the vehicle's engine.

Liddie's head bobbed. "I'm gonna swing. Me and Betsy."

Anne glanced in her rearview mirror. If only Ben was as easy to distract. She'd watched him with the dog, and he had seemed to come alive when feeding him and cleaning out the water bucket. He looked as happy as when playing with his Lionel caboose. She hated to crush his spirit, and prayed she wasn't, but he needed to accept responsibility for his lie and to learn the lesson.

She parked in the back of the library, close to the back stairs that went up to the second and third floors. "Ben, go ahead and start dusting, then sweep the floors," she said as she helped Liddie from the backseat.

"Okay, Mom." He drudged up the stairs behind her, dragging his feet. But at least he wasn't giving her an attitude.

Liddie danced into the house first, heading straight to her room. She returned in a moment with her ragdoll. "Me and Betsy are ready to swing, Mommy."

"It's *Betsy and I*, sweetheart." Anne smiled as she grabbed her laptop. "Okay, honey. Let's go." She glanced at Ben. "I'll be outside with your sister if you need me," she said.

He didn't answer but at least nodded his head.

She followed Liddie down the stairs. In the backyard, Alex had hung a tire swing from the large live oak tree. Adjacent to the back stairs, he'd put the old picnic table up. Anne sat down and opened her laptop. She smiled as her daughter jumped in the swing, holding tight to her doll.

Anne smiled and waved at Liddie, then opened her e-mail program. She zipped up her windbreaker and flexed her fingers.

The first few e-mails that loaded were from users on the historical message board. She opened the first one and read:

Don't trust users PAHISTEXP and IKNOWPAHIST. They've been kicked off several sites because they are notorious for claiming they have artifacts they really don't. Look elsewhere. Good luck.

She could vouch for IKNOWPAHIST's habit of doing that. He's the one she'd met at the Pittsburgh library and learned the hard way about him.

The next two e-mails were from other users on the board, basically warning her of the same thing. She e-mailed all three back with her thanks. Even if it was too late.

"Look at me, Mommy." Liddie had tucked her doll inside her sweater and swung higher, her legs kicking out the other side of the tire.

"Oh, my. That's too high, Liddie. You're scaring me." She smiled.

Liddie giggled. "It's not too high, Mommy."

"Hold on tight," Anne said.

The fourth e-mail she came to was from Dana Munroe, with an attachment. She opened the attachment first. The picture loaded slowly. It was a little grainy, but it was obvious the map in the picture was not the same as the map Anne had found.

All the research she'd done online showed that William Scull was rumored to have drawn several maps that Lewis and Clark used during their expedition assembly period. Both Dana Munroe's and the map she found could be authentic. Especially since Dana's had already been examined. Anne e-mailed Dana back, telling her just that.

"I'm going too high again, Mommy." Liddie drew her attention.

Anne stood, wrapping her arms around her waist. "Oh, Liddie. That's too, too high." She put her hands over her eyes. "I can't watch. It's too scary."

Liddie giggled and pumped herself higher.

Anne glanced up the stairs toward the third floor. The muffled sound of the vacuum drifted down. It was a beautiful day and the kids needed the fresh air. All too soon, winter would be upon them, limiting their time outside.

But Ben had to learn.

She ran toward Liddie and gave her a gentle push on the swing.

"Thanks, Mommy. Now I'm flying!" Liddie said. She leaned her head back, shaking her head so her hair swished back and forth.

Anne smiled. She'd done the same thing as a child, loving the feeling of flying. Of being free. Of feeling the wind blowing through her hair. Alex used to push her so high, high enough that he could run underneath her. She'd hold out her arms, not holding on to anything, using her legs to grip the swing tight.

She turned back to the picnic table. When had she lost that sense of adventure? That sense of daring?

With a shake of her head, Anne checked her e-mail again. Ah, a response from Dana Munroe: *I still think you're trying to con people. If you're not, prove it.*

Anne replied: *How?* She sent the message, then clicked on the last e-mail in her inbox. An automated response from the ancestry site she'd listed queries on. She clicked the link to go to her open queries.

She chewed her lip as she leaned closer to the screen and read. Megan's mother, who died several years ago, was named Isadora. Anne considered the bookplate in the book she'd found the map in: *Isa* and *es*...Isadora Rhodes?

Staring absently as Liddie slowed her swinging, Anne wondered. Could it be that Alfred Rhodes really *did* steal the map and pass it down to his son, who passed it to his son, and whose wife stuck it in a book for safekeeping? Perhaps no one in this generation of the family was even aware that the map was in the book, so it was given away, or sold at a yard sale, anything. Sometime down the road, the book landed in the possession of Brenda Hodges, who donated the book to the Blue Hill Library.

Anne took off her glasses and pinched the bridge of her nose. If that were true, it would devastate Megan. If true, it could implicate her family for three generations back.

She put her glasses back on and closed the site. The indicator that she had another e-mail lit up. She opened her inbox to find Dana's response: *Let my expert inspect the map you found.*

Anne quickly typed an answer: *Fine. As soon as my expert examines it and makes a determination, if he states it's authentic, we will have an expert of your choosing verify.*

"Mommy, me and Betsy are getting cold. We're ready to go in for some hot chocolate." Liddie stood beside the picnic table. Her little face was flushed with fresh air and sunshine.

"It's *Betsy and I*, honey. Okay. Give me just a second." Her e-mail indicator popped up. "You go on ahead, Liddie. I'll be there in just a minute."

"Okay." Liddie clamored up the stairs.

Anne checked her inbox and read the response from Dana: *Maybe you aren't trying to con after all. We'll see if you follow through. Let me know what your expert says as soon as he's done with his inspection and we'll take it from there.*

Her fingers flew over the keyboard. *Will let you know as soon as he inspects and makes a determination. I take it to him in less than two weeks.*

She shut the laptop and headed upstairs.

The phone rang just as she shut the door behind her.

Ben beat her to the phone. "Hello." In the space of a second, his face fell. "Yes."

Anne stopped and stared at her son. He looked like he'd just been kicked in the gut.

"Here's my mom." He held the phone out to her, looking as if he was about to cry.

"Hello?"

"Hi. I'm Emily Colbert. I think you found our dog? I saw the flyer you put out at the diner."

"Yes. That's your dog?"

"It looks like Duke in the picture. He got out of the yard a couple of weeks ago. We found his collar stuck on the fence. He liked to dig out. My Zoey is just heartsick."

"I understand." Anne watched Ben plop down on the couch and tuck his chin to his chest.

"When we saw your flyer, Zoey started crying. She's been praying someone would find her dog and take care of him until we could find him."

"He's a really good dog," said Anne.

Ben toed the edge of the rug under the coffee table.

"Yes, he is. So, what's your address? We'll come right away and pick Duke up. Zoey had me call you from my cell at the diner. She doesn't want to wait a minute more."

"I understand." Anne gave the library's address then hung up. She moved to sit beside Ben on the couch. "You need to go get the dog," she said.

He looked at her, fresh tear tracks down either side of his face. "They didn't take good enough care of Ranger, Mom. He didn't even have on a collar," he said.

"He dug out from their backyard, honey. His collar got stuck on the fence."

"Then he could've been choked to death," he said.

She pressed her lips together and smoothed his bangs, right where the cowlick always popped up. "He belongs to a family. It sounds like they love him and miss him very much." Anne stood. "You need to go get him from Alex's. They'll be here soon."

Ben shot up and ran out the door.

She wished she could take the pain from Ben, but she couldn't. This was part of growing up. Part of being responsible. She could only pray he was mature enough to understand that you had to do the right thing, even if it hurt.

"Mommy, do we have to get rid of Ranger?" Liddie appeared in the doorway, clutching Betsy.

"He's not ours, honey. He never was."

"But Ben loves him. So do I," said Liddie. Her bottom lip protruded.

"So does his owner. Come here." She sat down and pulled Liddie into her lap. "He belongs to a little girl name Zoey. She loves her dog. She misses him since he dug out of her backyard. She's been so sad," Anne said.

Liddie blinked.

"How would you feel if your pet went missing? Wouldn't you want him back if someone found him?" she asked.

Liddie nodded.

"Ben did a good thing by taking care of a lost animal, but he should have told me. We could have put those flyers up sooner and had the dog returned to his family sooner, so that little girl wouldn't be so sad." She stroked her daughter's silky curls. "Do you understand?"

Liddie nodded.

Car doors slammed downstairs.

Anne stood. "Come on. I think they're here." She led the way down the stairs and met Emily Colbert.

"Hi, I'm Anne Gibson," she said.

Emily stuck out her hand to shake Anne's. "Emily. Thank you so much." She helped her daughter from the backseat, handing her two metal braces to help Zoey stand.

Liddie immediately went to the girl of about eight. "Hi, I'm Liddie."

"I'm Zoey."

"What's wrong with your legs?" Liddie asked.

"Liddie!" Anne's face went hot.

"It's okay," Emily said. "Zoey would rather people ask than just stare."

Zoey nodded. "I have cerebral palsy."

"Do you always have it?" Liddie asked.

Zoey giggled. "Yep. Always. Since I was born and I always will, right, Mom?" She looked at Emily.

"That's right, kiddo." She smiled at her daughter.

"It's part of what makes me special," Zoey said.

Liddie held out her doll. "This is Betsy. She's a ragdoll. She can't stand up at all, but it's part of what makes her special"

Woof! Woof!

Ranger, aka Duke, ran straight for Zoey. Ben ran behind him.

Duke stopped about a foot from Zoey, dropped to his belly, and then crawled to her. His tail wagged so hard that his entire body shook.

Zoey let go of her metal braces and sat on the ground, burying her face in Duke's thick fur. The dog rolled on his side and licked Zoey's face.

Anne caught the unshed tears in Emily's eyes. "She's missed him so much. Even had trouble sleeping." Emily ran a hand under her eyes. "I felt awful because I left him in the backyard while I mopped the floors. Usually I do it when Zoey is outside with him, but she was at therapy, so I just thought I'd take advantage…"

Emily shook her head. "I should've known better. He loves to dig, and I keep meaning to call somebody to reinforce the fence, but I forget." She smiled at Zoey and Duke on the ground. "I'll have to call someone immediately. We can't go through this again."

"I know someone who could probably recommend a good handyman who could help you out," Anne offered.

"Really? That'd be great."

Anne rattled off Alex's phone number as Emily entered it in her smartphone contact list. "Thank you so much. For everything," she said.

Ben hadn't moved. He remained rooted in the spot, his eyes never leaving Zoey and Duke.

"I'm afraid my son's going to miss Duke," Anne whispered to Emily.

"He and your daughter are more than welcome to come by and play anytime." Emily gave Anne her address. "Zoey would love it."

"We just might do that."

Emily smiled, then turned to her daughter. "Zoey, we have to go." She helped her daughter stand, handing her the metal braces. "Duke, car," she said.

Duke jumped into the backseat and sat where a harness attached to the seat belt.

Emily helped Zoey get settled, then went around and secured the dog's harness. She turned to Ben. "Thank you very much for taking care of Duke for us. I told your mom that you're welcome to come by and visit us any time," she said.

Ben nodded but kept his gaze on the ground. Anne could only imagine the size of the lump in his throat.

Sometimes doing the right thing hurt so, so bad.

CHAPTER SIXTEEN

That's hard for Ben." Mildred took another drink of water.

"It is," Anne said. "But he has to learn his lesson. He lied to Alex, and he deliberately went behind my back to disobey me."

Mildred nodded. "True, and I agree he needs to serve his punishment."

A long moment of silence passed.

"But?" Anne asked.

"Well, dear, it's not really my place..."

"I'm asking for your advice," said Anne.

Mildred picked at her salad. "It's just that I understand how Ben feels. He lost his father and felt compelled to become the man of the house, but he's still just a little boy. Not that he'd admit that," said Mildred with a smile.

Anne just nodded.

"And he's made strides in making friends, right? He and Ryan made up after their scuffle and are friends. He's at least trying," said Mildred.

"I understand that, I do," said Anne. "But he deliberately went behind my back to disobey me and lied about it."

"And you've punished him for that. He just needs the forgiveness and compassion to come sooner rather than later," Mildred said. "But that's only my opinion."

"I know. And you're right. I just need him to understand how wrong lying and deception are first," Anne said.

"Good. I know you'll find the right balance," said Mildred.

"I think it was good for him to see Zoey with Duke. At least he realized how much Duke was loved."

"I know Emily and Zoey. Sad thing," said Mildred.

Anne took a bite of her sandwich. "The cerebral palsy?" she asked.

"Not that so much as Zoey's dad left when she was diagnosed before she was even a year old. Couldn't handle that his daughter was not *perfect*, so he just up and disappeared," Mildred said.

"That's awful. He just left Emily alone with Zoey?" Anne asked. She couldn't imagine tackling an infant alone. Eric had been a great father.

"Yep, left her without a single word or anything. Just got in their car and was gone," Mildred said. "Emily was devastated, of course, but she did what she had to do. I don't think she ever gave up hope that he'd grow up and come back home to her and Zoey."

"Wow. That's...I don't even know what to say," said Anne.

Mildred wadded her napkin and set it on the paper plate. "But after all these years, I think she's finally accepted the fact that he isn't coming back," she said.

"That's so horrible," said Anne. She took her and Mildred's plates and put them in the sink. She wiped her hands on the dishtowel. "I'm just glad we were able to give Duke back to Zoey."

"That dog's been a saving grace to that kid, for sure," said Mildred.

Anne nodded.

"But I know it had to be tough on Ben."

"It was," said Anne.

"You know, he told Ryan that while he loved the dog, he knew Zoey needed him more," Mildred said.

"He did?" Anne asked.

Mildred nodded. "Sounds like he's showing a bit of maturity, doesn't it?"

Anne smiled and narrowed her eyes. "Hey, whose side are you on, anyway?" she asked.

Mildred held up her hands in mock surrender. "I'm not on anybody's side here, I'm just stating facts." She dropped her hands into her lap. "Although, I have to say, there are quite a few young dogs down at the humane society that sure could use someone who's coming into a bit of maturity to love them," she said.

Anne shook her head and laughed as she headed to the checkout desk. "Remi, why don't you go in the back and fix yourself a sandwich?" she asked. "I just bought some lunchmeat and cheese. The bread's in the cabinet beside the refrigerator."

"Thanks, Mrs. Gibson." Remi headed toward the refreshment area. "Oh, the mail came. It's on the desk."

"Thanks." Anne grinned at Mildred. "We have mail. Guess that makes us official and everything." She reached for the stack on the desk.

Mildred laughed and shook her head. "It's the little things that impress you, huh?" she asked.

"I guess," said Anne.

The phone rang.

"Blue Hill Library, how may I help you?" She set the stack of mail on the counter.

"Anne? It's Grace."

"Hi, Grace. How're you?" asked Anne.

"Good. Listen, I need to talk to you. I did some digging around like I told you I was going to, and I found something that might interest you."

"Really?" she asked.

"Yeah. Can you come by the *Gazette*?"

"I can't today, and I don't have anybody covering the library tomorrow. How about Wednesday morning?" Anne asked.

"How about I come by the library tomorrow morning? Would that be okay?"

"Sure. Of course," said Anne.

"Great. I'll see you around nine thirtyish."

"See you then." Anne hung up the phone.

"Everything okay?" Mildred asked.

"Yeah. Grace is just going to come by tomorrow morning for a visit. She found something she wants to show me."

"Interesting," said Mildred.

Anne flipped through the mail. "Look, here's the *Librarian's Quarterly*." She tossed the slip of a catalog across the counter to Mildred. "They usually have some great recommendations."

"I should write some recommendations for them." Mildred turned through the pages.

"You sure read enough to write some reviews, that's for sure," Anne said as she continued sorting the mail. She tossed two sale ads into the trash. She paused at the handwritten envelope.

No postmark, so someone obviously stuck it in the mailbox. Anne used the letter opener to open the envelope. A single piece of copy paper sat inside. She pulled it out and unfolded it. Her heart stuttered as she read the handwritten note:

Stop looking into the map or you'll be sorry.

That was it…nothing more.

"What is it?" Mildred asked. "You look like you've seen a ghost."

Anne handed the letter to her but took the envelope and went to the refreshment area. "Hey, Remi?"

"Yes, ma'am?" asked Remi.

She held out the envelope. "Was this in the mailbox, or did someone leave it at the counter?" Anne asked.

"All of those envelopes were in the mailbox when I checked."

"Okay. Thanks." She turned to go.

"Is everything okay? Was I not supposed to check the mail?" Remi asked.

"Oh, no. You're fine," Anne said. "It's all okay." She forced herself to give Remi a smile then returned to the checkout area.

Mildred handed her the page back. "You should call the police," she said.

"And tell them what?" Anne reread the note. "That somebody put a note in my mailbox?" She shook her head. "This isn't police business."

"It's a threat. Did you not read the *you'll be sorry* part?" asked Mildred.

Anne stared at the note. "From someone who doesn't even know correct punctuation?" She smiled.

"It's not funny," said Mildred.

"What's not funny?" Alex appeared in the entryway.

Anne turned. "I didn't even hear you come in," she said.

"I'm light on my feet like that." He grinned then took in Mildred's serious expression. "What's not funny?" he asked.

"Show him the letter," Mildred instructed Anne.

"It's just a stupid note."

"It's a threat," Mildred argued.

"A threat?" Alex turned to Anne. "May I see?" he asked, holding out his hand.

"It's no big deal," Anne said, but she handed him the note.

He read it, the frown on his face deepening. "Mildred's right — this is a threat," he said.

"I told you." Mildred faced Alex. "I told her she should call the police."

"Nobody's calling the police." Anne took the note from Alex's hands. "It's just someone trying to scare me. Maybe because I'm getting too close to the truth."

"The truth about what?" Alex asked. His eyes were narrowed into little slits.

"About the map. About the past," said Anne. "About what really went on in this town."

Mildred shook her head. "It's a threat, plain and simple. You should treat it as such."

"Listen to her," Alex advised. "This should go to the police."

"It's my decision to make, and I'm not calling the police over nothing more than a scare tactic," said Anne.

"So what are you going to do? Nothing?" Mildred asked, crossing her arms over her chest.

"No," Anne said. She took off her glasses and pinched the bridge of her nose. She put them back on. "I'm going to see if I can figure out who wrote this."

"How do you plan on doing that?" Alex asked.

She moved behind the counter and pulled out the plastic bin with the library card applications. "By looking through these and seeing if the handwriting looks familiar."

"You aren't a handwriting expert," Mildred said.

"No, but if I find something that looks similar, I can check a little further, now can't I?" said Anne.

Mildred shrugged. "Well, then. Let me help." She reached for a stack of cards.

"Thank you." Anne handed Mildred some cards. She turned to Alex. "Do you want to help?" she asked.

He shook his head. "Actually, I came by to replace the latches on the back windows. I'm wondering now if I should install deadbolts on all the doors," he said.

"Don't be silly. It's fine." Anne waved him away. "Go ahead and replace the latches," she said.

He let out a sigh. "I'd feel better if you'd call the police."

"Alex." She used the tone she used on the kids to let them know she was in no mood to argue.

"Fine. I'm going," he said.

An hour and a half later, Alex had replaced the latches and left, and Anne and Mildred finished going through the applications. They hadn't found a single card that resembled the handwriting on the note.

"It was worth a try anyway," Anne said. She replaced the bin under the counter.

"Time to pick up kids." Mildred stood.

"It is that time, isn't it?" Anne called for Remi, who was shelving returns up in the Fiction Room.

"I'll see you later." Mildred headed to the door.

"Thanks, Mildred. For everything," said Anne. "I'll talk to you tomorrow."

After telling Remi she was leaving, Anne drove to the school.

The bell rang and children spilled from the school.

Anne started her engine, and in minutes, Ben and Liddie scrambled into the backseat. Ben helped his sister with her seat belt, and they were on their way.

"It's Tuesday, Mommy," Liddie announced.

Anne grinned as she looked at her daughter in the rearview mirror. "Yes, it is. What's so great about Tuesday?" Anne asked, although she already knew the answer.

"It's payday!"

Anne chuckled. When she'd worked for the library in New York, her payday had been every Tuesday, so that was always the day she'd given the children their allowance. Even after she lost her job, she'd kept up the routine. "So it is, Liddie. So it is," she said.

Once home and in the kitchen, Liddie couldn't even eat her snack of Clementine Cuties. "Mommy, it's payday." She held her plastic piggy bank.

"Okay." Anne pulled out her wallet. She handed Liddie ten dimes. "How much is this?" she asked.

"One dollar. For dusting." Liddie scrunched her nose. "But Ben did the dusting this week 'cause he's in trouble."

Anne nodded. "But you still get paid because you would've done the dusting, right?"

Liddie nodded. She handed Anne back a dime. "Here's God's."

"Your tithe, you mean?" asked Anne.

"Yes, Mommy." She put the other nine dimes in her piggy bank. They made a clanking sound as they dropped. "Listen, Mommy. That's a lot of money," Liddie said.

"It sure is. Now go put your bank back up in your room."

Liddie skipped down the hall to her room.

Anne turned to Ben. She handed him a dollar and ten dimes. "Here's yours, Ben."

He opened his old cigar box that had been Eric's. He gave Anne twenty cents. "Here's my tithe, Mom."

"Good."

He carefully counted out ten dollar bills and handed them to her.

"What's this for?" she asked.

"I want to make a donation to the humane society," he said.

Her heart squeezed. "What?"

"I didn't realize dog food was so expensive until I had to buy a bag for Ranger—er, Duke. The humane society has to buy a lot of dog food, and cat food. They're always taking donations, so I want to make a donation."

Anne had never been more proud of her son than in that moment, but she wouldn't make a big deal out of it. She took the ten dollars. "I'll put it up until this weekend. I'll take you to the humane society on Saturday and let you make the donation yourself. How's that sound?" Ben nodded. "Good. Thanks, Mom." He carried his cigar box back to his room.

Anne blinked back the tears as she sent up a prayer of gratitude for her son having learned a very valuable lesson.

Later that afternoon, after Remi had left and the kids were finishing their homework, Anne went through the library with glass cleaner and a lint-free rag. She polished all the glass display cabinets until they shone.

Finishing her task, she headed back upstairs. She and the kids enjoyed a simple dinner of a beef, potato, and cheese casserole before she got them bathed and in bed.

Sitting alone in the living room, a creak sounded. Faintly. She realized she'd dozed off. Had she been dreaming?

Before she headed to bed, she went to plug in her cell. Rats! She must have left the charger down in the library. Anne wrapped her robe tighter around her, unlocked the door at the top of the stairs, and stubbed her toe.

"Ouch!" She covered her mouth with her hand and went very still, hopping on one leg. A minute passed. Two. Good, at least she hadn't woken the kids.

She carefully went down to the library. Darkness engulfed her as she felt her way to the desk. She unplugged the charger and slipped it into her pocket. A piece of paper lying on the floor snagged her attention.

Lifting the sheet, she held it close to her face to read it. It was the printout of the day's activity. It must have fallen off the printer, but how had she missed it when she was picking up earlier?

Then the data hit her. Her heart dropped. Only returns? Not a single checkout? That couldn't be right.

Anne pulled up the program on the computer and requested the report again. It returned with the same results. No one came in and checked out a single book.

Could the people Wendy told her about really have followed through with their threats? Was the library being boycotted?

CHAPTER SEVENTEEN

The temperatures had dropped dramatically, dipping down into the low forties. The weather forecast called for heavy rain and cold. Just what Anne didn't need. Gloomy weather always put her in a funk, but it was usually a busy time for a library. Maybe the weather would drive some of the fine folks of Blue Hill in to checkout a new book.

Anne parked in her regular spot, rushing toward the library front door, then wondered why she rushed. It wasn't as if anybody stood there, waiting to get in. She hadn't even gone into the library this morning before taking the kids to school. Why depress herself if the library was being boycotted?

She unlocked the front door, turned the sign in the window to OPEN, and then headed to the checkout desk. She reached for the drawer to store her purse and realized it was already open.

Odd. She usually closed it very well when she took her purse out and took it upstairs. Anne shook her head and slipped her purse in the drawer and shut it soundly.

She pulled the scrunchie from her wrist and pulled her hair up into a ponytail. She needed to get it trimmed. If only she had time.

After turning on the computer, she moved to the other side of the area. She froze. Something wasn't right. But what?

She made a slow turn, letting her gaze linger. Not a book was out of place. The storage bins were neatly stowed under the counter. The —

Wait a minute. The storage shelves under the divider to the entryway weren't closed all the way.

Somebody had been in the library! She moved to the display case. Sure enough, there were some smudges, much like fingerprints. Without a doubt she knew now since she'd just polished that exact case last night after closing. No one would have been in the library since.

The map!

Anne rushed over and pulled open the reference desk's top drawer. The sheets of paper on top of the acrylic sheet might not have been as she'd left them — she couldn't exactly remember.

She eased up the acrylic sheet and let out a heavy sigh. The map was still there.

But someone had definitely been in the library.

She picked up the phone and dialed Alex's number. He answered before the ring ended. "Anne. What's wrong?"

"Can you come over? Someone's been in the library."

"Are you safe? Are you okay?"

"I'm fine," she said. "But I know someone's been in the library."

"I'm on my way."

Anne paced as she waited for Alex to show up. She went by the front door. It had been locked when she came in. She moved to the back door past the refreshment area. The door was unlocked. She was positive it had been locked last night.

192 | Secrets of the Blue Hill Library

"Anne!" Alex's voice thundered in the front.

She rushed to meet him. "I think they came in through the back door," she said.

He followed her and inspected the doorknob while she shivered against the frigid chill. "I don't see signs of it being picked, but that's not saying much," he said. "These types of locks are pretty easy to pick. I'll install some deadbolts."

She nodded, not arguing with him this time.

He led her to the checkout area and eased her into a chair. "Tell me how you know someone was in here."

She told him about the printout on the floor last night, the desk drawer, the storage shelves, and the fingerprints.

"Those shelves?" he asked, pointing at the glass display case.

She nodded.

He crossed the floor, then bent and studied the shelves. "I think you're right."

Anne joined him. "Can you see fingerprints?"

Shaking his head, he pointed at one. "See how it's smudge-like?"

"Yeah," she said.

"Looks like what would be made by someone wearing latex gloves."

"One way to find out." She went back to the desk and opened the first aid kit. She pulled out a pair of gloves and slipped them on. "Here goes nothing." She reached out to the unmarred bottom part of the sliding glass shelf and pressed her hand against it, then removed her hand.

The mark she left on the shelf looked almost identical to the ones above.

"Looks like you're right," she said.

"Hmm." Alex leaned in closer.

"What?" Anne asked. She pulled the glove off her hand and stuck it in her pocket.

"Well, the print you left is a little smaller than the one above it," said Alex. "So, I think we can rule out a kid leaving the print."

She crossed her arms. "Well, no kids have been in here since I cleaned the shelves last night."

"What I'm saying is, that print could've been left by a man or woman." He straightened and led the way back to the checkout area. "Is anything missing?"

She shook her head. "I don't think so. The important stuff's here. The map's still here."

"Tell me again about last night."

"I must've fallen asleep in the living room. I thought I heard a sound, but I could've been dreaming or it could've been one of the kids turning over in their bed. Anyway, I forgot I left my phone charger in the library so I went to get it." She paused. "Oh."

"What?"

"I stubbed my toe at the top of the stairs. I called out, but apparently not too loudly since I didn't wake the kids." She shook her head. "I came down stairs and got the charger, but then I saw the printout on the floor. I'm now certain it wasn't there when I'd been in the library earlier cleaning up, after it closed."

"You probably scared off whoever it was when you stubbed your toe," he said.

She nodded.

"You should call the police."

She blew out a long breath. Alex was right, she probably should call the police. But nothing was missing that she could tell, and there'd be a report.

"Anne?" Alex asked. He stared so intently at her that she had to force herself not to squirm under his scrutiny. "You're going to call the police, right?"

"I don't think that's the best idea," she said.

"What? Why on earth not?"

She told him what Wendy had said about the talk of boycott. Then she told him about not a single item being checked out yesterday. "I don't want to stir up more trouble. I can't take a chance on isolating any other person in town."

"That's ridiculous. Someone's broken in. With that threat you received yesterday and now this…surely you can see it isn't safe."

"There's no proof someone broke in, Alex. Really, what do we have? A note with no identifying marks that could've been written by anybody. Things moved in the library, but someone could easily say it's just my imagination because there's no sign of forced entry," she said. "And the finger smudges? Again, someone could say that I just thought I cleaned that glass, but was mistaken."

"Anne, you know all that's not true."

"Yes, Alex, I do. And I know you believe me. But what about the rest of the town?" Anne asked. "The people who think I'm just trying to stir up trouble? The folks who want to boycott the library because of me?"

"You should call the police anyway."

She shook her head. "It'll just make a bad situation worse."

They exchanged stares.

Finally, he let out a huff. "Fine. But I'm going to go get some deadbolts and install them right now."

"Fine." But she was already talking to his back.

She undid paper clips at the desk, her mind going in too many different directions. Who'd break into the library and take nothing? What were they looking for?

The map was the most logical answer, but it was still in place. Maybe Alex was right and she scared them off when she stubbed her toe and called out.

"Hey." Grace smiled as she carried two paper coffee cups with sleeves. "I took the liberty of stopping by the diner and grabbing us some coffees. It's gotten cold out there." She set the cups on the counter and dug in her pocket, dropping four little creamer cups beside them. "I sweetened mine there. Figured that was easier than getting enough sugar packets."

"Thanks." Anne picked the coffee cup off the counter and took a sip to test the temperature of the aromatic drink. "I really need it today." She took a long pull off the coffee, despite its scalding temperature. The warmth snaked all the way down into the pit of her stomach.

"Are you feeling okay?" Grace asked. "You look a little peaked." She shucked out of her coat before she sat across from Anne. "I hope you aren't coming down with a cold. The cold snap after some warm days always makes people get congestion."

"I feel okay."

"Then what's going on?" Grace asked.

Anne filled Grace in on everything that had happened lately. "But I can't call the police because there's no proof," she said.

"I agree with Alex," said Grace.

Anne shook her head. "Anyway, what did you have to tell me?"

"Remember I told you that I'd do some digging?" Grace reached down and opened her purse. She pulled out a little notebook.

Nodding, Anne took another sip of her coffee.

"Well, I did."

"You found something?" Anne asked.

Grace grinned and nodded. "An old interview with Alfred Rhodes from 1913 that never made it into the paper."

Anne set the cup on the desk. "Really?"

"Really." Grace nodded. "So old, I immediately put it in archival safe folder and placed it in a safe place...just in case."

"So what was the interview about?"

Grace looked at her notes. "I wrote down the important stuff. According to Alfred, the map was never real to begin with. He claimed the map was been forged by Isaac Jones, the man who helped start the Blue Hill Historical Society, and that he, Alfred, knew about it and went along with it."

"Isaac Jones?"

Grace nodded. "Yep, Garret Jones's great-grandfather."

"Did Alfred say why they forged the map?" asked Anne.

Grace nodded. "He said it was to be an interesting enough item to gain attention, since the town nearly voted against a society all together. But the item couldn't be too much a deal or experts would be crawling all over the place and the authenticity would be examined and that it was a fake would be easily determined."

The map was a fake?

"Anyway, Alfred claimed that once the society had been formed, he'd had an attack of conscious and planned to come forward with the truth, but before he could, Isaac Jones found out Alfred was about to blow the whistle so he took the map and reported it stolen, then accused Alfred of stealing it," Grace said.

Anne didn't know what to say.

"I know." Grace took a quick sip of coffee before continuing. "Even though there was never enough evidence to actually charge Alfred, the townsfolk all believed him to be the thief and wouldn't listen to his claim of the truth."

"Could that even have happened like that?" Anne asked.

Grace closed her notebook. "I would normally say no, but in this instance…"

"You think he might've been telling the truth?"

"Well, I don't know. But there's enough doubt in my mind. I mean, take this interview for example," said Grace. "This was newsworthy. Why didn't they run it? Why hide the interviewer's notes in the bottom of an old box about the case?"

"This is crazy."

"I know." Grace took another sip of her coffee, then stood. "Anyway, I've got to get back to the paper, but I wanted to let you know."

Anne stood and gave Grace a quick hug. "I'm glad you did. And thanks for the coffee. I really needed it."

Grace hugged her back. "Think about calling the police. Just think about it."

"I will," Anne said. She smiled.

"I'll talk to you later. Oh, and don't forget to check out today's edition of the *Gazette*." Grace tossed the paper on the counter, then headed out the front door.

Anne watched her go. What if Alfred Rhodes was innocent? She chewed her bottom lip. She needed to know. What would proving Alfred innocent mean to Megan?

Isaac Jones. *Isa es*. Was there a connection? Could Garret Jones shed any light on his great-grandfather's actions?

Pulling up Garret Jones's profile in the computer, Anne called him. It went to voice mail. "Mr. Jones, this is Anne Gibson over at the library. I've just heard something interesting regarding your great-grandfather and the map. I'd like to get your input. If you could call me back, I'd greatly appreciate it." She hung up the phone just as Alex returned.

He waved the plastic bag at her. "Deadbolts. For all the doors. No arguments this time," he said.

She smiled. "Fine. No arguments."

* * *

"I'm finished," said Ben. He hopped down from the stool in front of the library's public computer. He picked up his notebook and shoved it into his backpack.

Anne looked up from the newspaper. Grace had put the article and photo of the library's grand opening on the first page. Sadly, only a handful of people had been into the library today. Was she under a boycott?

"I did all my online research." Ben grinned.

She stood. "Well, good. Your sister's in the Children's Room upstairs. Take her with you to the third floor, okay? I'm going to lock up."

Ben nodded and started to leave but stopped when he heard Caleb Granderson's voice. "Hello, there, Ben. Enjoying your caboose?" He wore a tan, calf-length duster, the kind depicted in old western movies.

"Yes, sir."

"Good." Caleb turned to Anne, gesturing to the older man with thick glasses behind him. "Mrs. Gibson, this is Mr. Parsons, an expert in antique maps. We've come to look at yours."

She took a step back. "I'm sorry, but no."

Caleb stepped around the counter, getting into her space. "He's an expert and can look at it right here and give you his determination. No charge."

Anne took another step back. "I said no."

"Come now, Mrs. Gibson. What's the matter? I'm just trying to offer you a friendly service."

She turned to see Ben standing at the stairs. "Take Liddie upstairs. Now," she said.

He didn't hesitate.

"Mr. Granderson, I appreciate your offer, and Mr. Parsons, but my answer is no," Anne said. "I already have an expert."

"Oh, just a quick peek? Come now, what's the problem?" he asked.

Her back pushed against the standing reference desk. Her pulse spiked. "I told you, I'm not interested." Why was he being so demanding?

"I'm happy to just take a glance at it, Mrs. Gibson. I won't even touch it." Mr. Parsons stood right beside Caleb.

"No." She recognized the footfalls in the entry, and relief washed over her.

"Why so secretive, Anne? Just a look. What's the harm in that?" Caleb asked.

"Because she said no."

Caleb and Mr. Parsons turned in unison to face the much taller Alex Ochs.

And he looked anything but cordial at the moment.

Chapter Eighteen

Anne's breathing finally returned to normal.

Ben stood in the corner of the kitchen. "You okay, Mom?" he asked.

Anne forced the smile despite her anger. "Sure, honey. Go on up. I'll be behind you." Ben hesitated, then gave a serious nod before heading toward the stairs.

"Want to tell me what happened?" Alex asked. He handed her a glass of water from the refreshment area.

She took a sip. The coolness eased her overall discomfort. She'd always been able to take care of herself in every situation. "I'm not real sure." She told him about meeting Caleb at the flea market, and their brief conversation.

"He was so nice and affable when he sold me the caboose." She took another sip of water. "But today...he came in all but *demanding* I let his guy inspect the map. I kept telling him *No, thanks,* but he didn't care. He just kept on."

Her hands had stopped trembling. "I wasn't so much scared by him. I was more angry that he would come into *my* library and make demands."

"Well, you looked like you were handling the situation just fine when I came in." Alex took the glass from her, washed it out, and set it in the draining rack. "Just consider me your back-up."

"Thank you." She stood, smoothing her blouse. "Speaking of your coming in, how'd you know there was an issue?"

"Ben."

"Ben?" The fast image of her son's face at the stairs when Caleb had turned from genial to jerk in less than sixty seconds popped into her head, followed immediately by Ben's serious expression from just a moment ago.

"Yep. He called me. Said that a man wouldn't leave you alone and to come quick before you took his head off."

Ben...he sure took his role as the only man in her life to heart. He shouldn't. He didn't need to. She'd have to talk to him about that. No child should have that responsibility set upon their shoulders.

"So, I came on over," Alex said. "To save some poor guy from your wrath."

She smiled. "Ben was scared I was going to go after Caleb? That's funny."

Alex flashed her his roguish grin. "I'm more disappointed I didn't have to save you," he said. "Didn't you know knight in shining armor to save a damsel in distress duty comes along with my standard contracting agreement?"

She couldn't help but chuckle. As children, she'd demanded they play just those roles more times than she'd read *Goodnight Moon* to the kids. Except she hadn't been a damsel in distress but a princess locked away in a castle, kept at bay by a ferocious dragon, waiting for a gallant knight to come and fight the dragon alongside her.

She curtseyed. "Well, thank you kindly, sir."

He made a sweeping low bow. "All in a day's work, m' lady."

The tension evaporated like the warm temperatures of the day. Alex went serious. "All kidding aside, Anne, we need to talk about some security around here for you and the kids." She might be stubborn, but she would do anything to ensure Ben and Liddie were always protected. "What do you suggest?" she asked. "I don't want security bars or special locks or doors that will mess up the historic architecture lines of the house. Aunt Edie would've never wanted that."

"I agree. Since Edie's bequest left specifics on restoration work being kept in the era and style of Victorian, I understand." Alex leaned against the counter. "I was thinking more along the lines of an alarm system."

She'd had one at the apartment in Brooklyn, of course, but here in Blue Hill? "Do you think that's really necessary?"

Alex nodded. "I do. For a slew of reasons."

"Aside from keeping the kids safe?"

"Well, the back staircase is a direct point of entry to your living quarters," he said.

True. While she'd wanted their private entrance at the back of the house, it did make the door a vulnerable security point coming off the secluded backyard.

"All the entrances that face the back of the hill allow easy access to the house with little visibility of approach," Alex said.

Anne thought about Liddie swinging. Beyond the grassy area of the hill, one couldn't see very far as the hill sloped dramatically. That's why she wouldn't let Liddie play out back alone. It would be too easy for her to go a little too far and stumble, then she'd roll down the hill. And that's where the abandoned tree house sat. The front of the house had a steep knoll as well, but in the spring, it was covered in bluebells, thousands of them. It certainly looked less daunting.

Alex continued. "And if that map is authenticated, or if you acquire any other valuable artifacts for the library, you need to insure its safety."

She hadn't really thought about that.

"I'm sure your insurance will give you a better rate with an alarm system too," he said.

"Okay, okay." She held up her hands. "You're right. I need an alarm system."

He grinned. "Good. So I can set up an appointment to have it installed?"

"Sure. Whatever is needed," she agreed.

"I'll make the call in the morning."

She stood and gave him a spontaneous hug. "Alex, thank you. For the renovations, for being so kind to Ben, for being there for me." She let him go. "I really appreciate everything you've done for me and the kids."

"You are most welcome. Now, I think I'd better get home. Ryan will be sneaking chocolate if I'm not back quick enough." He nodded at the back door. "I'm going to bring up some firewood to the back porch, and then I'll lock everything up before I leave."

"Thanks, Alex." She rushed up the stairs to find Ben and Liddie sitting on the couch in the living room. Liddie held Betsy so tight, it was a good thing the doll was a ragdoll. Ben's face was paler than when he'd had the flu.

"Hey, you two," she said.

"Mommy!" Liddie said.

Both kids jumped up to hug her.

"Hey, hey…I appreciate the attention from the world's best kids, but I'm fine." She gave them both a squeeze, then sat in the chair opposite the couch.

"Mom, when Mr. Granderson kept getting in your face, I—"

She shook her head. "You were right, Ben, I was angry with Mr. Granderson."

"I saw that mad face of yours," Ben said.

"Yes, because he was invading my personal space. Everybody has boundaries of their personal area, and he stepped into mine," she said.

Ben's little brow furrowed. "Oh. I thought you were about to let him have it."

"I was fine, honey. He was just being…a bit demanding, and I was angry, but I can control my temper when I have to." She gave them both a big smile. "I don't want you to worry about this." The last thing she needed was for the kids to start having fears. Once those started, she'd be hard-pressed to reassure them.

"I'm sorry I called Alex then, Mom." Ben ducked his head.

"No, you did the right thing." How could she stress her point? She leaned forward, resting her elbows on her knees. "If you ever think there's cause for concern, Ben, for any of us, it's okay to call Alex. Just his showing up made Mr. Granderson leave without me having to order him to go. That was nice that I didn't have to lose my temper."

"So I did good?" Ben asked.

"Yes, you did the right thing." She smiled as Ben's expression lifted. "It's always nice if I don't have to be curt with a customer. The library is my business, so I don't want to have to be the bad guy." She leaned over and mussed Ben's hair. "I have to be the bad guy at home with you guys enough."

Liddie giggled, then hopped up and skipped around the living room. "My mommy's the bad guy. Where's your black hat?" she asked.

Anne laughed, so did Ben. She moved beside him on the couch. "You did really well, Ben. You showed a great bit of maturity in first off, minding me when I told you to leave, and secondly, calling Alex." She hugged him. "I'm very proud of you," she said.

"You know, Mom…"

"Yeah?" she asked.

He grinned, the smile reaching his eyes. "If we had a dog, we'd have some extra security."

"Ben!" She laughed with him, shaking her head.

He jumped up and chased Liddie through the house, both of them whooping and hollering.

Anne smiled at their antics, but the worry in Ben's face made her realize her son wasn't as oblivious to what was going on as she'd thought.

What else had he picked up on?

After dinner, Anne and the kids enjoyed a family sitcom together before baths. She tucked Liddie, and Betsy, into bed after prayers, then headed to Ben's room.

He sat crossed-legged in the center of the bed, holding a piece of paper.

"Well, don't you look all serious?" Anne sat on the bed beside him. "What's this?" she asked, nodding at the paper.

"I don't want you to get angry, Mom."

This must be serious. "Okay."

"Promise you won't just get mad and say no? Promise you'll at least think about this?" he implored.

Must be very serious. She nodded. "I promise."

"Okay." He handed her the piece of paper.

She scanned the handwritten note:

I, Benjamin Eric Gibson, promise that if my mom lets me have a dog, I will take care of it. I will give all my allowance to help buy his food. I will take him for walks. I will give him a bath when he needs one. I will let Liddie play with him. I will mind Mom when she tells me what I have to do for him. But most of all, I will love a dog.

Anne looked up from the paper to find hope twinkling in her son's eyes. She gave a brief nod. "I'll think about it," she said. "But I don't want you badgering me about it. I'll make up my mind in my time. All right?"

He nodded, then knelt beside the bed. "Dear God, thank you for Mom and Liddie. And Alex and Ryan. And thank you for keeping us all safe." He peeked at Anne, then blinked his eyes closed tight. "And thank you for letting Mom think about me getting a dog. Amen."

She pressed her lips together so she wouldn't smile, then leaned down and tucked the covers around her son before kissing his forehead.

After turning off the light and shutting the door, she checked the thermostat, turning the heat up before heading to her bedroom.

She set Ben's letter on her vanity while she changed into her pajamas. The letter beckoned her to take it, consider it, make a decision.

But what was the right decision?

* * *

Ben's eyes widened as she pulled into the parking lot of the humane society Wednesday after school. Ominous clouds hung low in the air, and late September wind gusted through Blue Hill.

"Mom?" Ben asked. Hope tinged his voice.

Anne turned off the engine and twisted to face the backseat. "Ben, you've impressed me with your choices lately. From recognizing the cost it takes to care for a pet and be willing to help with the responsibility of that, to instead of whining for what you want, presenting facts and a solid commitment plan, you've shown a level of maturity that I'm very proud of," she said.

Ben blinked several times. "Does this mean I get a dog?"

She laughed. "Yes, Ben, that means you're getting a dog. I filled out the adoption papers this morning after I dropped you off at school. You just have to pick out the one you want."

Her son was out of the backseat before she could even get her door opened to help Liddie.

"Can I have a kitty, Mommy?" Liddie asked. "I'd love it and take care of it and everything."

Anne shook her head as she undid the seat belt. "No, honey. Maybe when you're older and show you can accept the responsibility, we'll talk about it," Anne said. "Remember, Ben is four years older than you."

"So when I'm big like Ben I can get a kitten?" Liddie slipped out of the booster seat and onto the pavement.

"When you're as old as Ben, we'll discuss if you're ready for a pet of your own. It's a lot of work," Anne said.

Anne and Liddie trailed behind Ben into the humane society. He all but ran into the building.

"I'm here to pick out my dog," he announced to the worker behind the counter.

The girl smiled and nodded at Anne. She'd been the same one who'd taken Anne's paperwork earlier. "Well, young man. What kind of dog are you most interested in? Big or small? Active or more of a lap dog?" She moved from behind the counter. "Young or older?" she asked.

Ben's face went blank.

The girl laughed and put her arm around his shoulder. "We'll break it down easily enough. The most important thing is to select a dog you connect with. This will be your best friend, so you want to make sure you have an instant connection." She shot Anne a wink then led Ben around the corner. "Now, in here, we have our puppies..." Her voice trailed off as she moved out of hearing.

"Mommy, can I at least look at the kitties?" Liddie asked as she pointed at the cages along one wall, each housing a cat or a couple of kittens.

Anne nodded.

Liddie rushed and knelt beside a cage with three kittens playing. They immediately stopped pawing at each other and stuck their paws through the metal gate to reach Liddie. She giggled and crooned.

"Anne?"

She turned and smiled at Megan. "What are you doing here?" Anne asked her.

"I volunteer here every Wednesday afternoon. What about you?"

"Letting Ben pick out a dog," Anne said.

Megan laughed. "Well, I believe every kid needs a pet." A haunting look glimmered in her eyes. "If it weren't for my old hound dog, my youth would have been totally miserable."

Anne smiled. "I'm glad I ran in to you. I have something to tell you. About the map and your great-grandfather."

Wariness coated Megan's face. "What?"

"Through some research, an interview with Alfred has been discovered."

"An interview?" Megan asked.

Anne told Megan everything that was in the interview Grace found. "And I left a message for Garret Jones. Maybe he can do some verification." Anne squeezed Megan's arm. "It's possible that if everyone gets together, the truth can come out."

Megan's eyes shimmered under the cheap overhead lighting of the humane society. "Thank you, Anne," she said.

"I haven't done anything. And we don't know anything for certain yet." But she was happy to see Megan smiling. "I'm inviting Garret Jones over tomorrow afternoon at six, right after the library closes. Would you like to come?" Anne asked.

"Oh, yes. What you're doing is more than anyone else has done in decades. I really, really appreciate it." She blinked the tears free. "I can't even begin to tell you what the possibility of clearing my family's name, after three generations, means to me."

Anne shook her head. "We don't know anything for sure just yet."

"Oh, I understand. But just the possibility…" She smothered Anne in a hug. "Thank you for trying."

"Mom, come meet my dog," Ben said as he peeked around the corner.

"I'll see you tomorrow at six," Anne told Megan before taking Liddie's hand and joining Ben.

He stood beside a dark brown dog, whose head reached Ben's hip. "What do you think of him?"

The girl who'd helped Ben looked at Anne. "While we can't know his exact breed one hundred percent, this one's definitely got a lot of Labrador in him. He's about nine months, so he'll get a little bigger, but not too much. He's already been neutered, is housebroken, and has already stopped whining during the night.

"He's a favorite with the volunteers because he's so eager to please." The girl bent down and rubbed the dog between his ears. "Labs are great with kids, will play alongside them, but aren't too hyper," she said.

"Can I have him, Mom?" Ben asked. "He loves me already. I can tell." He shifted his weight from one leg to the other, back again, and then knelt beside the dog and buried his face in his neck.

The dog licked his ear. Ben laughed. A real, full-belly laugh.

Anne couldn't stop the grin from spreading across her face. "Of course. He seems perfect," she said.

The girl nodded. "Excellent. I'll just put his indentifying information in the paperwork you filled out earlier, and you'll be good to go. I'll be right back." She removed the plastic tag from the dog's collar.

"Can I pet him?" Liddie asked.

"Sure," Ben said.

She tentatively stuck out her hand. The dog nuzzled it. She giggled. "I like him. What's his name?" Liddie asked.

"I don't know." Ben studied his dog as Liddie stroked his ears. "What do you think I should name him?" he asked his sister.

Liddie took a step back, tilting her head to the side. "Hershey. 'Cuz he's the color of a chocolate bar."

Ben grinned. "I like it." He reached down and placed his forehead against the dog's head. "What do you think, boy? Is Hershey your name?" he asked the dog.

The dog wagged his tail, shaking his whole rear end then pawed at the floor in front of him.

Ben and Liddie laughed.

"Then Hershey it is!"

Chapter Nineteen

The rain beat down on Blue Hill like a child throwing a tantrum. The cold temperatures and tumultuous rain filled the Thursday afternoon with gloom. It matched Anne's hesitation.

"I'll call you tonight before bed, okay?" Anne kissed Liddie good-bye, choking on her own tears. This was the first time Liddie had spent the night with friends away from home. Anne was having a harder time with it than Liddie, who skipped off with two of Wendy's kids.

Anne normally wouldn't have agreed, but Liddie was so excited because school was out tomorrow for a teacher in-service date, and one of Wendy's kids had just gotten an indoor tent, and they were all eager to have an inside campout. Besides, she'd talked with Garret Jones this morning and he agreed to come by the library at six.

Wendy laughed. "She'll be fine."

"I know. And it's good for her to be doing something special with friends since the excitement of Ben's new dog is all about him," Anne said.

"Much jealousy?"

"A little. It helped that Ben let her name him." Anne shrugged. "Still, she's very aware Hershey is his dog and she doesn't have a pet."

"Well, we'll take her mind off that for the time being." Wendy grinned, then nudged Anne. "Go. We'll be fine. I promise to call you if she so much as asks for you, okay?"

Heart still aching, Anne nodded. "Thanks."

She got back in her car and let herself cry just a little. She'd bawled on Ben's first day of school, and came close to doing the same when Liddie started this year. Kids growing up was harder on the parents than on the kids, it seemed. At least for Anne. She wanted to hold them close, love and cherish them, yet give them the space to learn and grow into the amazing potential they had.

She made the quick drive back to the library, where Alex and Ryan were helping Ben enforce the back-porch area for a dog run for Hershey. She'd stressed to Ben quite explicitly that Hershey could not sleep at the foot of Ben's bed. He had to sleep in the back-porch's run. She'd even rounded up an old comforter and pillow for the dog.

Upon returning to the library, a welcoming popping sound greeted her. She wandered into the Nonfiction Room to find a roaring fire. The two oversized upholstered chairs had been moved slightly closer to face the fireplace, creating a warm and cozy atmosphere.

Anne herself wanted to sit down and read in front of the fire on this cold and wet afternoon, but instead she went to the door to the back porch.

Ben and Ryan played with Hershey and a ball while Alex worked on the door. She knocked on the glass and waved at them.

Alex stepped inside, leaving Ben and Ryan on the run. "It's bitter cold out there."

"It is. Thank you for the fire. It's lovely," said Anne.

"Thought you might like it."

"Would you like a cup of tea?" she asked.

Alex made a face. "How about hot chocolate instead?"

"I'm sorry. I don't think I have any cocoa."

He chuckled. "That's okay. We need to get home soon to start dinner." He held his hands out in front of the fire. "Got Liddie all settled over at Wendy's?" he asked.

"Unfortunately, yes."

"I understand," said Alex. "First time Ryan went on a sleep-over, I didn't get more than an hour's worth of sleep the whole night."

"I love that she's comfortable enough to stay away from me for the night, but it's bittersweet," she said. "I don't think it hit me so hard when it was Ben. Maybe because Liddie's the baby."

Ryan and Ben came in from the porch.

"Hey, Mrs. Gibson, me and Uncle Alex got the new latch all put in on the door," Ryan said.

Alex smiled at Anne. "What Ryan means is that we installed a new latch on the screen door. I reinforced the grate over the screen, too. Just in case Hershey tries to go exploring on his own," he said.

"Ah." Anne nodded. "Thank you both. Very much."

"Well, Ryan, we need to get home," said Alex.

Ben and Ryan said their good-byes, then Alex grabbed his umbrella and they left.

Anne and Ben ate sandwiches in front of the fire.

The rain kept coming down in sheets. Anne turned to Ben. "Will you please bring in a few more pieces of wood for the fire?"

she asked. It was almost time to close the library. She'd need to get ready for Garret's and Megan's arrival.

Lord, please let this go well.

"Okay, Mom," said Ben. Out the door he went. He was back in a few minutes, setting three logs of wood in the holder beside the fireplace.

"Why don't you go on upstairs and get your shower and turn in? You'll have to get up early to take Hershey on a walk," she told Ben.

He grinned. After telling Hershey good night and asking one more time if the dog could sleep in the house, then accepting her refusal, he kissed Anne and headed up the stairs.

The front door of the library opened. Anne moved to the front entry and smiled at the woman who was leaning her dripping umbrella on the welcome mat. She must really need something to brave this weather to come to the library. Especially this close to closing time.

"Hi, may I help you?" She smiled as the woman faced her.

"Are you Anne Gibson?"

"Yes," she said.

"I'm Dana Munroe."

Anne went still. The slight of a woman before her, standing no more than five feet tall, with her red hair close-cropped in a pixie cut, looked nothing like the Dana she had spoken with on the phone. Anne didn't have the words to respond.

"I'm here to apologize and explain, if you'll allow me," said Dana.

This should be interesting, Anne thought. "Let's go by the fire. It's bitter cold out." Anne led the way to the Nonfiction Room.

Once seated, Dana faced Anne. "I'm truly sorry for being such a bully toward you on the phone. I got emotional and I said things I didn't mean."

Anne nodded. "I understand. We can all say things we don't mean when we're upset."

"If you'll indulge me, I'd like to explain." She let out a long breath. "I've been a Pennsylvania history collector for over a decade now, taking over my father's business when his heart condition rendered him unable to work full-time a couple of years ago," said Dana. We never imagined he'd have to retire so early.

"The map I have is authentic, but the person who authenticated it back when my father first acquired it has now been accused of authenticating fake antiques in order to drive up prices on the real items." She pulled out some papers from her purse. "I have the authentication papers here, for what they're worth."

"If you're sure your map is real, why not just have someone else authenticate it?" Anne asked. That seemed the most logical answer to her.

"I will have to eventually, but right now…" Dana's face flushed but probably not from the fire. "Right now, I just don't have the extra money to put out. You see, Dad needs a pacemaker and his insurance won't cover it because his heart disease is a pre-existing condition. Medicare hasn't kicked in for him yet, so all the expenses are coming out of our savings. I've been managing to pay for his doctor visits and medication, but I'm saving every penny I can for the pacemaker operation."

Anne's own heart fluttered. She knew she was blessed that her parents were in great health. They enjoyed a very active lifestyle in Florida. She couldn't imagine what it would be like if one of them were to need a medical procedure and they couldn't pay for it. Especially with all the decreases in medical coverage and benefits.

"The good news is my map is about to be loaned to a private collection that features artifacts from Lewis and Clark's expedition," Dana said, drawing Anne back to the conversation. "The fee the private collector will pay will cover the down payment of the operation, which means we can go ahead and schedule it." Dana paused and stared into the fire. "But there's bad news too. For years, I've been in competition with a man named Caleb Granderson."

"Oh, I know Mr. Granderson," said Anne.

Dana stared at her. "You do?"

"Oh, yes." Anne nodded, recalling the way he tried to bully his way to see the map she'd found. "His methods don't impress me," she said.

Relief marched over Dana's features. "He does like to threaten and try to intimidate. At least that's been my experience."

"Exactly," Anne agreed.

"Well, if Caleb gets his hands on another map authenticated to have been used by Lewis and Clark, he'd offer it to the private collector at a lower price than mine," said Dana. "I can't afford to pay another expert to certify my map, much less get in a bidding war against Caleb."

Anne didn't know what to say.

"This is all more information than you needed to know, I'm sure, but I felt like I owed you an explanation. And a huge apology. I shouldn't have ever threatened to tell people you were a con artist. I didn't know you. I'm sorry," said Dana.

"It's okay. I understand," Anne said. Had she been in the same situation, she might've lashed out too.

Dana smiled, revealing a really pretty girl. "Thank you for understanding, but it's not okay. I was wrong to speak as I did and I'm sorry."

Anne grinned. "Apology accepted."

"Hello? Anne?" Megan's voice called out.

"In here." Anne stood and hugged Megan as she entered. She introduced Megan to Dana.

The introductions were barely made when a male voice sounded in the entry. "Mrs. Gibson?"

Anne moved to the Nonfiction Room's doorway. "In here, Mr. Jones."

"Please, call me Garret," he said.

"And I'm Anne." She ushered him into the room. "This is Dana Munroe, and you know Megan Rhodes."

He nodded at each woman, then turned back to Anne. "Now, what's this all about?" he asked.

"Perhaps I should leave," Dana stood.

"No. Please, stay." Anne pulled up one of the wooden chairs from the corner for Garret to sit. She knelt beside the coffee table between the two comfortable chairs, and slowly began to tell them about the interview with Alfred Rhodes that Grace found.

Everyone was silent as she finished, the only sound was the crackling of the fire.

"Well, that's quite interesting." Garret crossed his ankles and stroked his moustache. He stared directly at Anne. "Do you believe this interview is legitimate?" he asked.

She hesitated. She didn't really know these people, certainly didn't know Alfred or Isaac, but she knew Grace.

"I think so. I can't think of any logical reason why someone would go to the trouble to write out such an interview and then hide it away for so many years," said Anne.

"I think I should see this map you've found. If it's a forgery, I should be able to tell rather quickly." He straightened in the chair. "I'm a curator, you know," Garret said.

Dana spread out the papers she held. "According to an expert on William Scull and his maps, he determined back in 1915 that William Scull always placed a double-line infinity symbol under his name." She looked at Anne. "Does the map you found have that?" she asked.

Megan's face lit with hope.

Now was the time. Anne stood. "Let me go get the map and we'll see," she said.

She cautiously removed the map from the drawer, keeping the acrylic sheets under and on top of the map. Then she slowly walked back into the Nonfiction Room. She carefully spread the map out on the coffee table.

Everyone leaned forward, studying the map.

"It doesn't have Scull's infinity symbol," Dana announced.

"It's a fake, isn't it?" Megan asked.

Garret continued to inspect the map. He moved closer, to where his nose practically nudged the map, then stood to look down at the map. He tilted his head right and stared and then turned his head to the left.

"Garret, it's a fake. You have to tell people Alfred never stole an authentic map because it was forged to begin with." Megan's tone came out desperate.

"I'll do no such thing." Garret made eye contact with Anne. "I need to take the map to my office for a better inspection," he said.

"Why don't I take the map to an independent expert, just so there's no question," Dana offered.

"The map's already going to an independent expert next week. The appointment's already been made," said Anne. Her pulse thrummed.

Garret leaned forward. "Truly, Anne, I can probably eliminate your costs to have this inspected and appraised."

"It's a fake. We know that because there's no symbol under the cartographer's name." Megan's voice cracked. "My great-grandfather was telling the truth in that interview. All these years...everyone's thought my family vile and nothing more than thieves. This proves Alfred didn't have anything to do with stealing an authentic map," she said.

"I can't confirm that, Ms. Rhodes. I'll take the map back to my office and inspect it in detail." Garret reached for the map.

"No. I'm taking it to the expert I've already chosen." Anne reached for the map—

Bam!

The porch door slammed open. Hershey ran into the room, soaking wet. He shook, throwing water everywhere.

The books! Anne moved to grab his collar.

Hershey took off running. Anne gave chase.

She ran through the History Room but slipped as she rounded the corner into the front entry. Hershey's nails tapped on the stairs as he ran to the second floor.

"Hershey!" She chased him up the stairs. He stopped at the top step and shook again. Water flew against the wall.

"Come, Hershey," said Anne.

But the dog ran through the open door leading to their private quarters and down the hallway.

She was out of breath by the time she reached the top of the stairs. Ben held Hershey in the living room. "What happened?" he asked.

She pointed at the dog. "Take him…downstairs…on the porch." She caught her breath. "Make sure both doors are closed securely." She let out another puff of air. "He somehow got outside to get all wet then got back in the house. You'll be helping me mop tomorrow," she said.

"Okay." He held Hershey's collar. "I'm going to dry him off with an old towel before I bring him down." He stared at her a bit cautiously. "So he doesn't get anything else wet." Anne nodded. He'd gotten enough wet already.

The map!

A door slammed. Footsteps echoed off the walls.

She rushed down both flights of stairs to the Nonfiction Room. Anne burst into the room. The group no longer huddled around the map. She found only Dana in front of the fire.

"Dana," she said. "What's going on?"

Dana knelt in front of the fire. The edges of something curled into ash.

Anne's gut jerked. No. It couldn't be.

"Where are Garret and Megan?" Anne asked.

Dana remained silent, just staring at the bright orange flames.

Anne stared the coffee table.

Empty.

No! No! No!

"Where's the map?" she asked Dana.

Dana pointed at the fire.

The map? "No!" Anne gasped as the clump dropped into a black ball. With tears in her eyes, Anne turned to Dana. "What happened?"

"Megan said something about taking the map to an expert along with Garret's great-grandfather's handwriting sample to prove he forged the map." Dana couldn't stop staring at the fire. "Garret told her she was reaching for anything to cast blame on someone other than her great-grandfather."

"What happened to the map?" Anne all but hissed.

Dana finally looked at Anne, her eyes glazed over. "Garret jerked the map away. Somehow—and I still don't know exactly how it happened—the map went into the fire." Dana shook her head. "Megan tried to grab it, but it was already burning fast." She shook her head again. "I'm sorry, Anne."

Raised voices in the entryway grabbed Anne's and Dana's attention. Anne raced from the room to find Megan and Garret almost nose-to-nose.

"You burned it on purpose," Megan accused.

"Why on earth would I do that?" Garret asked. "I'm a curator. I appreciate historical artifacts, and for all we know, that map was authentic."

"You burned it so your family wouldn't be exposed as forgers," said Megan.

"That's ridiculous." Garret took a step away from Megan.

"Did you know your great-grandfather forged the map, Garret?" Megan stepped right into his space, causing him to stumble back a couple of steps. "Did you? I bet you did." She kept advancing...

Garret kept retreating.

"All these years, you've known my family was innocent of any involvement in the dissolution of the historical society, yet you allowed the entire town to believe my family was responsible. That's reprehensible," said Megan.

Garret pointed a finger in her face. "You stop right there, woman. I knew no such thing, nor do I believe my great-grandfather was a forger," he said. "There's no proof except the accusations of Alfred. Accusations that weren't even substantiated enough for the paper to print."

Megan backed up.

"You are bordering on slander, missy. I'd caution you to watch your words." He brushed past Megan and out the door. The rain swallowed his figure.

Megan bent her head and covered her face with her hands. Her shoulders shook as she sobbed silently.

Anne understood Megan's emotion. She wanted to cry herself. It was all over. The map was gone.

And the truth might never be revealed.

Chapter Twenty

Friday brought clearing skies and warming temperatures to Blue Hill, but the gloom of the previous evening still lingered in Anne's heart.

She couldn't believe the map was gone. Real or fake, she'd never know for sure.

She put in a call to Mr. Bridges to cancel his examination of the map. Megan would never get the opportunity to clear her great-grandfather's name.

It was so unfair.

"I'm taking Hershey for a walk," said Ben. He carried the leash.

She nodded, still aching for the injustice of it all. If only there was some other way to find out the truth.

A thought popped into Anne's head. *The book...donated by Brenda Hodges.*

It might be a dead end, but on the other hand, it might lead to some information. Anything was better than what she had left— nothing. She owed it to Megan, and all the residents of Blue Hill, to do her very best to try and uncover the truth. Healing from the shadows of the past.

Opening the Internet browser on the computer at the checkout desk, Anne accessed the Blue Hill registry. Once it loaded, she conducted a search for Brenda Hodges. The system searched.

God, please let me find something. So many people deserve answers. Let Your truth be shown, Lord. Amen.

A little *ding* sounded as the system loaded the search result. Anne cleaned her glasses, then read.

Brenda Hodges, a lifetime resident of Blue Hill was a registered nurse until her recent retirement.

Ahhh. That's why the name rang a bell—she was one of the nurses who checked in on Aunt Edie every couple of days back when she'd been diagnosed with diabetes. Anne recalled Aunt Edie had spoken highly of Brenda and said they'd become friends, sharing their love of reading and history.

"Good morning, Mrs. Gibson," said Bella. "I think the sun's trying to sneak out." She smiled wide as she bounced into the library.

"Hi, Bella." Anne hadn't even heard the girl come into the library. "You're in quite a good mood today."

The girl nodded, grinning. "A great mood. I love the air right after a hard rain. It smells good." She laughed. "My mom says I'm just weird, but I love the smell. Wish I could bottle it and use it as an air freshener."

Anne would have to agree. The air did smell cleaner and fresher, and most air fresheners smelled unnatural. She closed her active Internet window. "I have a couple of shipments scheduled to come in today, so if you could go ahead and start the process, that'd be great." She passed Bella the invoice she'd been e-mailed.

"I'll get right on it," Bella said. The girl was a bundle of energy—energy Anne sometimes wished she still had.

It would be nice to keep up with the kids' nonstop going. Some days when she fell into bed, her limbs vibrated with exhaustion.

She shifted in her seat, refocusing. If she could find out where Brenda was now. If she was still in Blue Hill, or close by, maybe she could talk to her, find out if she remembered *The Journals of Lewis and Clark*, and maybe she even remembered something about the map that had been tucked inside.

There was only one person Anne could think of who might know how to find Brenda. She pulled out her cell and dialed.

"Hi, Anne." Mildred's voice was like a sail in a choppy storm. "I was just thinking about you. How're you doing?"

"I've been better, that's for sure," said Anne.

"Uh-oh, what happened?"

Briefly, Anne told Mildred about last night's fiasco.

"Oh, that's awful." The dismay was evident in Mildred's voice, even over the phone connection. "What are you going to do now?"

"I can't just let it go. I'm going to go at it from a different angle. The only angle I have left. The book."

"Smart thinking. Do you know who originally owned the book?" Mildred asked.

"I found the donor's name in the inventory from Aunt Edie's estate. Brenda Hodges. She was a nurse and a friend of Aunt Edie's." Anne smiled as Ben walked through the room on his way to the stairs, his cheeks flushed from playing outside with his dog. He wagged his fingers at her in a wave. She waved back.

Anne continued. "My problem is, I don't have any idea how to locate where she is now, if she's even still in Blue Hill. I thought maybe you might know how to find that out."

Mildred laughed softly. "I can do you one better—I know where she lives. Brenda Hodges lives at Blue Hill Retirement Center. The one right off Main Street," she said. "I saw her not even a week ago at the grocery store."

"She lives in that upscale place with all the English ivy?" Anne asked. That building was a newer addition to town, and not in keeping with the Victorian architecture of the rest of Blue Hill. That wasn't to say the building didn't look charming—it was in its own way, it just didn't fit in with the rest of the quaintness of the area.

"That's the one. Brenda moved there, oh, I guess it was about a little less than a year ago, give or take a few months," said Mildred.

"That's perfect. Thanks, Mildred."

"Anytime. Let me know how it goes."

Anne couldn't wait. She called Wendy. "Hey, I know you said you'd bring Liddie back about midmorning. I was just—"

Wendy laughed. "Stop worrying, mother hen. She just finished breakfast and brushed her teeth. We're working on putting her stuff back in her duffle as we speak. We should be there in a few minutes," she said.

"Good, but what I wanted to know was if you could watch the kids here for a little bit while I run out to the Blue Hill Retirement Center to speak to someone?" asked Anne. "I hate to ask, but it's important. I shouldn't be gone long."

"Sure, but what's going on?" asked Wendy.

Anne told her about last night and the map being destroyed, and then she told Wendy about her conversation with Mildred. "I really need to talk with Brenda and see if she remembers anything about the book we found the map in. It's the only lead I have left to getting to the truth," she said.

"We're on our way," said Wendy.

Within half an hour, Anne had kissed and hugged Liddie relentlessly, received the shipment of donated books from a national writers' organization and handed it off to Bella to complete bringing the books into inventory, and then driven to the retirement center.

Now, as Anne walked up the steps to the front of the beautiful building, excitement thrummed through her every vein. Something inside her, a gut instinct maybe, told her that she was on the verge of uncovering a clue.

To what, Anne didn't exactly know. But she sure was anxious to find out.

A woman about Anne's own age of thirty-four sat behind a huge, beautifully ornate desk. "Welcome to Blue Hill Retirement Center. How may I assist you?" she asked.

Anne smiled at the woman, who had a couple of strands of gray mixed in with her blonde hair. "I'm here to see Brenda Hodges," Anne said.

"One moment." She lifted the receiver on the phone beside her, punched a couple of buttons, and then swiveled away from Anne. "Ms. Hodges, there's a lady in the lobby to see you." A pause. "Certainly." She returned the receiver and smiled up at Anne. "She'll be down in a moment."

"Thank you." Anne moved away from the desk, taking in the décor of the lobby.

An oversized chandelier hung in the foyer over the front entrance, the crystals dancing in the light. Several canvases of oil paintings, depicting playful scenes from a French-era picnic, adorned the walls.

"Hello?"

Anne turned. "Are you Brenda Hodges?" she asked.

The woman who smiled and nodded didn't look old enough to be retired. Her brown hair pulled back into a braid lying along her spine to nearly her waist barely had any visible gray. Her face was smooth, nearly wrinkle free, just a couple of lines in the corners of her eyes. "I am, and while you do look a little familiar..."

Anne held out her hand. "I'm Anne Gibson."

Brenda's eyes widened. "You're Edie's niece. I should have recognized the resemblance immediately," she said. She shook Anne's hand, and that's when Anne caught the telltale signs of aging in her arthritic fingers.

"I am," said Anne.

"You look like her. In your face structure," Brenda said.

Anne didn't know what to say. She'd never seen the resemblance, but she'd take it as a compliment. Aunt Edie had been quite striking.

"Come on to my suite," said Brenda. She led the way to the elevators, stepped inside, and pushed the button for the third floor. "I wanted to attend your grand opening, but unfortunately, a friend got sick and I wanted to sit with her."

"I completely understand," said Anne.

The elevator doors opened silently. Brenda stepped off, going to the right in the hallway that resembled a plush hotel. "How's the library? I heard you completed all the renovations and it looks really nice."

"It's almost complete. There are a few areas we're still working on, but I'm pleased with how it's turned out," said Anne.

"That's great. Edie loved the thought of Blue Hill finally having a library. I know she'd be thrilled with what you did." Brenda stopped at a door and punched in a code on the oversized keypad, clearly a consolation to Brenda's bent fingers. A click sounded, then she turned the knob. "Welcome." She waved Anne in before her.

Anne wasn't sure what she expected, but the living area held two small loveseats, a recliner, an entertainment center, and a table with a stained glass lamp. The overall effect was quite cozy and welcoming.

"Sit down, please. Can I get you a cup of coffee or tea?" Brenda asked.

"No, thank you." Anne sat on one of the loveseats. It seemed to cradle around her.

Brenda sat in the recliner. "I'm sure you have a reason to come over here to see me, so go ahead and ask what it is you're interested in asking."

Heat spread from Anne's neck.

"Oh, honey, I don't mean to make you uncomfortable. It's just that over my lifetime, I've found it's useless to beat around the bush. Just get straight to the point. It's quicker and less chance of misunderstandings," said Brenda.

232 | *Secrets of the Blue Hill Library*

"I can appreciate that." Anne sucked in air then slowly exhaled. She took the book out of her purse and handed it to Brenda. "Do you remember this book?" she asked. "You donated it to the library."

Brenda's gnarled hand smoothed the old, cloth cover. Tears welled in her eyes. "I'd almost forgotten about this book, and the owner."

Anne eased to the edge of the loveseat. "Can you tell me its story?"

"Wow. It's been a while." Brenda leaned back into the recliner. "Back in 1985, I worked in hospice." She shook her head. "I considered the assignment as part of my ministry."

Anne could only imagine. She was so thankful God hadn't called her to the medical field. She wouldn't have been able to stand the pain of the patients. But hospice? Her heart wouldn't have been able to withstand the unbearable and constant loss.

"Anyway, I had one particular patient who was only forty-eight, younger than most in the hospice system, battling an aggressive and debilitating bout of Alzheimer's." Brenda's gaze took on a far-away look. "He had brought a few history books with him when he moved in. He and I shared a passion for history, and I'd been delighted to read those books to him."

Anne's heart ached for the young man with such a dreadful disease.

"There is no set case of Alzheimer's, each person is affected differently," Brenda said. "For him, he couldn't recall why certain items evoked strong emotions, but there were two items he couldn't let out of his sight. If he couldn't see them, he'd become agitated. Very agitated." She paused, as if the memories were washing over her. "Those two items were an old pipe that still held the sweet, woody smell of pipe tobacco and this book."

Brenda ran her hand over the book again. "When he passed on in 1994, I kept the pipe and book, since his son said to donate his personal effects to anyone who wanted them." She smiled at Anne. "He was a very special man, you understand."

Anne nodded.

"I kept the book and pipe until last year, when I sold my house and moved here." She leaned forward a little, as if about to share a secret. "I was tired of cleaning that old house, to be honest."

"I can understand that." Keeping three floors of Aunt Edie's house tidy was almost overwhelming to Anne. It seemed as if the only way to stay on top of the chores was to do at least an hour's worth every day.

"Anyway, your aunt was my friend, and when I learned of her bequest, I donated his book for the library," said Brenda. "I figured there were many more young minds that would enjoy this book." She handed it back to Anne.

"That's quite a story." Anne handed the book back to Brenda. "I have to say, I'm intrigued by the nameplate, which is torn. Perhaps you can shed some light on it? Any idea who the *Isa es* is?"

Brenda opened the book and stared at the plate. "I don't really know for sure. The man I knew who owned the book was Samuel. Samuel Jones," she said.

Anne went very still. "His son, the one who told you to donate his personal effects to anyone who wanted them...was that Garret Jones?" she asked.

Brenda nodded. "Of course it was Garret." She handed the book back to Anne. "You know, in times of lucidness, Samuel was eaten up with remorse."

Anne gripped the edge of the book. "Because of his relationship with his son?" she asked.

"No. Even when Samuel was clear and in the present, he never really asked for Garret or anything," said Brenda. "I think their relationship had wasted away some time before Samuel's mind was stolen by the disease."

"Then what do you think caused Samuel's remorse?" Anne asked.

Brenda shrugged. "I can't say for sure, but he'd mention something about an offshore account, although whenever I asked him about it, his mind would go blank."

An offshore account? "But he seemed remorseful about this account?" asked Anne.

"He'd say he could only hope one day he could give the account to Donald to make it up to Paul." Brenda shook her head. "But that could have been the disease talking. He never had any friends named Donald or Paul come and visit him."

Donald? Paul? Could he have meant Paul Rhodes? Anne thought hard about a name she had discovered on the ancestry site. Megan's father's name was Donald. Could Samuel have found out the truth about Isaac and Alfred and the map and wanted to make things right with the Rhodes?

Brenda sat up on the edge of the recliner, shoulders squared. "Now, why don't you tell me what this is all about?" she asked.

Anne slipped the book back into her purse. Where to begin? The beginning. "Are you familiar with the Blue Hill Historical Society?"

Chapter Twenty-One

What was he doing here? Anne climbed out of her car and stared at Alex sitting in his truck parked in front of the library. He opened the door as she approached.

"Hey, I was hoping to catch you," he said.

She gave a closed-mouth smile. "Um, what're you doing sitting out here?"

"Waiting for you."

"For what?"

"Grace found something else. She wants you to see it now, so I volunteered to come get you," Alex said.

"Why didn't she just call my cell?" asked Anne.

"She did. Said she left two voice mail messages."

Anne dug in her purse and pulled out her phone. Sure enough, three missed calls were registered, as well as an indication of voice mail. Odd, she hadn't heard the phone ring. "So, what did she find?"

"Something about the embezzled money. Wants you to see what she found and get your opinion." Alex grinned. "I'm supposed to take you there now. Wendy's got the kids and Bella's got the library."

She shifted her purse strap onto her shoulder. "Then let's go."

Alex grinned as he opened the passenger door for her. "Hop in."

She checked her phone while he started the truck and backed out of the parking lot. She must have accidently put the phone on silent. "Did Grace tell you what she found?"

He shook his head as he turned at the stop sign. "Nope. Only that she thinks it's important and wants you to look at it."

Now she was really curious.

"So, how'd your meeting with Brenda Hodges go?" he asked.

She shot him a *how-did-you-know?* look.

He grinned. "Mildred told me."

"Ah. Good." She told him everything she'd learned, finishing just as they pulled into a parking space in front of the *Gazette*.

Alex came and opened her door for her before she could get her seat belt retracted. He held her elbow as they made their way up the steps. He opened the door to the newspaper office for her.

"Is that Anne?" Grace rushed into the front area. "Good, you're here. Come on." She motioned them back toward her office.

"What's so important?" Anne asked as she and Alex sat down in front of Grace's desk.

"Look what I found." Grace passed a folder to Anne over the desk.

With Alex leaning to look over her shoulder, Anne opened the folder. Inside were four pieces of paper. The first one was a bank statement on a savings account in the name of Samuel Jones, dated April of 1990. Interest acquired year-to-date reflected the amount of nineteen dollars and twelve cents. The ending balance was four thousand, two hundred, seventy-one dollars and eighty-two cents.

Anne looked at Grace and raised a single eyebrow.

Grace nodded. "Keep looking," she said.

Anne turned to the second page, also a bank statement. Same savings account number as before, same owner listed of Samuel Jones. This one was dated June of 1990. Interest acquired year-to-date reflected the amount of six hundred, fifty-seven dollars and seventy-seven cents. The ending balance was two thousand, six hundred, forty-four dollars and ninety-one cents.

What? Anne glanced at Grace, who nodded.

"Wait a minute...the ending balance decreased, but in two month's time, the year-to-date interest increased by about six hundred dollars?" Anne asked.

"Look at that next page." Grace crossed her arms over her chest and leaned back in her chair.

Anne flipped the page. A statement from the bank records, notating that in the second quarter of the 1990 fiscal year, the interest on savings account was approximately two point one percent.

Alex scratched his head. "I'm not following."

"The town's money was embezzled back in 1990," Grace reminded him.

Suddenly, Anne understood. "Thirty thousand dollars was embezzled, and two point one percent of thirty thousand dollars is roughly six hundred dollars," she said.

Grace grinned wide and nodded.

"How did you get these?" Anne asked.

"I did some digging around. Found these in the back of the last microfiche folder," Grace said. "I guess you didn't look in the pockets of the back of the folder, Anne."

Anne shook her head. "I didn't."

"It makes me wonder who had all these documents. The interview and now this," said Grace. "Like someone at the paper had been trying to piece together the mystery, but just didn't have all these pieces."

"Maybe not," Alex said.

Anne turned to the last page. It was a copy of the bank's issuance of an SAR form. Reporting a cash deposit of over ten thousand dollars into Samuel Jones's account.

"What's that," Alex asked.

"It's a Suspicious Activity Report." Anne pointed at it. "Whenever someone makes a cash deposit over a certain amount of money, this report is filled out and put into the customer's file. Just in case there's ever any issue, the Justice Department and IRS have documentation."

"It doesn't list the amount of the deposit on this particular piece of paper, but it shows that it was deposited in early May." Grace rocked in her chair. "But the question is, where did the money go? Obviously it was pulled out of the account in late June, but there's no itemization on these papers to know where it went." Grace leaned over her desk. "I've checked with my sources at the bank, and there's no way to get those records now. They're gone. We'll never know where the money went."

Anne snapped her fingers. "An offshore account."

"That's a bit of a reach, don't you think?" Alex asked.

She chuckled, then told them what Brenda had said about Samuel's remorse and comments about the offshore account. "What if he took the money he'd stolen from the town and stuck it in an offshore account, then years later felt bad about it and wished he could give it to the Rhodes family to prove Paul's innocence, but he couldn't because he was already sick with Alzheimer's? That would make sense."

"But how did Samuel steal the money? Paul was the town's chief financial officer," Alex asked as he rested his elbows on Grace's desk.

"I can do some digging," Grace said. "See if there was a connection between Samuel and the town or Samuel and Paul. Anything that could explain Samuel having access to the money." She ran a hand through her wispy bangs.

"That's a good start." Alex sat up straight. "What else?"

"I think I'm going to ask Garret to come to the library again." Anne nodded as she thought about it. "Maybe I can get more information out of him."

"I'm not sure that's such a great idea," said Alex.

"Why not?" Anne asked. "He might know about his father's offshore account." She held up a finger. "Actually, when Samuel passed, I think everything went to Garret. He probably *owns* the account."

"Which is exactly why you shouldn't press him on it." Alex pointed at her.

"Alex has a point," Grace agreed. "If that money's still there and he's planning on using it for his retirement, he won't take too kindly to you bringing up the fact that you believe it was acquired with ill-gotten funds taken from the town of Blue Hill."

"I'm just going to ask him a few questions, not accuse him of stealing money." Anne's back stiffened.

Grace flashed her a soft smile. "And you were just having Megan and Garret over last night for a friendly discussion and the map ended up being destroyed," she said.

Anne's face stiffened.

"Now, now." Grace held up both her hands. "Don't get riled up. I don't say that to offend, I just don't want you caught in the middle of something. You never expected Garret to be physical enough to destroy the map. I don't want him to surprise you in other ways. More dangerous ways."

"Exactly." Alex nodded.

Anne shook her head. "You two are something else. Garret panicked last night. Megan got in his face." She grinned as she mentally replayed their argument in the entry last night. "For such a little thing, she was quite intimidating. I think he panicked and then felt like she jumped on him like a lioness hunting, so that's what caused his destroying the map. I don't think he intended to do that."

"I'm sure it wouldn't panic him in the least for you to even insinuate the offshore account was created with the town's embezzled funds. Wouldn't cause him a flicker of worry, right?" The muscles in Alex's jaw flexed.

She'd forgotten how sarcastic he could be when he tried, but it was also nice to know that he and Grace were worried about her.

"I think you're making this more intense than it is. Garret won't be expecting me to mention the offshore account—he'll think I invited him over to talk about the map. I'll have the element of surprise," said Anne.

"I don't like it," said Grace.

"I don't either." Alex stared at Anne hard enough to make her want to squirm.

But she didn't. Instead, she laughed. "You don't have to like it. I'm a big girl, quite capable of taking care of myself, you know? Remember, Ben thought I was going to light up Caleb."

"This could be dangerous, Anne." Grace leaned over her desk, her eyes so serious. "You're talking about destroying this man's name, his reputation, not to mention possibly causing him to lose thousands of dollars. Yeah, it could turn a lot more dangerous than you think."

"Garret might be covering up for his family's and his own actions, but he's hardly violent." His stately demeanor, pointy chin, and super groomed moustache didn't exactly evoke a sense of alarm in Anne. She couldn't imagine anyone being fearful of him. "He might have burnt a piece of paper he knew to be worthless, but that's hardly a reason for panic," said Anne.

Alex crossed his arms over his chest. "I wouldn't have picked that gangly Caleb Granderson as someone who could threaten anybody, yet when provoked, he did," he said. "Although, I don't think he expected you to come charging back at him."

"Anne, please listen to us. I've reported on people who seemed unthreatening but who snapped when pushed over their limits in some way." Grace tapped a pencil against her desk. "Please don't make me become an insomniac because I'm up worrying about you."

They weren't going to let it go. Anne sighed. "Okay. How about I invite Garret over, and if he agrees, you two can be there? How's that sound? Surely you can't think he'd be a danger to all three of us?"

"If you're determined to confront Garret, then I think that's the only way." Grace nodded. "And we'll need to record it."

"Record it?" Anne stared at her friend. "Whatever for?"

"Because if he confesses to something, I can print it in the paper. It would help Megan in her quest to clear her family's name," Grace said.

Good point. "I'll try to find a recorder or something," said Anne.

"I have a digital voice recorder," Grace offered.

"Why don't you go ahead and call him?" Alex asked. "Set up a time so we can be ready."

"Okay." Anne pulled out her cell phone and dialed Garret's number. It rang once. When he saw her number on his caller ID, and considering his behavior last night, he'd probably let it go to voice mail.

It rang a second time. She readied to leave a message.

"Hello, Anne," he said.

"Garret." For a moment, she couldn't think straight.

"I'm glad you called."

"You are?" she asked.

Grace rushed from around her desk and put her head close to Anne's, listening. Alex did the same.

"I wanted to apologize for last night," said Garret.

"For burning the map?" Anne asked.

"The act was unintentional on my part, I assure you. I'm still not sure exactly how the map got into the fire. Megan reached for it, I did, and I believe even Ms. Munroe did as well. All I know is it somehow ended in the fire. A devastation to us all," said Garret.

Grace rolled her eyes.

"Especially to me, since it was my property." Anne paused. If he had even a sliver of doubt of the map being a fake, he'd argue the point here that if it was the real map, it would actually still belong to the Blue Hill Historical Society.

"I do apologize, Anne," he said.

So he probably knew the map was a fake. Was Megan right — had he known it all along and let the Rhodes family bear the responsibility for stealing something that was as worthless as a blank piece of paper?

"Well, there are a few things I need to conclude about the destruction of the map," Anne said.

"Really? Such as?"

Think fast, Anne, think fast. Her mouth was drier than ever. She glanced at her open purse and spied her wallet. The kids' new insurance cards were sticking out. "Insurance," she said.

"What?" Garret asked.

She had to keep going. "You know, the map was considered library inventory since it was found in one of the donated books now belonging to the library. Now that it's been destroyed...well, I should have documentation in case anyone questions where it went." *Lord, it's not really a lie. The map did belong to the library and I do need to have documentation of what happened.*

Garret was silent for so long she thought he might have hung up, except she could still hear him breathing.

"I've already talked to Megan," Anne said. That wasn't a lie, she had. Just not about any such thing as insurance. Then again, she hadn't said *what* she talked to Megan about.

"I see," Garret said.

Anne licked her lips with a dry tongue. "I'd really appreciate it if you could find your way to come by the library today." She glanced at Grace and Alex and shrugged. "Say about...."

Alex held up six fingers.

"Six. Could you come by around six this evening?" Anne held her breath.

"Well, eh...I suppose I could swing by." His voice grew more confident sounding. "Anything to help the library, of course."

"Oh, thank you, Garret. I really appreciate this." Could this be called gushing?

"You're most welcome. I'll see you at six," Garret replied.

She hung up the phone.

Grace giggled. "Insurance? That was brilliant."

Alex nodded. "And you didn't even lie. Everything you said was the truth. It was just how you strung it all together that was a bit misleading."

She hesitated. She tried very hard to live by the principles in God's Word. She hadn't lied, but she'd skirted the truth. She thought of Ben and Ranger, aka Duke. No, that was different. He'd flat-out lied to Alex when he'd said she knew about the dog.

As if reading her mind, Alex grabbed her hand and squeezed. "It's fine." He nodded. "No worrying over this, okay?" he said.

She smiled.

"Okay, well then, we need to get ready." Grace tapped her pen again. "I'll dig out my digital recorder and check the batteries. We don't want it going dead in case Garret starts telling us some juicy tidbits," she said.

Anne waved her finger in the air, drawing an outline around Grace. "This whole crazy-investigative-reporter thing is kind of scary."

Grace laughed. "Well, you never can tell. He might know more than we even suspect. If he gets to talking..."

Alex stood. "Ready to head back to the library?" he asked Anne. She nodded.

Grace stood as well. "I'll be there about five-fifteen or so, just in case he's early. I don't want to scare him off."

Scare him off…oh. "Grace, park behind the house, so he can't easily see your car when he arrives," Anne said.

Grace nodded. "Good thinking." She rubbed her hands together. "It's been a while since I've done any real sleuthing." She grinned at Anne. "You're a good influence on me."

Alex snorted and shook his head. "You're a reporter, Grace. Isn't sleuthing what you do?" he said.

"There's not a whole lot of sleuthing to do in Blue Hill," said Grace. "Usually."

"Well, this is definitely something to look into," said Anne. "I don't know if I'd call this going undercover or not."

Alex hesitated. "You realize we should probably call the police," he said.

"For what? To tell them we suspect Garret's up to his eyebrows in this?" Anne asked.

"She's right. There's no proof of anything. Not that would convince law enforcement," Grace said.

"Okay, okay." Alex pulled the truck keys from his front pocket. "Come on, let's go. Maybe we can sweet-talk Wendy into watching all the kids for us so we don't have to worry about them."

Anne snapped her fingers. "Let's stop by the diner on the way home. She's partial to their cream pie."

"It'd work on me. I'm a sucker for sweets." Grace wiggled her eyebrows. "I'll see you both in a few hours."

CHAPTER TWENTY-TWO

The front door of the library whooshed open, pushing in a gust of cooler air that blasted down the entry and winded to the checkout area.

A shiver skidded down Anne's spine. It didn't seem to matter that Alex and Grace were just in the other room, barely out of sight. She suddenly felt very alone.

She whispered a prayer, then planted a smile. "Hello, Garret."

His normally composed demeanor seemed a bit off as he approached her. "Hi, Anne. Isn't this weather crazy?"

She motioned him toward the Nonfiction Room, falling into step alongside him. "Come, get warmed up by the fireplace."

The fire was a nice touch Grace had suggested. *"Let him feel cozy and comfortable, then move in for the kill and start pressing him for details,"* she'd said. Alex hadn't exactly agreed, but he'd built the fire for them anyway.

Anne sat in one of the chairs, waving him toward the other. "Please, have a seat."

He hung his jacket on the back of the chair before sitting. "I have to say, Anne, I'm relieved it's just us two. Last night felt, to me, like an ambush of sorts."

"An ambush?" She glanced at the digital recorder hidden on the bookshelf closest to the chair she'd left for Garret. She couldn't see if the ON indicator was lit, but Alex and Grace had assured her the voice-activated device had new batteries and was working as it should. "Why on earth would you feel like that?" Anne asked.

"Well..." he picked nonexistent lint from the front of his slacks. "Megan Rhodes is a sweet girl, I'm sure, but she refuses to face the truth about her family's past actions. It's sad, really. I almost feel sorry for her," said Garret.

Anne struggled not to react. Alex had warned her to keep her emotions in check. He'd reminded her how clearly her face reflected her emotions, so to be extra careful.

"Funny, she says the same about your family's past actions," Anne said. "Especially considering the missing infinity symbol under William Scull's name. According to experts, that's Scull's cartographer identifier mark. That would render the map a forgery."

He cocked his head. "Perhaps. Then again, we weren't able to inspect the map closely before it was lost."

"Lost?" *Don't react. Don't let him get to you.* Anne took a deep inhale. "It wasn't lost; it was destroyed," she said.

"Yes, a most unfortunate accident." He smoothed the crease in his pants. "Now we'll never know."

And yet, if she'd had any doubt before, his reaction firmed up Megan's suspicions. Now was the time to, as Grace had worded it, "move in for the kill."

"No, we won't," said Anne. She leaned back in the chair, hoping she looked as relaxed and unintentional as she'd planned. "I do wonder, however, about that interview with Alfred Rhodes."

Garret let out a humorless, nasally laugh. "Fiction. Nothing more than a fantasy with a bit of wishful thinking mixed in. By someone in the Rhodes family, I'm sure. Probably Paul Rhodes." He leaned closer to Anne. "In case you don't remember, Paul Rhodes was accused of embezzling town monies."

Anne's heart pounded. "Yes, about that. There was never enough evidence to officially charge Paul, was there?"

He tapped a finger on the end of his nose, as if pondering the means to bring about world peace. "No, I don't believe there was. No matter, everyone in town knew he was the guilty party."

"Really? I heard it a little differently," she said.

He shifted in his seat to face her more fully. "Do tell."

She uncrossed her legs and stretched them out in front of her, crossing them at the ankles. A totally at-ease posture, she prayed. She pretended to stare into the fire but snuck stares at him from under her lowered eyelids, through her lashes.

"I heard the money mysteriously went into an offshore account," she said as she concentrated on watching his face for even the slightest nuance of change.

There! That split second of fear and anger washing over his face before he regained his stony expression. If she hadn't been looking for it, she would have missed it.

But she had been looking, and she caught it.

"An offshore account? How ridiculous," he said. "Do people really have offshore accounts?" He'd corrected his expression, but even now, his posture was too straight...too rigid.

She had him on edge, and he didn't even realize it.

"Sure, people have offshore accounts." She smiled, staring straight at him. "Most people don't realize they're traceable."

He stroked his moustache. "Is that so?" he asked.

"Sure. Some people think once they put the money in an offshore account, there's no tracing certain amounts of money back to them." She smiled wider. "But they'd be wrong."

"How's that?" He continued to stroke his moustache, but she detected a slight tremor in his hand now.

"Well, let's just say, purely hypothetically, of course, that someone had received a large amount of money. Oh, just for ease in mathematics since that's not my best subject, let's use a nice round figure of, say, thirty thousand dollars."

He stopped stroking his moustache and dropped his hand into his lap.

She was all in—no other option but to keep going. "Upon deposit for any amount over ten thousand dollars, the bank is required by law to fill out a certain report and put it in the customer's file."

His eyes widened. "Is that a fact?"

"It is. And even if that money was put into a regular account for less than sixty days, the amount of interest accrued and paid to that account holder is documented. Even turned in to the IRS," said Anne.

His face grew paler by the minute.

"So let's go back to that thirty thousand dollar deposit," she said. "There's that bank report record. Then there's the record of the interest accrued and paid, which would be easy enough to figure how much money had been deposited based upon the interest rate. So much documentation."

She sat up, curling her legs under her. "You know, I heard somewhere, I can't remember exactly where, that with enough documentation to justify a reasonable suspicion of theft, the United States government could subpoena offshore account records. Isn't *that* interesting?"

He gulped loudly. Then again. "That is interesting," he said.

"Something else you might not know...if someone received money, say through a legal means like through an inheritance, but knew that those funds were acquired from ill-gotten gains and didn't report it, that's a crime." She playfully slapped the arm of the chair. "And if a large sum of money was shifted to an offshore account and taxes were never paid on that money, well, that's a federal crime."

Garret's Adam's apple looked like a piston pumping.

"And, here's a final little tidbit for you. Say I found out about someone who was in such a situation and I reported them, the United States IRS would pay me ten percent of any funds they collected."

She leaned even closer to him. "So in my hypothetical situation, let's say that thirty thousand dollars might have been in an offshore account for over twenty years, gaining interest to be valued at fifty thousand dollars or more... Why, I could receive a check from the IRS for about five thousand dollars," Anne said. "For doing nothing but following a money trail and reporting it."

He remained silent.

"Some might say that's not a lot of money, but I say when you're doing the right thing, money isn't the most important thing."

His eyes narrowed. "What, exactly, are you getting at, Mrs. Gibson?"

Ah…now his true colors would come out.

"Did you ever wonder about your father's offshore account, or did you already know your family had taken the money Paul Rhodes was accused of embezzling?" Anne asked.

"Wha—how dare you? That's absurd." His back went straight as a rod and he shot to his feet, moving to stand behind the chair.

"Is it? You deny owning an offshore account you acquired from your father?" She held up her hand and stood as well. "Before you answer that, maybe you ought to consider that banks might keep records, even ones going back to May and June of 1990," she said.

He opened his mouth, paused, then clamped it shut. He gripped the back of the chair with both hands.

"I know the interview with Alfred is accurate, that Isaac Jones forged the map. And Alfred's explanation of why he forged it makes sense," Anne said. "I even understand why Isaac claimed the map was stolen when he did and accused Alfred of stealing it."

She smoothed the cloth of the chair, pausing for effect. "What I don't understand is why Isaac or your grandfather or even your father didn't destroy the map so no one would ever know it was a forgery. Why take the chance of being discovered later, like now?" She held her breath.

Would he take the bait and talk?

"What do you want? Money?" Garret asked. "I can pay you a lot more than five thousand dollars."

Anne didn't know what to say. She hadn't considered what she'd do if he actually admitted everything. Think fast, think fast. "Let's sit back down, Garret," she said.

Lord, please let the recorder be working.

She sat back down in the chair, staring directly into the fire. If she made eye contact with him, would he be able to read her bluff? Tell she had no clue as to what she was doing?

The chair's cushion made an *oomph* sound as he returned to his seat.

Struggling to look at ease, she forced her hand to dangle off the arm of her chair. She smiled into the fire. "Tell me, Garret, have you known from childhood about the map?" she asked.

"No. I didn't even know the map was a forgery until I became the curator for the historical society."

Pay dirt!

"And I can't give you a reason why Isaac didn't destroy the map," he said. "I wish I knew." He leaned his head back against the back of the chair. "I *really* wish I knew."

"Why didn't you destroy it when you found out about it?" Anne asked.

"Because I couldn't." He leaned forward. "Don't you see? I never had it. When I became curator back in 1983, the society wasn't doing so well. I was trying everything I knew to bring funds into the society, but nothing seemed to work. My father came to see me one day, and that's when he told me about the map."

Garret stared at the fire, lost in his tale. "Dad told me Isaac had hidden the map at his home. He'd passed it down to my grandfather, Walter, who passed it down to my father. Each man having some reason for not destroying the one thing that could destroy our family. We'd all seen, in each generation, how the Rhodes's name had been raked through the mud."

Anne kept silent, pressing her lips tight and praying the recorder was getting Garret's story.

"When Dad told me about the map, he had an idea," he said. "What if the map was suddenly *found* after almost eighty years? Found in an old box at the courthouse. Found in the basement of the church's hundred-year-old building. Anywhere, but that it was found."

Garret smiled and looked at her. "Think about the publicity. Can't you see the headlines: *Stolen Map Recovered After Eight Decades*? The media would eat it up, and not just local or regional, but larger cities. They'd all focus on the Blue Hill Historical Society. I'd be exalted as the curator who brought the map home."

Anne forced herself not to reveal her thoughts. *This man was delusional.*

"With the media attention, I could have organized some splashy events around the map and raised funds and donations to keep the society going for years to come. It was a brilliant plan," he said.

"What happened?" Anne asked.

Garret jerked his attention to her, almost as if he'd forgotten she was there. "Well, we had to wait several years after I was named curator, to avoid suspicion," he said.

She nodded, as if she not only understood, but was in agreement.

Hershey whined at the door.

"But just a year later, Dad began showing early signs of his disease," Garret said. "Oh, we didn't know it was Alzheimer's then. Who would've since Dad was just in his forties?" He bent his head and stared at the ground. "He just began forgetting little things at first. Not really a problem, just an annoyance."

Even knowing the awful secrets Samuel had kept and the harm he'd caused, Anne felt sorry for the man. No one should have to endure such a disease.

"Somehow, Dad stole money from the town." Garret shook his head. "No one ever questioned the fact that Dad sat on the town council for years. When he took early retirement, no one ever changed the signature cards. Or the pin numbers on the accounts. He stole the money and put it into his savings account. He told me a few weeks later and I panicked, telling him to get it out of the bank. He did, and put it into an offshore account."

Anne couldn't resist asking the logical question. "But what about the map?"

"I never knew where Dad hid it. When the society got in dire straits and was about to fold, I tried to get through Dad's Alzheimer's haze, but it didn't work. He couldn't remember. Didn't even know what I was talking about," Garret said.

Garret grabbed the poker from the hanger by the fireplace.

Anne started, then let out a lungful of air when he stabbed the logs in the fire. Sparks burst like a fireworks display. Garret hung the poker back up and sat back in the chair.

"I had to move Dad into a full-care medical facility soon after. I tore his house and belongings apart, looking for the map. I never found it. I assumed Dad, whether under the influence of the disease or in a moment of lucidness, had destroyed the map," he said.

He rubbed his hands against his legs. "I was okay with that. The society dissolved, which some blamed on me, labeling me a failure as well, but I could at least let the past go. I could at least take the secrets to the grave with me. In a few decades, Blue Hill would totally forget about the society, the Jones's and the Rhodes's."

He sighed and stared at Anne. "But then you had to go and find the map."

She leaned forward. "I bet that made you extremely nervous," she said.

"Oh, I was upset, all right. I almost had a fit when you told me that you'd found someone to examine the map. Knowing it was a fake, I needed to get the map and destroy it before your expert could appraise it."

Garret wagged a finger at her. "But you were smart enough not to let me have it right off the bat."

"No, I wouldn't."

He grinned. "I sent you a warning letter. I wondered how it affected you."

She forced a smile although the icy claws that gripped her chest. "That was you? Touché, Mr. Jones."

He gave a nod of his head and wore that confident smile of his, like he was proud of trying to scare a widow living alone with her children. "I even snuck in here and tried to find the map, but I had to leave when you almost caught me."

It *was* him, and she had scared him off when she'd stubbed her toe! A creepy feeling snaked up her spine. He'd been in the library. Her space. When she and the kids were right upstairs. What would he have done had she caught him?

Maybe Grace had been right. Maybe she wasn't safe with him. Maybe he had too much to lose and she was too much of a liability.

He grinned, the kind that made the goosebumps pop up on her arms and the hairs on the back of her neck stand at attention. "Did you even know someone had been here?" he asked.

She nodded. "Yes, and you wore gloves."

He raised his brows.

"You left smudges on the display glass that I'd just cleaned that afternoon after I closed the library," she said.

"You didn't call the police?"

She shook her head. "No need. I started figuring things out." Like there was no evidence, but he didn't need to know that much information.

"Did you?" he asked.

"Of course. It wasn't too hard." Well, not when all the pieces started coming together. "When we found Alfred Rhodes's interview, that was when I pretty much knew," she said.

"Yet you left me in the room alone with the map, suspecting it was a fake and I knew it?" He tsk-tsked. "Not a very bright thing to do, wouldn't you agree?" he asked.

A siren wailed in the distance.

"Actually, it was a very smart move. Knowing it was a fake, it didn't matter what you did to it, I just needed you to try something to confirm what I was pretty sure was the truth." She smiled, even though her palms sweated. "It would have been stupid of me to leave you alone with the map if I thought there was a chance it was authentic."

"Touché to you, Mrs. Gibson." He twisted, facing her head-on. "So, again I have to ask you, how much do you want for your silence?"

CHAPTER TWENTY-THREE

The tension in the Nonfiction Room felt as oppressive as an elephant on her chest.

She hadn't prepared a response for his question. As a matter of fact, she hadn't thought through a response if he'd confessed.

And confessed he had. With more culpability than she'd imagined.

Now what?

"Well, I haven't really thought about a number. I—"

The siren screeched just outside the library.

Garret jumped to his feet. "What's going on?" He jabbed his finger in Anne's direction. "You called the police? It's my word against yours." He took a step toward her.

Alex stepped out from behind the row of bookshelves, holding the digital recorder. "Not exactly, Garret. Not only did Grace Hawkins and I hear every single word you said, but we also recorded it." He stepped beside Anne and took her hand, squeezing it. "When he'd said enough to thoroughly incriminate himself, Grace slipped back into the other room and called the police."

She held tight to Alex's hand, drawing strength from him.

Garret's eyes narrowed into little slits. His hands balled into fists at his side.

"What's going on here?" a policeman asked.

Grace led the policeman into the Nonfiction Room. She handed Anne a bottle of water.

"I'm Jake Passton with the Blue Hill Police Department." The policeman repeated his question. "What's going on here?"

"We have a recording you need to hear, Officer Passton." Alex held up the digital recorder. "This man, Garret Jones, confessed to numerous crimes."

"This is nonsense. I'm not going to stand here and listen to their nonsense." Garret moved to leave.

Officer Passton put a hand on Garret's shoulder. "I think maybe you should wait here for a moment, Mr. Jones, until I can sort out what's what."

Garret puffed out his chest. "I have things to do, sir. You do what you have to do, and if you need me for anything, I'll be at home."

"Well, it seems like maybe we should head on down to the police station and figure everything out." The police officer grabbed Garret's arm. "Let's go, Mr. Jones."

Alex slipped the recorder into the front pocket of his shirt. "We'll secure the fire and the library and follow you, Officer Passton."

The policeman nodded, then led Garret out of the library. Garret wasn't going quietly, either.

"You can't hold me. I've done nothing wrong. I demand you release me at once," Garret was saying.

Anne stared after them, shaking her head. "That man is truly self-deceiving. He knew everything was wrong, even had remorse, although he probably didn't even recognize it as that. And even though his guilt wasn't enough for him to actually do the right thing, he was able to convince himself that by just keeping quiet and letting the secrets die when he did, he should be admired."

Grace gave her a hug. "I was a little worried about you, pushing him like you did. And when you kept asking him questions and getting him to answer, well, I have to admit, I was a bit jealous. Are you sure you aren't a journalist hiding out as a librarian?" Grace asked Anne.

Anne laughed. "I wasn't really scared, not really, but he managed to shock me a few times."

"I never thought he'd confess to everything." Alex bent and addressed the fire. He steadied what was left of the logs, then leveled the embers so none would roll out.

"I know." Anne took a sip of water. "I kept thinking he'd tell me I was crazy, but when he asked me how much it would take to keep me silent, I knew he wouldn't turn back."

"I called Wendy and told her everything. She said to tell you both not to worry about the kids. They were making homemade pizza," Grace said.

"Well, let's head on down to the police station. I can't wait to hear Garret try to get out of this," Alex said, then led the way to his truck.

"I still can't believe we did it." Anne grinned into the darkness of the cab of the truck. "Megan's going to be thrilled," she said.

"I can't wait to run the article in the paper this Sunday." Grace grinned wide enough that the white of her teeth shone in the dashboard lights. "It'll not only clear the Rhodes family name but will expose the truth."

Anne smiled to herself. That's all she'd wanted — to uncover the truth. Maybe there was hope yet that Blue Hill could finally move out of the shadows of the past.

Once at the police station, it only took them fifteen minutes into the playback of the recording before Garret asked for a lawyer. The police left him with the phone to make his call in the interrogation room and escorted Anne, Grace, and Alex out.

"What do you think? Is the recording enough to charge him?" Anne asked.

The detective who'd sat in on the playback nodded. "Oh, but yeah. I'd be willing to bet, however, that his attorney will talk to the District Attorney and work out some sort of plea agreement. With a recorded confession, Jones would be stupid not to take anything they offer him," he said.

Grace handed him her business card. "I'll call tomorrow for a status, if that's okay. For this week's paper, of course."

He took the card and set it on his desk. "There might not be anything new until next week." He shrugged. "But you never know. If he has a good attorney who isn't afraid to work deals on a weekend…"

"By the way," Anne said, "there is an abandoned tree house down at the bottom of Blue Hill. I've seen some young boys hanging around there smoking, sometimes even during school hours."

The detective nodded. "We got a report of that very thing just last week. We'll be following up," he said.

"As a parent, I would want someone to let me know if it was one of my children," Anne said.

"I understand," he said.

"Thank you. For everything." Anne offered her hand.

"No, thank you." He shook her hand, and Grace's, and Alex's.

As soon as they walked out of the station, Anne dialed Megan's number.

"Hi, Anne. What's up?" Megan asked.

Even though Megan couldn't see her, Anne couldn't stop the smile. "Are you sitting down?"

* * *

Blue Hill Gazette

Alfred Rhodes Proven Innocent, A Hundred Years Later

Anne smiled as she reread the headline for probably the tenth time. Garret had pled guilty to conspiracy to commit fraud, and breaking and entering. He was awaiting sentencing, but most in town were calling the judge, demanding he serve some time.

The townspeople were outraged over the century-old secret. Most felt guilty over the way they'd treated Megan and her family. Several of the women in the Garden Club pulled together a quick wedding shower for Megan. Alex thought it might be too little, too late, but Megan had loved it.

To celebrate, Anne had a fund-raising party at the library. It seemed everyone in Blue Hill showed up. Anne had accepted quite a few checks already.

Dana Munroe led an elderly man toward them. "Anne, I want you to meet my father, Jeffery Munroe," she said. "Dad, this is the lady I told you about."

He shook her hand. "Dana tells me that because of your investigation, her map got some serious attention." He nodded. "I thank you," he said.

"No thanks are necessary. Have you tried the punch?" Anne asked. The attention had begun to embarrass her. She didn't do anything any of the town's residents wouldn't do to expose the truth.

As Alex led Mr. Munroe to the refreshment area, Dana gave Anne a big hug.

"Dad's right. Because of what you did and the article Grace ran in the paper, the private collector called and upped what he was willing to pay to exhibit my map in his collection. It's more than enough money to pay for Dad's pacemaker surgery, and even his treatments after."

"I didn't do that," Anne said. Heat enfused the back of her neck.

"Maybe not, but it wouldn't have happened without you." Dana gave her another quick hug. "So, thank you. And anytime you want to borrow the map to display here in the library, you just let me know."

"I will." Anne smiled as Dana headed back toward the refreshment area to join her father.

"Mrs. Gibson," Bella appeared beside her. "Do you have any more napkins?" she asked. "We're running low."

"A whole new package. Bottom cabinet on the right," said Anne.

Bella rushed back toward the refreshment room.

Anne smiled and made polite chatter with people as she wandered through the Nonfiction Room. She felt so warm,…so welcome. She'd come *home*.

Grace rushed up and grabbed her arm. "Oh my goodness, you aren't going to believe this," she gushed.

Anne laughed. "Remember who you're talking to? I'll believe anything."

"True." Grace giggled. "I just got a call from the *Pittsburgh Tribune*. They're going to run my article in their Sunday edition. With *my* byline!"

Anne hugged her. "Oh, Grace. That's awesome. Congratulations."

Grace's face glowed. "Thank you, Anne."

"I didn't do anything," said Anne.

"Yes, you did. You didn't just accept the rumors and old stories. You kept digging and digging until you got to the truth." Grace tapped the end of Anne's nose. "If you ever want to write some articles for me, the invitation is always extended."

Anne nudged her, warmth spreading throughout her whole body. "Thanks, but no thanks. I'll leave all the Pulitzer dreams to you."

"Mom, Coach Pyle told me they were going to start a new baseball team this spring," Ben said, nearly running her over in his excitement. "And I'll be old enough to play on it."

"Ben, you interrupted Ms. Hawkins," Anne said.

Her son turned to Grace. "I'm sorry."

Grace shook her head. "No worries. I was finished talking anyway." She headed toward the History Room.

"That's great, Ben." Anne planted a kiss on her son's cheek. "Have you checked on Hershey and made sure he has plenty of water?"

He nodded. "Ryan and I just did when we finished walking him."

"Good," said Anne.

"Okay, I've gotta go tell Ryan. He'll want to play on the team, too." He rushed off to the stairs.

Anne smiled after him.

"Mrs. Gibson."

She turned around. "Hello, Mayor Bultman. How nice of you to come," said Anne.

"Of course. I wouldn't miss it." He straightened. "However, I'm also here on official Blue Hill business."

"Let's step into the checkout area. It's a little more private," she said.

Once there, she waited.

"The town council held its meeting yesterday. After much debate and consideration, they determined that since there was no real map to begin with back in 1912, the reward money is nullified," the mayor said.

Anne went very still.

"Therefore, we elected to remove the money from the escrow account and put it back into the town's account."

Her mouth dried up.

"Because of your role in uncovering the truth, we've elected to donate the money to our new Blue Hill Library," he said.

"Oh!" Speechless, Anne covered her mouth with her hand. "I don't know what to say."

"Say nothing right now, my dear. We'll have an official check presentation ceremony next week, just like a big press conference."

He patted her shoulder. "Don't you think that will bring a lot of tourists into Blue Hill?"

It was always about something, but she didn't care. "I do. Thank you, Mayor Bultman. I appreciate it."

He nodded and moseyed out to mill with the people.

"Anne, dear, I'm impressed," said Mildred as she joined Anne in the hallway.

"Thank you, Mildred," said Anne.

"Edie would be so proud of you," said Mildred. "I know I sure am." She gave Anne a warm hug.

"I am, too," Coraline echoed from behind Mildred. "You're a blessing to this town, Anne Gibson. A true blessing."

"Thank you," Anne mumbled as tears caught in her throat.

So many people offered gratitude and acceptance. Anne smiled as Mildred and Coraline moseyed into one of the rooms. Those two women had certainly come to mean a lot to Anne. They were so loving and generous, and she couldn't imagine them not being a part of her life.

She glanced down toward the other end of the hall, catching Megan and Grace chatting—two women she was proud to call friends. Each of them unique but offering much.

Emily and Liddie raced down the hall, Wendy on their heels. Anne couldn't stop her smile. Wendy, in her take-charge way, had charged into Anne's heart as well.

Anne leaned against the counter, the wood digging into her hip. So many wonderful people who helped to make her feel right at home in Blue Hill. Again.

"Psst."

She turned, then laughed to see Alex hiding by the back stairs. "What are you doing?" she asked.

"Come on." He motioned her over.

She glanced over her shoulder at the crowd. No one was watching. She tiptoed to him. "What's going on?" she asked.

"Come on." He took her hand and led her to the narrow balcony in the back of the house, right off her bedroom. "Do you remember this?"

She nodded, breathing in the fresh air. "I do."

Many, many times, they'd played hide-and-seek, ending up in this exact place. When Alex had completed the actual construction when he'd renovated, he'd made sure this special place had remained intact. It was one of her favorite spots in the house. A place that was all hers.

"I wanted to tell you how proud I am of you," he said. "You kept to your guns to dig up the truth, and you did. You cared about the people of Blue Hill, and I'm really proud of you."

It had been a long time since someone she cared about told her that.

"You solved a decades-old mystery, exposed the truth, and paved the way for Blue Hill to begin healing."

She joined him at the rail, staring out into the backyard. It felt natural. It felt right.

He gave her a little nudge. "You did good."

"It's *well*. I did well." she teased, but she nudged him back. "Thanks."

The comfortable silence of two longtime friends settled over them in the moonlight.

Hershey ran across the yard. Ben, Ryan, and Liddie in pursuit, followed by two of Wendy's kids. Screams and children's laughter filled the evening air.

Anne smiled. Yes, she was home.

ABOUT THE AUTHOR

Emily Thomas is the pen name for a team of writers who have come together to create the series Secrets of the Blue Hill Library. *Shadows of the Past* was written by Robin Carroll. Born and raised in Louisiana, Robin is a Southerner through and through. Her passion has always been to tell stories to entertain others. Robin's mother, bless her heart, is a genealogist who instilled in Robin the deep love of family and pride of heritage — two aspects Robin has woven into each of her sixteen published novels. When she isn't writing, Robin spends time with her husband of twenty-plus years, her three beautiful daughters and two handsome grandsons, and their character-filled pets at home — in the South, where else? She gives back to the writing community by serving as Executive Director for the American Christian Fiction Writers Association. Her books have finaled or placed in such contests as the Carol Award, Holt Medallion, RT Reviewer's Choice Award, Bookseller's Best, and Book of the Year.

An avid reader herself, Robin loves hearing from and chatting with other readers. Although her favorite genre to read is mystery/suspense, of course, she'll read just about any good story. (Except historicals!) To learn more about this author of Deep South mysteries and suspense to inspire your heart, visit Robin's website at www.robincaroll.com. Facebook: www.facebook.com/robincaroll. Twitter: www.twitter.com/robincaroll.

A Conversation with the Author

Q. Do you see your personality as being more like Anne Gibson or Wendy Pyle? Why?

A. I'm definitely more like Wendy in that I have a "take charge" attitude. I'm a HUGE organizational freak. I'll admit it, I'm addicted to spreadsheets and flowcharts. That's even how I write. I don't think I could write without using OneNote to track my characters and timeline.

Q. Anne and her friend Wendy share a great love of books, as did Anne's great-aunt Edie before her. If you could join in on a book club session with Anne and Wendy, what book would you most like to discuss?

A. I would love to sit down and discuss *The Stand* by Stephen King with them. I love the book because of the great characterization. I'd love to get Anne's and Wendy's thoughts on the characters, too. I bet we'd have quite the lively conversation.

Q. What is your favorite childhood reading experience? Can you tell us how this experience most influenced your life?

A. My favorite reading experience as a child was, hands down, the Trixie Belden series. My "treat" was when a new book in the series came out. I loved Trixie and Honey and the rest of the Bob-Whites. I still have the original series. I think I write mysteries/suspense stories because of my early love for mysteries.

Q. *Which scene in this story was the most challenging or rewarding for you to write?*

A. While I had plotted most of the book, one scene went "off the outline" while writing it, and it really grabbed my heart. It's the scene where they meet the stray dog's owner. That one really put a lump in my throat.

Recipes from the Library Guild

Green Jell-O Salad

0.6 oz. (large) package lime Jell-O
10.5 oz. (small) package tiny marshmallows
8 oz. package cream cheese
3.5 cups of boiling water
20 oz. (large) can crushed pineapple
12 oz. carton small curd cottage cheese

Put Jell-O and marshmallows in a bowl, add hot water, and mix well. Mix cream cheese with a little sweet milk and mix well. Add to Jell-O mixture. Add pineapple and cottage cheese. Chill in square pan.

From the Guideposts Archives

The following "His Mysterious Ways" article by Cecile Goosby Evans originally appeared in the May 1996 issue of Guideposts *magazine.*

I have no sense of direction. Friends joke that I couldn't find my way out of a paper bag without a clearly marked map. To get someplace without writing down specifics each time, I must travel the same route on a daily basis for weeks.

However, not even this seemed to help me get Sean, my six-year-old, to kindergarten every day. His school was located on one of many small residential side streets, all of which looked alike to me. Hence, my dilemma each morning was which street to turn down to get to the school.

One morning I noticed that the house on the corner of the street where I needed to turn had a huge clay pot in the yard. I realized I could use it as a landmark to steer me in the right direction. For months afterward I silently praised the occupants of that house for this makeshift turn signal. It became an ongoing family joke that if the people who lived there were ever to move and take the clay pot with them, Sean would have to transfer to a new school!

The day did come for Sean to change schools, and even though I had prayed over our decision, I still worried whether we had made the right choice. Then, the morning of Sean's first day at the new school, I had to drive past that now-familiar corner. I glanced over, then looked again in astonishment. The clay pot that had been my turn signal for so long was gone. In its place was a large For Sale sign. Sean and I had been given the best directions of all.

Read on for a sneak peek of another exciting book
in *Secrets of the Blue Hill Library*!

Unlocking the Truth

Overnight, autumn had splashed brilliant hues of yellow
and orange on the trees lining the streets of Blue Hill,
Pennsylvania. From her kitchen window, Anne Gibson had an
excellent view of the rolling hills. She took a deep breath of
contentment. She enjoyed the peaceful Monday morning
routine as her two children readied for school. The smell of
brewing coffee signaled a fresh day with a clean slate to fill
spending time with her family and working on the house and
library she'd come to love.

"Mom!" A resounding crash sounded below and footsteps
pounded on the stairs. Anne nearly dropped her coffee mug as
their big brown dog burst into the kitchen. Paws flailed on the
polished wood floor as it slid into Anne's knees. With an *oomph*,
she caught the animal.

Her nine-year-old son Ben skidded to a stop behind him.
"Sorry, Mom."

Anne tugged on Hershey's collar, making him sit. "What
happened? Are you okay?"

"I went to feed Hershey on the back porch and he almost knocked
me over getting into the house. I think he wanted to see you."

"Hmm." Anne suspected that, although Hershey had a nice dog house and run in the backyard, he considered himself a member of their family with equal rights to the house.

"What was that crash?"

Ben's hazel eyes widened. "Oh, uh, you know those books that were in the hall?"

"Yeah?" Anne had stacked several piles of books outside the Reference Room while she'd put another coat of paint on a shelf. Aunt Edie bequeathed the beautiful Queen Anne Victorian to the people of Blue Hill and appointed her niece to turn the first floor and a good portion of the second into a needed library for the town.

"They all tipped over," Ben said. "I can go pick them up if you want."

Anne sighed. She shouldn't have left open the usually locked door between their living apartment to the second-floor library area this morning when she'd returned a book to the Fiction Room that she'd read last night. "You won't have time for breakfast if you do. I'll take care of them later. Take Hershey back downstairs and then wash your hands. Hurry, okay?"

Ben grabbed Hershey's collar and pulled the reluctant Lab out of the second-floor living area and down the back stairs. Anne smiled as she turned to the sink to wash her hands. She hadn't wanted to take in a pet so soon after moving back to Blue Hill from New York. They had experienced so many changes since her husband had passed away, but Ben had wanted a dog so badly. Shortly after their move to Blue Hill he'd helped a stray dog find its rightful owners and continued to beg for one of his own. He'd even written up a signed contract of commitment to take care of a dog. Anne had been so impressed with the maturity and responsibility her son showed, she took him to the Blue Hill Humane Society and, together, they'd picked out Hershey.

"Liddie, sweetheart, you need to come eat." Anne poked her head in her daughter's room. Her five-year-old sat on the bed surrounded by discarded clothing. "Why did you change clothes?"

She rubbed her neck. "The shirt itched me."

"Itched you?" Anne picked up the long-sleeved blouse they'd just bought. She felt the collar between her fingers. "Well, it is a little stiff. We'll just wash it again and then it should be okay. If you're going to wear short sleeves you need to take a warm sweater or sweatshirt. It's going to get colder this afternoon."

Liddie nodded and rubbed again.

"Let me see." Anne lifted Liddie's soft brown hair and examined her neck. The pink skin did look slightly irritated. Poor baby.

"Mom! The toast is burning!" Ben yelled.

Anne dashed back to the kitchen as the smoke alarm went off. She had been using Aunt Edie's old toaster, which was almost as much of an antique as the house itself.

Charcoal slices smoldered. Anne grabbed a potholder and snatched up the bread, threw them in the sink, and turned the water on. Ben coughed as he climbed on a chair and poked the smoke alarm button until it stopped.

Anne pushed the window up, letting in the crisp air. The sound of barking rushed into the room. Hershey was chasing a squirrel around the backyard.

"Stop that, Hershey! Let the squirrel alone," Anne yelled. Hershey paid no heed but the squirrel leapt on the hundred-year-old oak, chattering all the while.

"Do you want me to go down and tell Hershey to stop barking?" Ben asked.

Anne glanced at the clock. They were officially behind schedule. So much for her peaceful start to the day. "Let's just eat. He'll stop soon." At least she hoped so. "Did you wash your hands?"

"Oh I forgot." Ben headed for the bathroom.

Anne quickly spooned up the oatmeal from the stove into bowls, sprinkled on some raisins, swirled a little honey on top and placed them on the table for the kids.

"Liddie," she called. "Come eat."

Anne eyed the ancient toaster, wondering if she dared trust it again. The more modern model she'd brought from New York was broken. Besides, the old silver 1950s toaster reminded of her of pleasant summer breakfasts with Aunt Edie. She tucked in another two slices and kept an eye on them as she finished the lunches. She placed the sandwiches and grapes into the lunch boxes, Liddie's Twinkle Bell, and Ben's Spider-Man, and clicked them shut.

Ben returned to the kitchen. "The faucet's dripping again."

Anne suppressed a groan. "I'll see if I can get it fixed." She spread peanut butter on the toast. Liddie still hadn't made an appearance.

"Liddie, come on, honey!"

Liddie shuffled into the room. She'd changed shirts yet again. The soft blue long-sleeved T-shirt was wrinkled, but Anne wasn't going to send her back to pick out something else. Liddie scooted onto her chair.

"Let's say the blessing. I think it's your turn, Liddie," Annie said as she took her children's hands.

Liddie shook her head, surprising Anne. Usually Liddie liked to say the blessing and offered to say one even if her brother got chosen instead.

"Ben?" She turned to her son who fidgeted in his seat.

Ben bowed his head. "Dear Lord. Thanks for this day and please bless the food. Please help me on my math quiz today. And please help Hershey stay out of trouble. Amen."

"Amen." Anne glanced at Liddie who poured milk on her oatmeal and dug in. At least she was eating. Anne supposed her little girl was tired from the church picnic yesterday. The children played hide-and-seek for hours. Her rambunctious kindergartener could run as fast as the boys in her class and did a good job keeping up with her brother too.

Anne passed the milk to Ben. "I didn't know you had a math quiz today."

Ben shrugged. "I forgot about it until last night."

"Are you ready for it?" Anne asked. Being in fourth grade, Ben didn't often get homework, but when he did, Anne tried to help him establish good study habits so he wouldn't struggle later on.

He shrugged. "Maybe."

There wasn't time to pursue the subject of trying your best versus just thinking maybe, so Anne filed it away for future discussion. There was so much more to parenting than she'd ever imagined and she hadn't expected to be doing it alone.

Talk was minimal as they quickly ate their food. Not Anne's idea of a relaxed breakfast, but they'd get to school on time if they left soon. She sent the kids off to brush their teeth and get something warm to wear. They descended down the two flights to the first floor, which housed the main library.

Liddie picked up something by the front door.

"What is it?" Anne asked, pulling a long navy sweater over her T-shirt and jeans.

Liddie shrugged and handed over a medium-sized manila envelope. Anne tossed it on the checkout desk and hustled the children through the door.

Crisp air greeted them as they crossed the wide porch to the sidewalk. The temperature had taken on a chill after a gorgeous fall day yesterday in the park. Their feet crunched through the piles of leaves.

Raking leaves would make a good job for Ben. Anne had spent many hours doing the same when she'd grown up in Blue Hill. When she was young, she would leap in the piles her father had spent hours raking up. Her dad, bless his heart, had never complained. One time he dove right in with her and buried her in the brightly colored pile.

"What are you smiling at?" Ben asked as they reached the car and Anne was helping Liddie into her car seat.

"Just remembering how fun raking leaves was with your grandpa. We're going to have to get started on our yard soon."

Ben made a face but Liddie looked up. "I want to rake leaves. Please?"

"We'll have plenty of opportunities." Anne waved to a neighbor as they drove down the street. Anne found a parking spot at the Blue Hill Elementary School, a tall, three-story brick building that was at least seventy years old. Anne attended here when the building used to house the high school. A few years ago a new high school had been built and this one was remodeled and converted to an elementary school. Ben separated himself from them as soon as they left the car. He had spied Ryan Slater and ran off with a "Bye!" flung over his shoulder.

Liddie stuck close and seemed to drag her feet when they reached her kindergarten room. Usually she charged right in.

"You okay, Liddie?" Anne automatically placed her palm on the child's forehead. No fever. "Are you tired?"

Liddie shrugged and slunk into the noisy room full of kindergartners. "See you later, sweetie." Anne gave her a quick kiss on the top of her head, reluctant to leave when Liddie seemed so out of sorts.

"Liddie!" Suzy, a little blonde girl waved. Liddie waved back and ran over to the table with lumps of brightly colored clay.

Anne turned back down the hall with relief, thinking again her daughter was just tired from her busy weekend. She drove toward home with a prayer that her children would have a good day.

When she reached home, she checked on Hershey, who was snoozing in the sun. She climbed back up the stairs, pausing on the second floor to look at the toppled stacks of books. They'd all have to be sorted again. She pushed them back against the wall and continued up to their apartment.

After cleaning up their breakfast mess, she checked on the bathroom faucet. It did have a slow leak. She wondered if she could ask Alex over to fix it. Or maybe he could refer her to someone who wouldn't charge her too much. She grabbed the kitchen phone and dialed. His voice mail answered.

Since Alex Ochs, her high-school boyfriend, had done renovations on the mansion, she knew the brief message she left wouldn't be a surprise. And since he now owned a contracting business and had been raising Ryan, his late sister's ten-year-old son and Ben's best friend, she hoped he'd be able to fit the small request from a friend into his schedule.

Anne brewed herself another cup of coffee and went downstairs to the library's checkout desk. She had a few minutes before opening the library to the public and decided to go through the stack of mail that had gathered since last Friday.

Anne took a sip from her mug and sorted through envelopes separating out the bills, a magazine, the manila envelope, and a card from her mother. Even though her mother was proficient with e-mail and on Facebook, she still sent cards and notes through the mail at least monthly. She slipped out a pretty, flowery card. Tucked inside was a photo of her father on the greens standing by a shiny blue golf cart. On the back of the photo her mother had written, "Dale's new toy."

Anne smiled, glad her parents were enjoying life in Florida where they'd retired five years ago. Her father had been able to take an early retirement from his position in the finance division of a steel manufacturer thanks to his company's buy-out offer.

Her mother's note was short and sweet saying how much she missed Anne and the kids and hoped they'd be up for the holidays. Anne set the photo aside to show Liddie and Ben when they got home from school.

She picked up the manila envelope next and slit open the flap. She pulled out an article that appeared to have been clipped from a newspaper. A black and white picture topped the page and a headline read:

Secrets and Betrayal in Blue Hill

Anne examined the photo, which seemed familiar. Was that the Blue Hill High School gym? A dense crowd of teenagers danced beneath hundreds of streamers hanging from the tall ceiling. In the background a banner stating "Homecoming Dance" was tacked on the wall above the band.

She read the opening sentence.

The night was supposed to be a celebration, but treachery delivered a blow that would change people's lives forever.

Anne quickly scanned the column and gasped.

The article was about her!

A NOTE FROM THE EDITORS

We hope you enjoy Secrets of the Blue Hill Library, created by the Books and Inspirational Media Division of Guideposts, a nonprofit organization that touches millions of lives every day through products and services that inspire, encourage, help you grow in your faith, and celebrate God's love in every aspect of your daily life.

Thank you for making a difference with your purchase of this book, which helps fund our many outreach programs to military personnel, prisons, hospitals, nursing homes, and educational institutions. To learn more, visit GuidepostsFoundation.org.

We also maintain many useful and uplifting online resources. Visit Guideposts.org to read true stories of hope and inspiration, access OurPrayer network, sign up for free newsletters, download free e-books, join our Facebook community, and follow our stimulating blogs.

To learn about other Guideposts publications, including the best-selling devotional Daily Guideposts, go to ShopGuideposts .org, call (800) 932-2145, or write to Guideposts, PO Box 5815, Harlan, Iowa 51593.